He looked at her. Really looked.

She felt his gaze as it traveled up her simple silk gown of palest green and then studied the ivory satin sash tied beneath her bosom.

"That is all wrong, my dear. Allow me." He pulled her close to him, undoing her sash with impatient fingers.

"You appear to have had much practice at undoing sashes, my lord," Juliet said evenly. "Another one of your talents?"

Alexander's eyes danced with mirth, and Juliet was quite mortified when she realized what she had uttered. "You look very nice this evening, my Juliet. I trust that we shall be able to convince these good people that we are indeed husband and wife. I fear my reputation may have preceded me. Do you think you can redeem me?"

"Do not mock me so, or no one will ever believe it," Juliet scolded.

She found him close once again, his fingers brushing her tender skin with careless regard. "They will believe what I wish them to believe, and *that* is that I do desire you. Make no mistake, my dear, when this evening is over, they will be convinced of it."

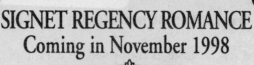

The Unexpected Wife

Emily Hendrickson

A SIGNET BOOK

SIGNET
Published by the Penguin Group
Penguin Putnam Inc., 375 Hudson Street,
New York, New York 10014, U.S.A.
Penguin Books Ltd, 27 Wrights Lane,
London W8 5TZ, England
Penguin Books Australia Ltd,
Ringwood, Victoria, Australia
Penguin Books Canada Ltd, 10 Alcorn Avenue,
Toronto, Ontario, Canada M4V 3B2
Penguin Books (N.Z.) Ltd, 182-190 Wairau Road,
Auckland 10, New Zealand

Penguin Books Ltd, Registered Offices:
Harmondsworth, Middlesex, England

First published by Signet, an imprint of Dutton NAL,
a member of Penguin Putnam Inc.

First Printing, October, 1998
10 9 8 7 6 5 4 3 2 1

Chapter 1

There was a wondrous tingle in the air; spring could not be so very far away. Juliet Winterton crunched through the thin layer of winter snow, sniffing appreciatively while she climbed the last few feet to the crest of the south-facing slope near her home. At the summit she paused, gazing upon a much loved view. Before her a drift of snowdrops swept down to meet budding crocus near the reflecting pool. It was a glorious morning at Winterton Hall.

Wrapping her arms about her, she heard the ominous crackle of the letter in the pocket of her rust-colored redingote. She shivered at the sound. The multiple capelets kept much of the morning chill from reaching her; rather, her shiver came from remembrance of the missive's contents.

As Juliet bent to collect a few of the pretty snowdrops, she considered what she must do as a result of that letter. It was all because of her stepbrother, drat his hide. Marius had been brief, conveying only the bare bones of his intent. He'd decided that their father must have died over in Russia—no one had heard a word from him in years. Therefore Marius had taken it upon his slim shoulders to arrange a marriage for his sister with his good drinking and gambling crony, Robert, Lord Taunton.

Juliet had no intention of wedding a man she had heard described as a rowdy good fellow. In the few times she had seen him, Robert Taunton appeared no better than Marius. After years of putting up with her miserable stepbrother, Juliet had no desire to wed a man just like him. Indeed, were there any men equal to her dear, and possibly departed, father? He'd been a man of principle, loving and kind to his only daughter. *He* would never have sanctioned a marriage between a mere baron—a drunken gamester at that—and Juliet.

She sauntered down the hill, deep in thought, vaguely aiming for the reflecting pool. What could she do? Normally, she would have turned for advice to her governess, Miss Pritchard, but that worthy lady had been called home; her parents had been taken severely ill. Juliet's maid was less than helpful, Pansy being the sort who shrouded herself with gloom and doom, forever seeing the unfavorable side of matters.

The one thing of which Juliet was certain was that she could not, indeed, must not marry Robert, Lord Taunton! Not that she'd mind being left in the country while her husband flitted about London with his friends. She adored living in the country, considering it far preferable to London, which she viewed with great misgivings.

Of course, she had to admit she'd not had the dubious pleasure of a come-out in London since her dearest papa had been detained in far-off Russia these past years. Miss Pritchard had described a come-out to Juliet in glowing terms, but Juliet had seen pitfalls in every sentence. It sounded more to her like a trial by peers, with judgments rendered upon rather superficial matters—like the gowns one wore or obtaining those plaguey vouchers to Almack's assemblies.

No, it was not being left alone that bothered her; it was that she would likely have children without her husband's comfort, that he would be more interested in spending money in the city or at the race courses than in improving his estate—if he followed Marius's example. She would be little better than a brood mare, with straightened circumstances in which to live to boot. It was a situation not to be tolerated—at least not if she could manage otherwise.

Which brought her to the crux of the problem—how to avoid the marriage.

Off in the distance she observed a traveling coach bowling along the lane, headed south. It was trailed by a fourgon bearing luggage and other necessities. The neighbors appeared to be off to London. Everyone was headed for the city, and by everyone she of course meant those of the privileged group of which she ought to be one. If only dear papa would return. In her heart Juliet refused to accept that he was dead. Surely she would have felt something, a premonition, a sense of loss?

Drooping slightly, she re-entered her home to find Mrs. Mullins, the housekeeper at Winterton Hall ever since Juliet could remember, awaiting her. The woman stood in the hall, hands folded across her ample expanse, looking for all the world as if Juliet had done her a grave injustice.

"Mrs. Mullins, is there a problem?" Juliet dropped her flowers, pulled off her gloves, and tossed them and her bonnet on the table in the center of the entry while awaiting the explanation she knew would come. She unbuttoned her redingote with chilled fingers, taking note that the housekeeper did not as customary urge Juliet to warm herself nor offer a hot drink. The predicament was indeed dire.

"Your stepbrother, miss. He sent a message to Mullins to have rooms prepared for him and his friend, Lord Taunton. He also wrote for Mullins to request the parson to present himself come next Tuesday for a wedding ceremony. Your wedding, miss, if I make no mistake." The housekeeper gave Juliet an affronted look, as though Juliet would deliberately neglect to inform her of such a momentous event.

"So I gather from the letter I received. I had no inkling of my stepbrother's intent, you may be sure, Mrs. Mullins. Indeed, I scarce know what to think." Juliet went on to soothe the woman's sensibilities while feeling as though a trap had been set and sprung for her. There appeared to be no escape. Yet there must be, if only she could be sufficiently clever. In spite of her brother's opinion of her, she had brains and would now use them.

Alone once more, Juliet walked to the library, settling herself in her father's great leather chair near the fireplace with the hope that while there she might be inspired with a solution.

In London, the elegantly handsome and polished figure of Alexander Barr, Viscount Hawkswood, impatiently trod the

steps leading from White's, his anger well concealed beneath a
veneer of sophistication. He had been on the town long enough
to have acquired a patina of town bronze sufficiently thick
enough to ignore the twitting of his friends and so appear
supremely undisturbed. But lately things had grown out of
hand. It was one thing to be the most sought after gentleman in
London; it was quite another to be hounded by Camilla
Shelford to the point where everyone expected an announcement at any moment. He had no intention of wedding the little
baggage, even if she was beautiful and possessed a reasonable
dowry. If anything like her mother, she would be a shrew of the
most objectionable sort once safely married. *That* was to be
avoided at all costs.

Worst of all, he could not go to one of his country estates, for
he was certain that wily young woman would follow, somehow
trapping Alexander into being forced to wed her. The same reasoning prevented him from visiting any friends who had remained in the country. *Blasted women!* They were all the same,
out to trap a husband in any way they could.

Alexander determined that when he decided to marry—and
that was a time off if he had his way—he would choose his own
bride and there would be no entrapments!

In the meantime, Alexander vowed to walk with cautious
steps. Miss Shelford would not catch him unawares. Just at that
moment, he caught sight of a familiar carriage tooling up Pic-
cadilly and hastened into the calm environs of Hatchards with
the comforting knowledge that if necessary he could slip out
the back door. He was not about to be trapped.

"Pansy," Juliet said with hesitant determination, "we must
leave here. I refuse to be trapped into marrying that dreadful
man."

The maid paused in replacing the garments she had just
ironed and bestowed a frown on her mistress. "And just where
do you be thinking you might go?" she demanded.

"I do not know," Juliet admitted wearily. She had remained
in the library until the dinner hour and was nowhere near a solution to her dilemma. "Only we *must* leave here, and I suspect

the sooner we go, the better. I fear if we wait too long, I may be easily caught. Time is of the essence. That is why we must go as soon as may be. I want you to pack my clothes, and I shall fabricate a reason for departing. I doubt I shall fool Mrs. Mullins, though," Juliet added pensively. "She has ever seen through me. But she'd not give me away to Marius, would she?"

"That she would not," agreed Pansy reluctantly. "I still don't see where you'd go."

Juliet took a deep breath and announced calmly, "Just leave that to me. We shall leave at first light." She went to the door, then turned to face her maid. "I intend to inform Mrs. Mullins that Miss Pritchard has requested I come to visit her."

Pansy gave her a doubtful look, but kept her thoughts to herself, for once. Resigned to her fate, the maid went to fetch a trunk along with a hatbox and her own valise.

With a view to traveling and the costs that might be entailed, Juliet went to the library safe and removed every pound therein—which fortunately proved to be a considerable sum. What her stepbrother would think of the missing money she preferred not to consider. He was unaware that she knew the combination to the safe. She had inadvertently overheard the series of numbers and carefully stowed that knowledge away in the back of her mind. How useful a good memory was at times!

Miss Pritchard's family lived to the north in Yorkshire somewhere. Her home was in some little village far north and west from the town of York. It would certainly confuse Marius should he seek Juliet there, for she intended to head south. That she had no *definite* plan was not to be revealed to the doubting Pansy. Something would turn up, of that she was certain.

Rather, Juliet hunted out her father's copy of *Patterson's Roads* and hoped it was not too horridly out of date for her use. South and west, she decided, wishing to avoid proximity to London. She would plan as she went, traveling when and where the spirit moved her.

Mrs. Mullins was another matter entirely.

"I'd not wish to see you haring off to visit your governess, no matter she is as kind and gentle as any lady might be," the housekeeper asserted. "Why, anything might happen to you along the way!"

Daughter of a vicar with a large family, Miss Pritchard had been an excellent influence on the exuberant Juliet. If the housekeeper was aware that Juliet fled marriage to Lord Taunton, her suppositions were not voiced. Her objections voiced, she had put no additional hindrance to Juliet's departure.

Thus it was that early the next morning after a substantial breakfast and a tearful farewell to Mullins and Mrs. Mullins, Juliet—along with Pansy, the trunk, hatbox, and Pansy's modest valise—was deposited at the main posting inn in the nearest market town by a most reluctant coachman. This good man thought it scandalous that Miss Juliet take a public conveyance of any sort when he could offer his services. It was only by means of cheerful guile that Juliet convinced him she would do well enough on her own with Pansy at her side.

"Doubtless there is no place to stable a coach such as this at poor Miss Pritchard's house. I'd not wish to embarrass her nor cause her any trouble," Juliet virtuously explained.

The coachman frowningly agreed and reluctantly turned the ponderous Winterton traveling coach around for his return trip to the hall.

Juliet breathed a sigh of relief when the coach was out of sight. Then she made her way to the proprietor of the inn and requested a post chaise. Once that was arranged, she directed the driver to head south in such a quiet voice that no one else heard her. That the inn proprietor had taken the notion she was headed into Yorkshire was deliberate on her part. He would tell Marius when and if he bothered to inquire, and her stepbrother would be lured in the opposite direction.

"I think you be daft, if you don't mind my saying so," Pansy grumbled when the chaise gave a lurch as it hit a pothole with some violence.

"Would you rather I marry a drunken gamester who would soon have my dowry spent and his estate quickly encumbered with debts, leaving me with a clutch of babies and no money?" Juliet demanded.

Pansy subsided into appalled silence at the horrible future projected.

At the next town of some size, Juliet requested with her pretty manners to be let down at a comfortable-looking coaching inn. She paid off the driver of the post chaise, handing over precisely what was due plus a modest tip—large enough so he was not disgruntled, but not so vast that he thought her a fool.

She thought this was what was called covering her trail—not that she believed Marius would do much serious looking for her. He seemed too indolent for such effort just to find his chum a wife he doubtless did not desire in the least. She suffered no illusions regarding her status in the marriage market. As a viscount's daughter with a goodly dowry as well as admittedly possessing a pleasing appearance, she was more than acceptable.

On the other hand, she had little to recommend her. She hadn't made her bow to Society, nor had she been presented at court. She knew of no well-born relative or older friend to sponsor her entry to the *ton*. It came from living such an isolated life and not keeping in contact with her late mother's friends. Well, that could not be helped at this point. What mattered now was to escape the clutches of Lord Taunton.

It was but a little matter to take the mail to the next town, then hire a post chaise to travel west to another sizable town, where they spent the night in a large and comfortable inn. She made as little fuss as possible, not wishing to be a memorable guest.

Thus she continued from city to city, alternating with the mail and the post chaise, far preferring the luxury of the post chaise to the dubious charm of the mail coach and those who traveled within.

"I be getting dizzy what with changing coaches and all," Pansy complained several days later after they had paid off the chaise and entered a small but clean-looking village inn.

Juliet had miscalculated. There was not only a distinct lack of accommodation to be had, but she doubted if the mail would stop here. Yet the hour was late, and she refused to travel by night, fearing a highwayman and the loss of her carefully guarded money. Even Pansy wasn't sure where all of it was hidden. Juliet had prudently divided it into a number of concealed places—her trunk, the sole of her left half boot, her reticule, and her large fur muff. Still, she preferred to keep the sum for her own needs, not hand it to some ruffian along with her pearls.

She sank into reflective thought while she consumed a cup of tea in the neat little parlor she shared with another couple, the inn not given to private parlors. The conversation of the other couple reached her ears.

"La," said the woman, "what a pity he never comes within hide nor hair of the house his dear grandmama gave him. 'Tis a terrible shame; such a waste of a good house it is," the woman exclaimed.

"Viscount Hawkswood doubtless has so many properties he can't remember this little place," her partner grumbled.

"Little!" the woman cried to Juliet's fascination. "I scarcely think it to be a *little* house, my dear sir. There must be at the very least eight bedrooms, plus a handsome suite for his use—and his wife if he has one, which I doubt."

"He could be wed for all we know—not that it is any of our business, may I remind you," her spouse testily responded.

"Well, I still say it is a dreadful shame that such a pretty house is closed up."

"You just want a viscountess in the neighborhood," the husband claimed with a wry twist of a smile.

"Now, Mr. Ogleby, the things you say!" she cried in affronted dignity.

At this point Juliet had a lightning inspiration. She rose from her little table and crossed to where the couple had sat in argument while consuming their coffee and rolls.

The gentleman rose from his place as she paused before them, looking at her with undisguised curiosity.

"I do beg your pardon," she said softly with her pretty manners and best smile firmly in place. "I could not but help overhear what you said about the house belonging to Viscount

Hawkswood. It is nearby? I am on my way there, and I must confess that I am completely at a loss as to where it might be." She bowed her head and contrived to look very humble as she added, "I dismissed the driver of my post chaise when he could not find the place."

"And now you need to reach the house before dark," the woman who was doubtless Mrs. Ogleby exclaimed. "And you are . . . ?"

"I am Lady Hawkswood. My husband has remained in London while I sought the tranquillity of the country. I do not care for the smells and noise of the city, you see," Juliet added shyly. She darted a glance at Mr. Ogleby to see if he swallowed her tale, and it seemed he did.

He exchanged a look with his wife, then said, " 'Tis not an easy house to locate unless you know the area. I daresay your driver was a stranger to these parts. Please allow my wife and me to escort you to your home."

"Oh, indeed, yes. You must be worn to a flinder, having traveled all the way from London!" Mrs. Ogleby cried, sympathy clear in her voice. She rose from her table, obviously pleased to make the acquaintance of the very woman she had so desired to see. She would be the first to have met the pretty Lady Hawkswood and would be able to lord it over Mrs. Tackley, who claimed to have known the old viscountess before she moved away.

Within less time than Juliet would have believed possible, she was ushered into a very neat landau with Pansy settled alongside the coachman. The luggage was to be brought later by the landlord's son, who looked smitten when he clapped eyes on Juliet. One shy smile from her and the trunk was stowed on his wagon with all speed.

"Now my dear, we will have you at Hawkswood Manor in no time at all," Mrs. Ogleby gushed.

Juliet merely smiled and permitted the older lady to natter on regarding the sights to be seen in this area as well as the many little assemblies and church-related functions that Juliet would doubtless want to join.

"Will Lord Hawkswood be joining you soon?" Mr. Ogleby inquired.

"No!" Juliet said emphatically, then modified her reply by adding, "I believe my husband finds the country not much to his liking." She fastened her gaze on her lap and thought she might just get away with the masquerade once she passed this hurdle.

The house was all that Mrs. Ogleby had claimed and more. The housekeeper met them at the door, ready to repel invaders if needs be, but was clearly thrilled to welcome the new mistress of the house. She bustled about, proudly pointing out the better points of the interior until Juliet espied a harp in the corner of the snug drawing room.

"A harp! Of all things delightful. I adore to play a harp," she said happily. Things were truly looking up. She had a roof over her head, a couple who accepted her in her new role, and a harp to keep her company. "Oh, I am so pleased I decided to come *here*!"

The Oglebys were obviously delighted to hear these sentiments and beamed a smile at the new resident of their little village. They left the young viscountess to settle into her new home and drove along the lane, discussing the startling turn of events.

"I think they must be separated!" Mrs. Ogleby declared in ringing accents. "Tell me, Mr. Ogleby, what man in his right mind would allow that pretty little thing to go off to live deep in the country all by herself!"

Her spouse agreed with surprising alacrity, considering his usual deliberate replies. He was not the slightest immune to a pair of long-lashed amber eyes set into a perfect oval face. Not that there was anything amiss with her mouth or nose, mind you. But her eyes were far and away her best feature, and Mr. Ogleby's elderly heart was captured. Of course, when he'd caught a glimpse of her chestnut curls he'd been fair gone. But her eyes had finished him.

"I cannot wait to tell Caroline Tackley that I have met Lady Hawkswood. She will be positively *green*," Mrs. Ogleby said with a decided purr to her voice.

*   *   *

Pansy found her mistress inspecting the upper floor by herself, having sent the housekeeper to prepare some sort of supper for her.

"And are you to be carted off to Bedlam—my *lady*?" the maid said with a snap.

"Can you think of a better situation than this?" Juliet replied softly. "We have a charming house in which to live. I certainly know what is expected of a viscountess—after all, my mama was one. And just think, Pansy—there is a harp for me to play. I was most sorry to leave my harp behind."

"There will be trouble," Pansy predicted.

"But for now we have a supper to come and good beds to rest upon, and I believe I saw a garden to the rear of the house. At least it will be a garden when I am done with it."

Knowing that besides her music her mistress liked nothing more than pottering about in a garden, Pansy admitted she had lost. "Just don't say I didn't warn you there'd be trouble when it comes," Pansy whispered in her parting shot as Juliet began her walk down the stairs to the ground floor.

The housekeeper had introduced herself as Mrs. Bassett and informed Juliet that she had been a maid when Lord Hawkswood's grandmother had been in residence.

"You see," Mrs. Bassett explained, "Lady Hawkswood lived here during the hot summers, preferring the cool of Wiltshire to the heat of the city."

"Is she still living?" Juliet thought to ask.

"Indeed, madam, though she rarely leaves her London home nowadays from what I have heard."

Juliet thought it might take a bit of time before she would become accustomed to being addressed as madam, or for that matter as my lady or Lady Hawkswood. Yet, had she married the odious Lord Taunton, she'd have been Lady Taunton by now—a more horrific situation she could not imagine.

So she quietly ate her modest supper, then discussed the hiring of servants with Mrs. Bassett.

"A cook and two maids ye'll be needing at once," the housekeeper advised.

"I wish to live simply, you understand," Juliet replied, thinking of life at Winterton Hall. "But I should like to have a gardener, please."

If the housekeeper hadn't been won over by Juliet's modest manners and her sweet smile, the request for someone to take in hand the grounds of the house, which she had overseen these past years, completed the job.

"The garden is sadly neglected. There never seemed to be the necessary funds to do more than scythe the lawn and trim a few trees," Mrs. Bassett happily explained.

Juliet went to her bed, feeling that her first day at Hawkswood Manor had been a success. It remained to be seen how the neighborhood would accept her. Perhaps her meeting with the Oglebys was fortuitous in more ways than one, for if she knew anything about women at all, it was that Mrs. Ogleby was a prattle-box of the first order. There most likely would be a goodly number of invitations to tea once the gossip had been avidly bandied about.

Juliet was not unaccustomed to village gossip; she'd known such all her life, living in the country as she had. It remained for her to make sure that certain bits of information were spread about in the village.

"I intend to let it be known that I expect to remain here alone and am content with my lot," she told Pansy as she crawled into the lovely and large bed in the room that belonged to the Viscountess of Hawkswood. "The last thing I want is for my supposed husband to be summoned or informed of my presence!"

"You do ask for trouble, miss."

"I expect you had best learn to say *my lady*, even when we are alone. I shall become used to my new name in time, I fancy," Juliet concluded as she snuggled beneath the fine lavender-scented linen sheets. "Consider the alternative, and you will accept that what I have done was for the best."

Pansy couldn't argue on that score, for she had no more liking for Marius Winterton than his sister did—even less. And truth to tell, she knew that her mistress would have been most miserable married to a man just like her stepbrother.

Left alone, Juliet pondered the change in her life. Was it terribly wrong of her to pretend to be someone else—a woman who did not exist? Even though she had not been to London, Miss Pritchard had seen to it that she was conversant with the latest fashions and in particular the marriages among the *ton*. Juliet's memory had never failed her in the past, and she could not recall a marriage for the viscount.

Then she frowned, for she did recall something about him. He was one of the premier gentlemen of London, much mentioned in the gossip columns. If her memory served her right, and it usually did, he flitted from one woman to the next with all the discrimination of a butterfly.

Well, it was a great comfort to know that his lordship would not deign to cross the threshold of this modest country house. Juliet doubted if he ever strayed far from the London scene, and if he did, it would not be to this remote village. Woodbury was too lacking in amusements of the sort to appeal to a man of his undoubted tastes. She shortly fell asleep, assured she was quite safe.

"I tell you, Harry, I am quite heartily fed up with the beauteous Camilla. Odd thing is, were she a retiring sort, I believe I could find her tolerable." Lord Hawkswood stared into the depths of his glass, wishing it were full instead of empty.

"Tolerable, old chap?" Harry Riggs cried softly. "I should wish a wife more than tolerable."

"A wife? Who said anything about a wife?" his lordship murmured with a chuckle.

"What do you propose to do about her?" Harry inquired.

"Find a bolthole somewhere she can't find me."

"That shan't be an easy task," Harry offered.

"There must be someplace that dratted woman won't go," Hawkswood said, frowning into his glass.

"I wish you well. Someday you will have to marry, you know," Harry concluded.

"Not now and certainly not to the estimable Camilla," came

the instant reply. "Perhaps my solicitor can think of a place."
With that vague notion, Lord Hawkswood bid his friend good
night, concluding this was coming to be the worst Season he
had ever known.

Perhaps Harry was right, he should marry. It might not be too
bad if he could find some acceptable chit and deposit her in the
country. Why, he might not have to change his ways in the least.
And on that happy thought he fell into a sound, if ignoble,
sleep.

Chapter 2

Juliet stretched, relishing the comfort of her bed, then blinked when—upon opening her eyes—she saw gold damask overhead rather than her own plain white ceiling. She turned her head, absorbing the details of the room she had so hastily perused the day before.

In the clear light of early morning, she could see that the golden hue was repeated throughout the room. The walls were hung with pale gold damask; delicate fruitwood chairs were covered with the same fabric; and only the rug that decorated the floor had white and celadon green as well as the lovely golden hue. It was most assuredly a room to cheer the heart.

Punching up her pillow, she settled back to study the portrait hanging above the fireplace surround. A young, very handsome boy leaned against an enormous dog, one arm draped lovingly about his pet's neck. The boy smiled out at the artist—and the world—with charm, possessing a grace that few boys had. Certainly Marius had never in his life gazed out with such self-possession and appeal. Juliet wondered who the boy might be and why this beautiful portrait had been left here, neglected and unappreciated.

"Ah, you be awake," Pansy said as she bustled into the room, carrying a pitcher of hot water. "I must say, 'tis a most agreeable house you picked to camp in, my lady."

"I am pleased you like it," Juliet replied with a grin. She pushed the luxurious covers aside and rose from her excellent bed, crossing to gaze out of the window at the garden—or what would be the garden when it was cleaned up and made to look presentable again.

"The trees are beginning to leaf out, and I do not doubt the primroses and daffodils are ready to burst forth in bloom. Ah, spring, Pansy! Traveling south has brought it to us sooner." With a light heart, Juliet submitted to the ministrations of her maid. Once dressed in appropriate garb for inspecting cupboards and crannies, she made her way to the ground floor.

Mrs. Bassett met her at the foot of the stairs, taking note of Juliet's simple morning dress with what appeared to be approval. Juliet had considered the ribbon-bound scallops marching down the front were rather a nice touch and the mameluke sleeves were something she and her mantua-maker had copied from an illustration in an issue of *The Lady's Magazine*. This morning she'd added a simple batiste betsy at her neck, thinking it made her look a bit more like a married lady about to spend a day overseeing her new home. Now her hand crept up to finger the delicate frills at the neck.

"Perhaps a bit of breakfast, Mrs. Bassett?" she asked, trying to sound like the mistress of the house.

"Of course, my lady. The breakfast room is the same where you had your bit of supper last evening." The housekeeper led the way to the pretty room where Juliet had hungrily attacked the simple meal last evening.

In the morning light she could see that the pale gold used in her bedroom decorated this room as well. Pale golden walls proved an excellent background for the rosewood table and chairs, while the carpet underfoot echoed the gold, with rust, celadon green, and darkest brown as accents.

Catching sight of herself in the mirror over the sideboard, Juliet turned to the housekeeper. "Perhaps there is an apron I might use today? I should like to go over the house with you to see what needs doing. There must be a goodly number of matters that have had to be put aside until you had more help or direction." Juliet ignored the minor detail that she had no business doing any of this. Were she to pretend to be mistress of the house, she had better act the role. She well remembered how her mother supervised the household, for Juliet had tagged along rather than remain in the schoolroom to be plagued by Marius.

Mrs. Bassett gave a pleased nod, then disappeared, leaving Juliet to her breakfast of toast and buttered eggs. Sipping her tea, Juliet reflected that her residing here was not such a terrible imposition. She had sufficient funds so she could at least pay for her food. As well, she would see to it that the house was kept in good condition. No doubt evenings would see her diligently mending sheets!

The morning passed swiftly. Juliet and Mrs. Bassett went through every cupboard and linen chest in the house. As they surveyed the lovely old linens, Juliet took time to note her surroundings. The house might be smallish, but each room was beautifully proportioned and lovingly decorated. As one who had chestnut hair, she was fond of gold and pale greens. It seemed that whoever it was that chose the colorways for this house liked them as well.

Her only moment of discomfort came when they entered the room adjacent to hers.

"This is, or would be, his lordship's room. What a pity he'll not be joining you." Mrs. Bassett hurried over to pull aside the deep gold velvet draperies, allowing the spring sunshine to flood the room.

There was a question in that last sentence that Juliet elected to quite ignore. Rather, she gazed about with curious eyes. She'd never been in a gentleman's room before. It was beautiful in an austere way—simple drapery and mahogany furniture with clean lines. The bed caught her gaze, for it was massive and very masculine.

Her lingering look, accounted by a romantic heart as being wistful, was noted by the housekeeper, who later told Cook it was a crying shame the young viscountess was left alone by that heartless rake off in London. Not that Mrs. Bassett read the papers, mind you, or knew much about the present lord, but it stood to reason, didn't it?

Juliet considered the furnishings in the room, intrigued by the shaving stand and an elegant Argand reading lamp on a small table with a comfortable-looking chair to hand. She wondered if the present lord enjoyed reading and rather doubted it. He wouldn't have time, given all the women he chased.

Several days passed in like fashion until Juliet began to feel as though she had lived here always. She learned which step squeaked, which chair was the best to sit in while doing her needlework, and bits and scraps about the former occupants of the house. It was with great interest that she discovered the handsome boy in the portrait was none other than the present Lord Hawkswood. She wondered if he was still as handsome and why that precious portrait had been left here. It was difficult to reconcile that handsome boy, his eyes so full of innocent love and trust, with the rake she read about in the gossip columns.

She also had the harp tuned and one string replaced. She spent a goodly number of hours contentedly playing music she discovered in a walnut canterbury. Many pieces were duets, witness to the interesting fact that whoever had played the harp also had someone who played the clavichord in accompaniment.

About a week after she had taken up residence in Hawkswood Manor, she had her first visitors. The Oglebys presented themselves at the proper hour for calling. Juliet could only thank Pansy for insisting that she put on a relatively new gown for the day, her other day dresses requiring a washing after her foray into the cupboards and chests. While the white muslin gown was utter simplicity, high at the neck with long fitted sleeves caught up in a puff at the upper arm, its plainness was redeemed by a brown velvet tunic trimmed with pearl beads attached to tiny embroidered silk roses.

Mr. Ogleby seemed much pleased by what he saw when they entered the drawing room to be greeted by a delighted Juliet. "How lovely to see you both again. I can never forget your kindness to one so very lost."

"I assure you that it was our great pleasure, my lady," Mr. Ogleby replied while he bowed over Juliet's offered hand.

"Dear Lady Hawkswood," Mrs. Ogleby gushed, "we trust you are settling in well? I waited to call until I felt you had matters here in hand, for I can imagine all that needs doing. Not that Mrs. Bassett isn't the most capable of housekeepers, but even the best need a guiding hand."

"Indeed," Juliet murmured, thinking Mrs. Bassett could

work circles around her, knowing all the while precisely what needed doing. However, knowing what needed to be done and having the authority to do something were two entirely different things. Not that Juliet had the authority, but she realized that certain matters had to be cared for else the house fall to rack and ruin. "Mrs. Bassett has been wonderfully helpful."

"Do say we are the first to hazard a call," Mrs. Ogleby ventured with a trace of hesitation in her manner.

"You are, and I am pleased to see you. The silence and lack of company can become a trifle wearying after a time."

Mrs. Ogleby, delighted to learn that she had the jump on that odious Caroline Tackley, beamed. "Well, we are here to change all that for you. I am having a small party come next Friday evening and would be pleased if you would join us."

Thinking that it would be a good way to become established in the little community, Juliet accepted with pleasure.

It wasn't until the Oglebys had left and she was once again alone that she realized the danger she faced. What if someone attended who knew the present Lord Hawkswood and that he was unmarried! She could only pray that the news from London rarely found its way into Woodbury or that the gossips did not realize the items regarding a certain Lord H and his many flirts pertained to her supposed husband!

Alexander smiled with relief at the news brought by Harry Riggs regarding a certain young flirt. "She has gone out of town, you say?"

"I have it on the best authority. My valet heard the news straight from the Shelford butler. It seems that the divine Camilla has acquired some spots on her face and cannot bear to be seen! Hence this hasty departure from the city to the rustification of the Shelford country home. I gather her mother is furious. The girl is much given to sweets, according to the butler."

"Which means she will be as grossly fat as her mother come another ten or twenty years," Alexander said with a knowing glance at his friend. "It also means I am free and do not have to look for an escape wherever I go. I cannot tell you how wearing it has been. Why, last week I was forced to slip through the kitchen at Lord Rutland's."

"Devilish bad luck to have a chit like Camilla Shelford enamored of you, old man," Harry said with sympathy.

"Not enamored of *me,* rather my title and money," Alexander corrected with a grimace. "It's as well my mother cannot read the tidbits in the gossip columns regarding my supposed flirts. As it is, my grandmother sends me strongly worded missives containing harsh scolds. She wishes to see me wed, and the sooner the better."

"Mothers and grandmothers are alike in that respect. I think it's the babies. Women dote on babies," Harry said with a reflective air.

Alexander absently agreed, thinking that infants were the last thing he wanted on his mind. The two men left his place with the air of gentlemen freed of an abominable cloud over their heads, facing the day with unalloyed pleasure.

"What a pity you do not have a child, Lady Hawkswood," the elegantly slim and fashionably gowned Mrs. Tackley said with the gracious condescension of one who has produced an heir and a spare—as they were wont to say—plus three lovely girls. "Children are such a comfort when one is alone."

Juliet noted that Mrs. Tackley managed to imply that Juliet was at fault for her supposed separation from the owner of the title and property. Lord Hawkswood might be a rake and a dashing man about town; he was also her presumed husband, and as such her lord and master. It would never occur to a woman such as Mrs. Tackley that Juliet had come to Woodbury on her own. His lordship must have banished her. The pity was enough to make Juliet grind her teeth in annoyance and frustration.

Thus it was that the following Friday evening she dressed with extra care and attention for the little party given by the Oglebys. Juliet guessed that only the cream of Woodbury society would be invited and that as the viscountess newly come she would be on display. She remembered how her mother had been feted and fawned over prior to her untimely death. Juliet was well primed on what she might expect.

Her pale green gown was again one of utter simplicity; Juliet had never cared for frills and fussiness. The low-cut neckline was edged in exquisite lace, as were the long sleeves. The gown fell from beneath her bosom to the floor in unpretentious grace. She wore her pearls, and when she gathered up a pretty paisley shawl and studied the result of her efforts, she was pleased by what she saw.

"Simple, yet elegant, I think," she said to Pansy with satisfaction. Even though she had never met his lordship, she knew an odd desire to show these people that she was worthy to be his viscountess. If he had put her aside, she wanted the local gentry to understand that it was not by her choice.

"Dear Lady Hawkswood," Mrs. Ogleby gushed when Juliet stepped into the spacious entry hall of the Ogleby manor house. It was immediately clear to Juliet that while Mr. Ogleby might not possess a title, he did have money in abundance. The house was beautifully decorated in excellent taste, all dating from sometime in the late 1700s Juliet guessed, and while the house was old, it was marvelously well kept. It somehow reminded her of Winterton Hall, and for an instant she was most homesick.

"How kind of you to invite me to your charming gathering," Juliet said composedly, smoothing her glove over the simple gold band she now wore on her left hand. She'd found the ring in a drawer of the library desk that second day and decided that it was most fortuitous, adopting it for her own when she discovered it a perfect fit.

"Allow me to introduce you, my lady," Mrs. Ogleby purred, ushering Juliet into the drawing room, exuding an air of importance. There followed a bewildering series of introductions that required close concentration on Juliet's part. What a pity she might not have arrived in advance so that she could have met all these people one or two at a time.

Mrs. Tackley, Juliet knew. The others she soon sorted out. Mrs. Ogleby unknowingly gave Juliet clues as to the importance of each person or couple by her manner and speech. It was admittedly an odd feeling to be led around the room and introduced with such deference. However, Juliet was surprised how easily she fell into her new role as Lady Hawkswood. She gave modest opinions when asked, listened well to all that was said, and in general tried to behave with seemly decorum, such as would have done Miss Pritchard proud.

It had been difficult to decide what to do about Miss Pritchard, for if her parents died or recovered, that dear lady might return to take up her post as governess-companion to Juliet. Substitute mother had been more like her position, and for that reason Juliet had deliberated long over a letter explaining what had happened.

At last, Juliet had composed a brief missive, begging Miss Pritchard not to reveal Juliet's location to anyone should she be asked. Since that dear woman had no fondness for Marius, it was doubtful she'd be inclined to assist him in his persecution of Juliet. As well, Juliet was not too specific regarding her address, preferring anonymity to discovery.

The dinner went well, and again Juliet blessed Miss Pritchard for her admonitions regarding proper etiquette at the table and suitable subjects for conversation. How lovely to discover that her neighbor at the table was an ardent gardener.

"Mr. Wyllard, I beg you will give me some advice on planting my garden this spring," Juliet said quietly between courses. "The admirable Mrs. Bassett has found someone to assist me with planting—but *what* to plant is the problem now. I would do it properly." Juliet bestowed a hesitant smile on Mr. Wyllard.

Since the gentleman was no more than in his thirties and certainly not immune to the charm of a pair of fine amber-hued eyes, he hastened to offer his services in garden planning.

When the ladies adjourned to the drawing room, leaving the gentlemen to their port and conversation, Mrs. Ogleby sought out Juliet.

"I am so pleased you appeared to get on well with Mr. Wyllard. Poor man, his wife died a few years ago, and he has been quite the solitary gentleman since then."

"He offered to assist me with planning a garden, for I know not what best to plant here. I trust that past plantings may be uncovered and perhaps restored. I do enjoy this sort of thing," Juliet said with quiet enthusiasm.

Mrs. Tackley joined them at this point, and Mrs. Ogleby turned to address her. "Caroline, you must agree with me that it will be a lovely thing for the gardens at Hawkswood to be restored to their past glory. Lady Hawkswood intends to undertake the task. Poor dear, it is a daunting prospect. I am so pleased that Mr. Wyllard has offered to help her. And"—Mrs. Ogleby gave Caroline Tackley a knowing look—"I believe it to be a kindness to poor Mr. Wyllard, get him out of that house and doing something once again."

"Indeed, Fanny, I do agree."

"I trust there will be no impropriety in his assisting me," Juliet said with an endearing little frown. "I'd not have the poor gentleman mortified by gossip."

"Never fear, my dear," Mrs. Ogleby said with a glance at Caroline Tackley. "We shall be in a position to stop it at once should we hear a whisper of insinuation. Is that not so, Caroline?" Looking at Juliet, Mrs. Ogleby added, "Mrs. Tackley is always knowing of the very latest that goes on in this area. She can be relied upon to scotch any hint of impropriety."

"I flatter myself that others listen to what I say and are guided by my suggestions," Mrs. Tackley said without a trace of pomposity. "Never fear, dear Lady Hawkswood, we shall guard your reputation—as well as Mr. Wyllard's."

Juliet felt as though she had waded through a swamp of verbiage, but a very necessary wade for all that. Kindly Mrs. Ogleby had most neatly obtained the aid of the worst gossip in Woodbury if Juliet knew anything about the matter. Having lived in a village atmosphere all her life, she well knew the power of a gossip, in particular one who was persuasive and convincing. Scandal broth was undoubtedly Mrs. Tackley's drink of life.

The following days brought a few changes. The various ladies came to call, enchanted to be invited to remain for tea and further conversation. Juliet was most careful to mention that Mr. Wyllard had graciously agreed to assist her with planning the gardens. She was inspired to add, "I am certain that my husband will be happy to see the gardens restored," giving the impression that her only wish was to please Lord Hawkswood.

That the ladies went home convinced that poor Lady Hawkswood was most hard done by and that her husband was an utter fool was unknown to Juliet, for not a word of their opinion returned to haunt her ears.

As to her relationship with George Wyllard, she was surprised to discover that they fell into easy conversation and very soon developed a casual bantering. It was the sort of friendship she had longed to know and thought Mrs. Ogleby an angel for her introduction.

"It appears that this bed contained perennials, perhaps daisies and aquilegia, foxglove and wallflowers—that sort of thing," George suggested one morning when they tackled the worst of the flower beds.

"Hmm, I suspect you have the right of it. I believe I see some foxglove leaves even now, and certainly that must be a daisy struggling to survive?" she queried.

"And do you agree that these other two were likely rose beds?" he added with a gesture toward a particularly thorny collection of plants.

"Indeed, I do agree. Oh, I am so pleased to have your help. The man Mrs. Basset located for me, Mr. Lumpkin, is quite good at digging, but no help at all when it comes to what I ought to plant." Juliet smiled at Mr. Wyllard and thought what a very agreeable person he was. Well to look at and nice to visit with, he was most soothing to her feelings. "Come, let us return to the house and look at the garden catalogs once again. They are so enticing with all those charming names for familiar plants."

If George Wyllard thought Juliet was extraordinarily charming in her fetching green muslin and a clever little chip hat worn especially for garden work, he gave no hint.

"A cup of tea would be welcome, my lady."

"I appreciate your company," Juliet said over their cups of bohea tea. "I feel the lack of close friends very deeply, you see." She offered him a ginger cream and sighed at the constrained life she lived.

"Your husband?" Mr. Wyllard offered hesitantly. "He remains in London?"

"I suppose so. I do not know him so very well, but I expect he finds country life terribly dull," she said in a vast understatement of the facts. "Some people do, you know. For myself, I wish nothing more than a garden and my harp."

"You do play, then? I was not certain that the presence of a harp meant you played it. I favor the clavichord myself," he said modestly.

"Oh," Juliet cried with delight and jumped up from her chair, running to the canterbury to hunt through the music. "There are several pieces here for clavichord and harp. Would you give me the pleasure of playing with me? I vow it would be most pleasing."

Mr. Wyllard set aside his cup and saucer to rise from the chair drawn close to where Juliet had sat and joined her. Perusing the first of the music, he took it to the clavichord and began to lightly play the melody.

"Very nice, I should think. I believe I am somewhat acquainted with this piece." He turned to give her a shy smile, and she returned it in kind.

"Well, then, shall we have a try at it?" She positioned herself by the harp and waited for him to commence. Shortly, the house was filled with the sounds of two fine musicians in total harmony. If there was a missed note or sour chord, it made no matter. There were none to hear except Mrs. Bassett and Cook, who thought it above all things wonderful.

When they had finished, Juliet sat quietly, her hands in her lap while she mulled over the duet. Then her face cleared, and she said with a sunny look, "I believe I should like to do this often, if we might. Think how we may amaze the others when we offer our music for their entertainment."

"You would have a party here? It is difficult to cart that harp about, and not everyone possesses such an instrument," Mr. Wyllard reminded her.

"Why not?" Juliet crowed with delight. "I owe a goodly number of people dinners and the like. What an excellent suggestion."

And so Juliet planned her little party, wishing she had the re-doubtable Miss Pritchard to advise her on a number of things. Mrs. Bassett proved to be enormously helpful, however, and Juliet soon felt more at ease with her preparations.

As well, she began to work with the ladies of the church, tending to calling on the poor and ailing as her own mother had been accustomed to doing. The property was too small to have tenants, but Juliet felt as though she was expected to do some charity work, and she could see how well her efforts were received.

"Poor Mr. Taunton," Mrs. Ogleby said one day, startling Juliet half out of her mind. "He's an elderly gentleman quite ignored by his relatives in spite of the fact that they will be happy to receive his fortune when he dies."

Relaxing a trifle, Juliet inquired carefully, "This Mr. Taunton has a son or nephew perhaps?"

"Indeed, a scapegrace of a nephew who never sets his eyes on the place from one end of the year to the other, for all he wants the inheritance." Mrs. Ogleby looked rather fierce at the notion of so contemptible a man.

"What a pity," Juliet replied softly, sorry for anyone related to the odious Robert Taunton in any manner.

"We shall visit him on the morrow. I feel sure a call from you will cheer his day considerably."

Juliet forced a wan smile to her lips, thinking that he wouldn't know the half of the matter.

Her duty call went well. Old Mr. Taunton would delight his nephew before too long, for it was clear he had not very long to live.

She was thankful that none of those upon whom she called with baskets of preserves or jars of soup were the sort to correspond with anyone in London. The very thought of having to part from this agreeable life was not to be considered. Then too, what Lord Hawkswood might say or do when he discovered her masquerade as his wife was too horrible to contemplate. He'd likely have her transported.

She pushed the disagreeable thought from her mind and

prepared for her party. It would be her very first, which she confided to Mrs. Ogleby the day before the event.

"My dear girl," Mrs. Ogleby cried, "how fortunate we are to be favored with the evening here. It has been many a year since the old lady entertained. I feel certain that your little dinner will bring back happy memories of days past. Do not worry about a thing; you will do just fine."

Juliet had invited all the cream of Woodbury society, the very people she had met when she attended that first dinner at the Ogleby manor house. The dinner proceeded well, with Cook excelling herself for her dear viscountess, so happy was she with a chance to show off her cooking skills.

Mr. Wyllard and Juliet were a smashing success with their duet. Miss Tackley sang tolerably well with Mr. Wyllard playing nicely for her. In fact, Juliet thought she might promote an interest in that quarter if it proved possible.

After the music Juliet served a light supper, and the guests sat around happily gossiping or conversing—depending on their given nature.

"I told you not to worry in the least," Mrs. Ogleby confided as she was about to depart with her husband. "If I do say so myself, Woodbury has a very elegant collection of agreeable people."

"You are so right," Juliet concurred, smiling with relief that the hurdle of entertaining so many had passed with what appeared to be reasonable success. She closed the door behind the last of them and wandered through the rooms, thinking that she was indeed lucky. Everything was utterly perfect.

"I intend to write the dowager viscountess and let her know what a nodcock her grandson is," Mrs. Tackley divulged to her good friend and enemy, Mrs. Ogleby, as they were about to enter their respective carriages. "Imagine a talented and kind girl like that left to molder in the country without even one child to comfort her!"

"Indeed," Mrs. Ogleby replied, not being on letter-writing terms with the elderly lady. "It would be good to see them together again." If they ever were in the first place, she added silently, unknowing how close she came to the truth.

Chapter 3

The cream of London Society whirled about the Hetherton ballroom in a sedate waltz, revolving like so many leaves drifting from autumn trees. Alexander stared at the scene with a harried look, one that was hastily erased when he was approached by Lady Hetherton madly plying her fan.

"You naughty boy, never tell me that you have at last become betrothed to Camilla Shelford. Rumors are circulating to that effect, you must know." She tapped him not too gently with her fan, a sign of her disapproval.

"I fear the rumor is grossly exaggerated, madam. I am not, nor will I likely become engaged to Miss Shelford." Alexander gave his hostess a speaking look, then resumed the bland expression he had worn since overhearing the latest rumor—an attempt, no doubt, by Miss Shelford to force him to the wall. The lady would find that he was made of sterner stuff than to yield so pitifully to her coercion. He would never marry her— not if he had to hide out in some godforsaken corner of the country.

"I am relieved to learn that," Lady Hetherton said quietly, her ire defused now that she had heard from Alexander himself that there was no truth to the rumor. "I scarcely think you two would be the least suited. Whatever is the girl about to be so brazen? Does she not know that the truth of the matter will out, in effect ruining her?"

"I have come to believe she is slightly mad, my lady. She is determined to have me, and while I am flattered at her choice, I must decline any reciprocation of interest. I refuse to be trapped into marriage with any woman, least of all Miss Shelford."

"She is here, you know. I could not deny her mother an invitation, for we have been friends this age and more. I do not wish to send you away, for you are quite the handsomest man here, but it might be safer on your part were you to leave. As a matter of fact, I would seriously think about traveling a bit. The rolling stone and all that, you know. If she can't find you, she can scarcely trick you, can she?"

Alexander listened to the quietly spoken words, acknowledging that Lady Hetherton spoke nothing but the truth. "It galls me to be compelled to leave what promises to be a brilliant Season, my lady. My only consolation is that I did not miss your annual ball. If I must go, allow me a dance before I vanish." Alexander summoned a smile for the older woman, who had always proven his friend.

Her eyes alive with mirth, she nodded her agreement and subtly guided Alexander to a corner of the ballroom far from where delicate, blond Camilla Shelford stood with her mother.

Later, on his way to his rooms, Alexander stared out of the window of his carriage. This entire farce was growing beyond him. Come morning he would consult with his solicitor as to possible legal action should it prove necessary. Doubtless it would make him look a fool, but better that than marriage to the willful Camilla.

The next morning Alexander made his way to the solicitor's office at an hour that guaranteed Miss Shelford would still be abed. It did not take him long to present his dilemma to Mr. Small, who sat rubbing his gray-frosted side-whiskers all the while Alexander talked.

"I do not think it in your best interests to consider legal action. A cease and desist order could bring unpleasant notoriety. Could you not take a tour of your estates?"

Alexander was not one of those peers who neglected his land. Once the Season concluded, he spent his time inspecting each and every estate to keep the land and property in good heart. "She will likely follow me. I tell you, the girl is not right in her head."

Mr. Small frowned, rubbing his chin until he brightened, appearing to have thought of something.

"Do you remember that smallish property your grandmother left you? A neat little manor house down at the tip of Wiltshire somewhere if I make no mistake." He rose from his desk to cross the room, where a wooden cabinet provided a plump file containing the most current papers dealing with the Hawkswood properties.

"Wiltshire?" Alexander queried softly. "I recall something to that effect, but I confess I've not had the time to go so far from the other estates. A smallish house does not command the attention Hawkswood Abbey does," he concluded, referring to his principal seat.

"Here it is," Mr. Small said cheerfully. He spread out a map and a few other papers on his desk.

Alexander rose to examine all before reluctantly assenting to the opinion voiced by Mr. Small. The village of Woodbury appeared to be the ideal place for a bolt-hole in which to hide until Camilla Shelford decided to turn her attention to some other poor chap.

"To think I should be reduced to this!" Alexander said with a grimace.

"It would appear to be as good a solution as any, my lord, and a good deal cheaper, not to mention easier on your reputation," Mr. Small suggested.

"I shan't inform anyone else of my plans, and I rely upon you to keep me informed of Miss Shelford's whereabouts," Alexander offered lightly. "I leave immediately, as soon as my man can pack. Remember, utter silence—unless there is need for communication of a sort, and in that case contact Harry Riggs. I'll leave his direction with you." Alexander immediately jotted down Harry's address, then turned to leave.

"Good luck, my lord," Mr. Small said as Alexander left the room and clattered down the stairs with great haste.

It took but a little time before Alexander saw his banker, acquired all he needed from that source, then informed his valet that they would be taking an extensive journey to the south of England. As that worthy valiantly suppressed a shudder,

Alexander offered the details while gathering a few papers he wanted.

"The hinterland, I expect one might call it," he confided with a sigh, thinking of all the delights of the Season he would be forced to forgo. That brought to mind the number of engagements that perforce must be canceled. Once his regrets were written, he handed them to his butler with instructions to send them out the following day.

Within two hours he was on the road, his curricle racing from the city quite as though he fully expected to see Camilla Shelford behind him with an archbishop in tow.

The greater distance he achieved, the more at ease he became, enjoying the lovely early summer scene as he passed green fields and patches of primroses and wild campion. Here was England at its best, fields sprouting, apple trees coming to blossom. The very air smelled of freedom.

Rather than stay at the best inns as was customary for him, he settled on quiet country hostelries, clean and respectable, but not apt to be frequented by his cronies or anyone he knew. The food proved to be filling, and often the home brewed was most splendid.

At Salisbury he felt sufficiently relaxed to spend some time prowling about the local sights, picking up a number of items he suspected might not be found in the village of Woodbury. Egads, the place was so small it was not even found in his copy of *Patterson's,* and he had thought every spot in the country was listed therein. It was a good thing he had Mr. Small's direction as a guide or he'd never have found the place.

Ultimately, he felt the urge to move on to the south and would have set off immediately had he not bumped into an old friend and accepted an invitation to visit a race course not far from Salisbury. The Downs were famous for their racing courses, and this one promised to offer excellent diversion. Once Alexander explained his predicament, Giles Dodsworth was only too happy to offer shelter and quiet anonymity.

"There is no one awaiting me; my time is my own." It occurred to Alexander that he possibly ought to drop the housekeeper a line to warn her of his coming, but figured that a single gentleman ought not cause that much of a stir. Besides, he didn't trust her not to let the surrounding gentry know of his coming, and he wanted to test the local waters on his own. He wanted no predatory females if he could avoid them. When the day inevitably came that he had to marry, *he* would select his wife.

"What a glorious day this is," Juliet cried in delight as she left the house to inspect the newly redone gardens. "Look, the wallflowers are doing well as are the aquilegia you brought me," she exclaimed to Mr. Wyllard. "Soon there will be blooms from one side of my garden to the other. And I owe it all to you," she concluded shyly with a demure glance at her companion. The sun gave a splendid glow to the garden as well as to Mr. Wyllard's ruddy countenance—the result of many hours spent supervising the planting.

In spite of his high color, he was a well-looking man, with darkish brown hair and thoughtful gray eyes. True, his hair receded a trifle and his face was a bit longish, but his excellent character more than made up for these slight defects. And character was important to Juliet. She desired steadfastness and decency in a man. Her stepbrother had revealed the other side of a man's character far too well to please her, and she wanted none of it.

However, Juliet was beginning to wonder if this masquerade was such a wonderful idea. She considered George Wyllard a very nice gentleman. He enjoyed music as did she, and his knowledge of gardening surpassed that of anyone she had ever met. Mrs. Ogleby had let it drop that he was tolerably well to grass, possessing an acceptable property and sound investments.

Juliet had not intended to look for a husband while in concealment from her stepbrother. That had been the last thing on her mind when she fled Winterton Hall that chilly morning. What a pity if Juliet came to love Mr. Wyllard and was trapped in an arrangement from which it would be near impossible to extricate herself. Why hadn't she thought of such a possibility? Pansy had warned her that trouble would undoubtedly follow from her foolishness, but Juliet had never considered what form it might take—certainly not falling in love with a gentleman such as Mr. Wyllard!

"Trouble, is what they are, my good fellow," Alexander exclaimed, lounging back in his chair in the Dodsworth dining room while studying his glass of excellent port. "Women are nothing but trouble. Take my word for it, you do not want to get involved with the lot of them."

"Oh, come now, there must be one or two who merit your attention," Giles laughingly declared.

"Attention, indeed," Alexander said with a sudden grin. "My name in marriage, I think not. At least, not at this time," he amended. "I imagine there is a fair charmer out there somewhere who might possibly capture my heart and hand."

"But you give leave to doubt it," Giles inserted, continuing the line of thought.

"Precisely," Alexander agreed.

"Perhaps I might put a wager on your chances—and then perhaps not," he amended at Alexander's sudden frown. "But I will suggest that you may find life unpredictable at best, my good friend. You never know what is around the corner."

"Indeed," Alexander mused. "Who would have thought a mere chit like Camilla Shelford could send me into hiding! Which reminds me, I had best continue on my way. Tomorrow I'll head south to Woodbury and seclusion."

"Never heard of the place myself," Giles said with a frown.

"A mere village by all accounts. It will be as dull as ditch-water without a doubt."

"Another party?" Juliet said with delight. "Life in these parts is scarcely dreary." That the local gentry had decided to do more than usual entertaining because of the presence of the supposed Hawkswood viscountess crossed her mind. What didn't occur to her was that they all felt sorry for her, sent to live quietly in the country by a heartless and very blind husband. Stupid as well. Stood to reason he must be shatter-brained to ignore such a nice girl.

The gentlemen of the area were all captivated by her, developing fatherly interest, so they claimed. The good ladies of Woodbury and that surrounding area had taken the modest girl to their collective hearts. Oh, if they could just get their hands on that viscount, the rake.

It was on a cloudy afternoon that the strange, dusty curricle entered the village. The driver, a handsome gentleman dressed in the first stare of fashion, seemed hesitant, certainly unacquainted with the area. He looked about him with a curious and searching gaze. At last he paused before the inn, the very same one where Juliet had met the Oglebys. He entered, then shortly left with a purposeful stride and an awesome frown. The children and old Widow Barnes took note, but didn't relay this uneventful tidbit to anyone.

"I must say," Alexander said to Randall, his valet, "this is a most unfriendly place in which to rusticate. I asked the way to the manor, and the man looked at me as though I were a poacher. Had a devil of a time persuading him to part with the information."

Randall, who had no high opinion of the countryside to begin with, looked suitably disgusted and murmured a sympathetic comment.

It was not long before they negotiated the lanes that led to the manor. Alexander was agreeably surprised when at their approach to the charming old house he saw sparkling windows and fresh paint. He must commend the housekeeper and caretaker—a Mrs. Bassett, by Mr. Small's notation. A lazy spiral of smoke proclaimed that the kitchen oven was in use, and, indeed, he could detect the aroma of freshly baked bread in the air. His nose twitched appreciatively at the smell, as did Randall's.

He entered the drive to the property and took note of the well-raked gravel, the abundance of late spring flowers and well-tended beds. Unusual to find such care for a never visited property. Truth to tell, he had expected serious neglect, even mildew and rot.

"Randall, take the carriage around to the back. I would enter the house before anyone knows I have come."

Seeing the wisdom of the element of surprise, the valet did as bid.

Alexander strolled along the graveled path, observing the neatly pruned trees and shrubs, beautifully planted beds, and knew a feeling as though someone lived there, resided permanently. *Amazing!*

He opened the front door without knocking first, wanting to examine the rooms without a housekeeper hovering at his elbow. The first thing that struck him was the vase of fresh flowers on the commode in the entry hall. He proceeded to the drawing room to note that everything had the same fresh look to it, as though the owner had just stepped from the room. There were flowers here as well. And his grandmother's harp looked as though she had just finished a tune. Then he espied the small worktable, a piece of needlework tumbling from the opening with the air of having been cast down but a moment ago.

Greatly puzzled, he decided that without any of the family about Mrs. Bassett had taken the house as her own, which was quite agreeable to him if she kept the place in such excellent condition. He returned to the hall to be greeted by a small exclamation of surprise from a short, plump woman.

"Lawks, sirrah, and who might you be?" The woman drew herself to her full height and held a mixing spoon as though it were a sword.

"Might you be Mrs. Bassett?" he queried before replying.

"Indeed, I am, sir. And you? I do not know you."

"No, you do not. I am Hawkswood, you see." He assumed his usual pose when announcing himself to a servant or one who was of an inferior position.

His statement brought a strange reaction. Mrs. Bassett gave him a suspicious look, then seemed to freeze. "It is about time you came," she said with a sniff. "Your wife is in the garden."

Alexander stiffened at her words. "My wife?"

"Indeed, my lord, and a sweeter lady never lived."

Stunned, Alexander turned at a sound from the end of the hall, where a door opened to allow a young woman to enter.

She was slender, with a halo of chestnut curls peeping out from beneath a scrap of a muslin morning cap, and wore a yellow morning gown of recent style. She hurried down the hall, a question on her face.

Alexander drew a sigh of relief that it was not Camilla Shelford, then noted that his supposed wife was a little beauty, her arms full of flowers and her cheeks gently kissed with the sun of past days.

"As you see, my lady, your husband has arrived." *At last* was unspoken, but the words hung in the air. Mrs. Bassett bustled off from the highly intriguing scene she would have loved to witness, but she knew her place.

"My husband?" the young beauty said in a breathless whisper as though she hoped it would be denied.

Furious, Alexander contained his anger, replying, "I am Hawkswood, madam." He was about to demand an explanation when she rushed forward to pluck at his sleeve.

"Hush," she cautioned. "Come into the library, where we can be private. I must explain."

He caught the scent of heliotrope as she hurried along at his side. She was a nice height and possessed no obvious defects. Her figure seemed excellent, and she dressed well if the yellow morning gown was any indication. Why was she here pretending to be his wife? He knew he'd never seen her before in his life.

Thrusting the flowers into a convenient vase only partly filled with flowers, Juliet turned to face the man who claimed to be Lord Hawkswood.

"I must explain." She clasped her hands before her, lacing her fingers together in a nervous gesture. "I never thought you would come here, you see. They said you never had and probably never would. I needed a place to hide."

"To hide?" Startled at these words, Alexander gestured to a pair of chairs by the window and drew her over to one, observing as he did her delicate bone structure and air of fragility— misleading, no doubt.

"I had best explain all. My name is Juliet Winterton, daughter of Viscount Winterton. Please know that I never intended to trap you into any sort of marriage, my lord. The last thing I want is to marry, especially one who is a rake." She gave him a pleading look, one that begged for patience.

Alexander winced at the way she said "rake," quite as though it were something nasty to be found under a rock. "So why are you here?"

Juliet took a deep breath, then plunged on. "My stepbrother decided to compel me to marry his good friend Robert, Lord Taunton. Marius had it all arranged, even to sending for the parson. Lord Taunton is a gamester and drunkard, a lamentable excuse for a man, as is my stepbrother if I may say so. After years of enduring Marius, I was not about to marry the same sort of man, if you follow my reasoning. So I fled." She threw up her hands at these words as though to say her actions were obvious.

"That does not explain how you came to be here posing as my wife. How did you know but that I was not already married?" Alexander shifted in his chair so he might better study Juliet, as she had introduced herself. Her eyes, he decided, were her best feature, long-lashed and a lovely amber color like aged brandy.

"First of all, I knew you were single. Your doings are frequently noted in the newspapers, my lord. And I must say, you do seem to go from one escapade to another with scarcely a letup." She gave him a scolding look such as he might have received from his mother.

"Go on," he said dryly.

"It was while Pansy and I were at the little inn in the village—I'd had a disagreement with the driver of our post chaise and dismissed him only to find that we were rather stranded. We heard some people discussing this house and you. They said you had never been here, nor were you likely to come."

"That doesn't explain why *you* are here. And how long, may I ask, have you been here?" Alexander rubbed his chin while he considered his options, wondering what Mr. Small would think of this mare's nest.

"First of all, I was looking for a place to hide from my stepbrother. I had traveled quite some distance and hunted for a situation where he would be unlikely to find me. This little village seemed perfect. It isn't even listed in my *Patterson's Roads*. So I pretended I was your estranged wife to have a place to hide." She exchanged a look with Alexander, then dropped her gaze to her lap. "As to the other, I have been here now for about two months."

"No brother as yet? It doesn't surprise me. I'd never have found the place had my solicitor not given me good directions."

"Why are *you* here, my lord? I do not mean to pry, but I would like to know. This is a rather odd place for you to be at the height of the Season, if you will pardon the observation." Juliet darted a glance at him, mindful of his height and excellence of dress. He was as handsome as his youthful portrait had promised. Only now he emanated a sort of leashed power the child had not yet attained.

Alexander thought that Juliet Winterton deserved as truthful and complete an answer as she had given him. "I, too, am in hiding. There is a willful, some say unbalanced, young woman who has taken it into her mind to marry me. I suspect she desires a title and the money more than my person."

"Oh." Juliet digested this for a moment, then said, "Well, I must say this is a wonderful place to hide. The house is charming, and Mrs. Bassett is a gem." Suddenly, she looked self-conscious. "I have done a few things—garden and mend and those sort of things a lady of the house is expected to do. I even gave a dinner. I have money of my own, so you need not think I have charged it all to you."

He merely raised his brows as though she were being silly.

Then it struck Juliet that she was actually a criminal; what she had done was punishable by law. She turned cold and said in a small voice, "I beg you, please do not turn me over to the magistrate. I will slip away and go to Canada or anywhere you wish, only I'd rather not to go court and prison."

"So you are aware that what you do is wrong?" Alexander studied the contrite face, the frightened eyes, and knew he could never expose her to such a fate. After all, she was fleeing a horrible marriage just as he did. Oddly enough, he did not doubt her tale; she had been too direct and straightforward to have been lying. Something about her eyes as well. She had stared directly into his with no sign of guile or evasion.

"Of course, but I could see nothing else to hand and this was extremely tempting." She managed a wisp of a smile, and Alexander discovered an enchanting dimple nestled beside the left corner of her mouth. A very delectable mouth, he perceived.

There were several minutes of silence in the room while the pair contemplated a possible solution.

"Let me sort this out. Mrs. Bassett and others believe I am your estranged husband. Correct?" He glanced at Juliet, who nodded vigorously in reply.

"True. I suspect they feel sorry for me, alone and unwanted as it were."

"Which undoubtedly places me in the role of a cad and a bounder to send my dear little wife to the ends of the earth while I live it up in the city." Alexander grimaced at the image that scenario prompted and winced at her eager agreement.

"I believe you have the right of it," she said in a subdued voice. "Mrs. Bassett is even now likely wondering if you are about to scold me."

"Perhaps we could help each other?" he mused and was startled at the instant flame of hope on her face. It was as though someone had lit a candle behind each of those remarkable eyes.

"How? Oh, I'd do anything to avoid marrying Lord Taunton. I will *not* be his wife and stuck in a country house with a cluster of babies and no money, for you must know that as a gamester and all he would go through my fortune in no time." She stretched out a dainty but capable hand to touch Alexander on the arm, then hastily withdrew it as though she had been burned by the contact.

Alexander cleared his throat at the image presented of Juliet surrounded by a cluster of babies and continued. "We can proceed with the deception as begun. You will portray a dutiful wife, and I the husband who is making an attempt at a reconciliation."

"We do not have to marry? I have no wish to marry you. Forgive me if you do not like that, but it is true." She gave him a clear look that revealed she spoke the truth, however uncomfortable she felt in doing so.

"No," Alexander replied gently. "I believe we can manage to avoid that distasteful state. We can take things day by day, see how we get along."

"There is a dinner party tomorrow evening at the Tackley's. I am invited, and I expect you had best make an appearance if we are to make a success of this. Must I pretend to be in love with you?" she said with a blush staining her delicate cheeks.

"Not if you find it disagreeable," he said and found he was rather put out that she objected to even pretending to be in love with him.

"And I shan't have to kiss you or hang on your arm?" she demanded in her direct manner.

"That does not appeal to you? There are many women in London who would leap at the chance," he found himself saying to his chagrin.

"Perhaps so, but I do not love you, and I could not kiss you if I had no love for you, you see."

"I am not encumbered with such nicety," he observed, "and if the situation arises where I deem it to our mutual advantage, I may kiss you. Is that acceptable?" Alexander thought this had to be the strangest conversation he had ever held in his life.

"Very well." She rose from her chair and took a step toward the door. "Why do you not settle into your room and we can discuss anything else that comes to mind over dinner. We dine later than country hours, yet not so late as London, I suppose." She looked troubled, but said nothing more.

"I would that you show me to my room. Somehow I believe Mrs. Bassett expects it of you."

Alexander watched Juliet square her shoulders as though preparing to do battle, then offer a decisive nod.

"Come, your room is clean and needs but fresh sheets and towels. No doubt Mrs. Bassett has seen to that even as we talked. It would not occur to her that you would sleep anywhere but in your own residence."

Alexander walked at Juliet's side up the curving stairs that led to the first floor and the bedrooms. As he anticipated, his room was adjacent to hers, and he smiled as she blushed when she saw him look at the connecting door.

"I do not believe there is a key for that door," she muttered.

"You may trust me, Juliet." He walked closer to her, touching her lightly on the chin so as to see her face more clearly. He could not resist those lips and touched them lightly with his own, smiling at her dazed expression.

"There was no reason to do that, my lord."

"Ah, but there was. I cannot have you going about looking like an unkissed schoolgirl. No gentleman would accept that of me. And you had best call me Alexander; all my intimate friends do."

"We may not be intimate, but I hope we might be friends," Juliet said in that small voice he found oddly appealing.

"Friends it shall be. Is it a bargain, then?" he asked, holding out his hand to her.

Hesitantly, she placed her slim hand in his. "Indeed! A bargain it shall be."

Chapter 4

He was mad, utterly, totally mad. Alexander rubbed a hand over his unshaven and shadowed chin as he stared out the window at the morning scene below. He absently took note of the splendor of the early summer garden, all the while wondering if his wits truly had gone begging. He—the man who had insisted that he would never be trapped into marriage, that no woman would trick him into that state—was well and truly caught. Never mind that she was a fetching little piece with those seductive amber eyes and that delectable dimple at the corner of a very kissable mouth. She was also a woman who thought ill of him, declaring she had no desire to marry him or any other man. He winced again at the memory of her contempt as she had used the word *rake*.

Blast! How would he ever extricate himself from this mess? He raked his fingers through his dark hair in frustration. Could they pull the deception off? He thought with hope that *if* no one came from town, and *if* no one read the papers, and *if* neither her family nor his got wind of this supposed marriage, they might each eventually go their separate ways. And pigs might fly.

On the other hand, Juliet was *not* Camilla Shelford! He imagined he could tolerate an alliance with the delicious and aggravating Juliet should it prove unavoidable. Their first test would come this evening at the dinner party given by some local gentry. Tackley, he thought Juliet had said. Perhaps it would be well to discuss how they would act? After all, if they were to play roles, they had parts to learn.

Randall entered the room, and Alexander turned to request

his clothes for the day and then submit to the valet's ministrations.

Juliet sank down on the pretty window seat in her bedroom. She gave an apprehensive look at the closed door between her room and *his*. Her pretend husband—Alexander—he was a rake, a womanizer, a man who would attract women like flowers attracted bees. Recalling his seductive voice, even when angered, she wondered how a woman resisted such a man. She sighed deeply. For a woman who had determined never to marry a rake she had put her foot in it this time.

What on earth could she do now? She was not so naive as to think they could emerge from this bumblebroth unscathed. But to what extent would she be punished and how?

Still, he was not Lord Taunton. There might have been gossip about Alexander in the newspapers, and he certainly was devilishly handsome—putting the chinless Lord Taunton totally in the shade. But the truth of the matter was that he appeared to live up to his reputation—kissing her because he didn't want an unkissed schoolgirl for a wife! Even were it true, he had promised to behave. Was she afraid he would or wouldn't do it again?

She drew her legs up, then wrapped her arms about them, resting her chin on her knees. Could they fool the people of Woodbury? Mrs. Tackley had known the viscount's grandmama. That was a danger. What other pitfalls lurked in their way she couldn't imagine, but she guessed she had best discuss the matter with Alexander. He had taken charge yesterday, and without a doubt he would take charge again. Truth be known—and she would never have admitted it to a soul—it was rather good to have another who knew her secret and was to help in one way or another.

Pansy opened the door, nudging it aside while balancing a tray upon which sat a cup of steaming chocolate and some buttered toast. "Morning," the maid said with her usual terseness. "Trouble is still here, I see. His man came down for hot water while I was getting your chocolate and toast. Nothin' but trouble, missy."

"You think I do not know that?" Juliet moved to accommodate the tray in her lap and munched toast and sipped hot chocolate in silence while Pansy nattered on about the day to come and what did Miss Juliet intend to wear to the dinner that evening.

"Not *Miss* Juliet, Pansy. Madam or my lady. And you must remember it, particularly now that his lordship is here." Juliet glanced again at the closed door and set the tray aside, the toast forgotten.

"Your yellow muslin, madam?" Pansy asked with a gloomy manner.

"That's better," Juliet muttered and proceeded to dress for the morning confrontation. That there would be one, she had not the least doubt.

When she marched down the curving stairs to the ground floor, she searched the area to see if Alexander was around. Then she nearly jumped out of her skin when a voice came from behind her.

"I am here, and as soon as we have broken our fast, we had better discuss what is to be done." Alexander joined her, keeping his distance as might be expected from a gentleman whose wife was not quite pleased with him.

Juliet thought back to various novels she had read. Not one of them dwelt with the problem of an estranged couple. In the future she would ignore all those Gothic books and look for something more helpful.

Pansy had added a frilled betsy over Juliet's gown, and Juliet found it very useful to occupy her nervous fingers. It was pointless to try to eat a thing, but she did manage to sip a cup of hot tea. Lord Hawkswood had no such difficulty, it seemed. He loaded his plate and ate a hearty meal, drinking several cups of coffee as well.

Randall brought in the latest London newspaper, one only four days old, and his lordship hastily scanned the paper for scandalous tattle about Society characters. His twisted smile indicated something amused him.

"Is there anything of import, my lord?" Juliet ventured to ask.

He folded the paper and handed it to Juliet by way of reply. It took but moments to spot the item that had caught his eye. "Lord H has disappeared, leaving Miss S in tears and on the hunt," she read softly. "No need to explain that, I expect."

"If you are finished with that tea, perhaps we might have our little discussion now?" He glanced at Randall, who left the room, taking the paper with him.

Alexander rose to escort his little "wife" to the library. He had figured that the room offered the greatest privacy while affording comfortable chairs in which to sit. He carefully closed the doors behind them when once inside and thoughtfully eyed Juliet.

She was nervous of him, perhaps afraid of the consequences of her actions—as she well ought to be. There was no point in recriminations now; it was too late.

"Well, my lady? You had best tell me what you have said about me to the local gentry. The more I know of our circumstances, the better."

Juliet gave his lordship, the man who insisted she had better call him Alexander, a wary look. "You may not like this," she cautioned.

"I don't like any of this entire mare's nest, but I had still best know of it." He leaned back in his chair, his chin propped on one elegant hand as he watched her, reminding her of a cat watching its prey.

"I said you preferred to remain in London. If I hinted you had more interesting things to do and more fascinating women to amuse you, that is most likely all," she confessed.

"You portrayed the little woman abandoned by a heartless rake who'd rather be anywhere but with you, is that it?" His eyes were all that revealed his anger with her and what she had said. Juliet had never considered gray eyes particularly expressive. Alexander proved her wrong, for his eyes snapped with his unspoken ire.

Juliet licked her lips and shredded the bit of cambric in her hands. "I suppose you could put it that way."

"So how do we proceed from this point? I have come to find you—they will think—and do I desire a reconciliation with my pretty little bride? I expect so," he mused. "What man after taking a look at you would accept that a man such as myself could leave you alone?"

"What does that involve?" Juliet dared to ask. His words had sent shivers up her spine for some reason.

"Think of it like a play," he advised. "At first you must pretend to be vastly annoyed with me."

"That should not be difficult," Juliet murmured.

"Quiet," he snapped, then continued. "You will have to appear to warm up to me by degrees, a slow process involving a bit of courting on my part."

"Courting?" Juliet inquired, seizing the one word that had leaped out at her like a red flag.

"Little presents, nosegays of flowers, my attentions, that is all," he said with what Juliet thought to be a very wicked little smile and a curious light in his eyes.

"What attentions? I want to be prepared." She bravely met his gaze, tilting her chin in mock defiance.

"Holding your hand, for instance."

He suited his words and picked up her hand. Only he didn't merely hold it, he subtly caressed it, minute moves that sent tingles up her arm and to her heart. *Mercy!* If this was holding her hand, she didn't think she would survive anything stronger. She had better learn the worst of it.

"And?" she asked without a quaver in her voice.

"I expect I ought to slip my arm about you when in public. Nothing ostentatious, of course, but little touches are a sign of affection between a couple."

"What should I do while all this is going on?" she queried, proud of her steady voice.

"At first I think you must tilt up your chin and ignore me with disdain as you just did now. I am certain you should be very good at that," he added wryly. "Then in time you must accept my little touches, perhaps even return them. It would give the impression that I am succeeding in my wooing and you are being an excellent wife."

"By all means I should be an excellent wife," she said with the same degree of sarcasm.

"Now, Juliet," he began, then stopped. Appearing to change his mind about what he'd intended to say, he shook his head and said, "No, you may appear mocking to begin with, for you do not trust me at the moment, do you?"

"In truth, or this bit of fiction?" Juliet said, thinking he understood her all too well.

"Both, I suppose," he said. Then he proceeded to outline a number of other things she ought to know about him and quizzed her gently about her past, learning a great deal more than she suspected.

"Is that all, *Alexander*?" Juliet rose from her chair when he appeared to have concluded his instructions.

"Dear Juliet, I shall likely think of something else, but I trust you have duties to attend to this morning."

"Indeed. Mr. Wyllard is coming to assist me with planning the rose garden."

"Mr. Wyllard?" Something about the way Juliet said the name alerted Alexander to trouble.

"A local widower who is an expert gardener. He has been enormous help to me these past weeks, offering advice and giving me special plants. Mr. Lumpkin, the man Mrs. Bassett found to serve as gardener, is not very helpful, although certainly useful."

"And Mr. Wyllard is . . . helpful, that is," Alexander concluded, vowing to put a spike in Wyllard's aspirations should it be necessary. Although why he should care was beyond him.

"He is above all things wonderful," Juliet said quietly. "He is most thoughtful and astonishingly knowledgeable about plants. He also plays the clavichord." She dimpled a smile at Alexander. "We often play duets together, he on the clavichord and I on the harp."

Alexander watched as she flitted from the room like a golden sprite. Oh, she definitely was trouble, and he wondered how she had managed to learn those wiles deep in the country with nary a gentleman to practice them on.

He strolled to the drawing room, but instead of studying the newspaper as he'd intended to do, he found himself standing at the window, watching as Juliet greeted a gentleman, obviously the famous Mr. Wyllard.

Hmm, Alexander thought, pretty dull stuff. The chap's garb was countrified, his hair receding, his manner looked to be slightly awkward as well. Yet little Juliet looked at the fellow with great respect and smiled at him in a way she'd not smiled at Alexander.

Retreating to a chair where he could read his paper as well as keep an eye on the proceedings in the garden, Alexander tried to concentrate on the news. His gaze kept drifting to the scene in the garden. This girl clearly needed a keeper. Did she realize how those smiles might impress a man? Did it occur to her that touching his arm in just that way was a flirtatious gesture, one she ought not use?

At last Alexander gave up trying to read and wandered from the house into the garden to confront the man he supposed must be his rival for Juliet's affections. Rival, that is, purely in assumption.

"Oh!" Juliet cried when he rounded the corner to where they debated the merits of several kinds of roses. "My lord, that is, er, Alexander." There was no way she could possibly have looked more flustered or guilty.

He strolled to her side, picked up her hand to place it tenderly on his arm, and smiled benignly at her. "My dear, will you not introduce me to your . . . gardener friend?"

Alexander caught the momentary flash of anger in her eyes as she looked up at him before she turned to make the introduction.

Mr. Wyllard looked properly impressed with his lordship in all his London garb—a coat from the finest tailor to be had, breeches that revealed an athletic form, and boots so polished he could see his reflection in them. When Mr. Wyllard brought his gaze to meet Alexander's, he took a step backward.

Alexander, without saying one word, made it plain to Mr. Wyllard that Juliet belonged to Alexander and that no poaching was to be allowed. He placed a hand over hers and gently patted it, looking down at Juliet with what was deliberately intended to be a possessive air.

"Perhaps we can discuss this later, at a better time," Mr. Wyllard stammered, giving Juliet a distressed look.

"I would not dream of interrupting a discussion on roses, my dear sir. What do you suggest? *I* believe fragrance to be important." Alexander dredged up from the back of his excellent memory some information given him by the head gardener at the Abbey to casually toss it out, thereby causing Juliet to stare up at him in openmouthed amazement.

"I had no idea you knew anything about roses, my, er, Alexander," she said, clearly awed.

Repressing a smile, Alexander patted her hand again and shrugged. "But then, did you try to learn about my interests, my dear?" He decided she was not to have it all her way. By Jove, a man could take so much, and he was not about to continue being pictured as the guilty party of this farce.

They continued to discuss the possible roses for the garden, Mr. Wyllard turning more and more to Alexander with suggestions and additional information as to what variety did well locally.

Just as Mr. Wyllard was about to make his departure, Juliet spoke up. "Have you forgotten we are to entertain this evening, George?"

He paled at her use of his first name, darting a glance at the formidable Lord Hawkswood before replying, "I do recall, my lady. If you wish, we could run through the piece now. I am entirely at your disposal."

The three of them left the garden to enter the drawing room, where Mr. Wyllard took refuge at the clavichord.

Juliet seated herself at the harp, placed so as to capture the morning sun on her music and thus on herself.

Rather than leave them, Alexander, in the spirit of the moment, lounged back in the one really comfortable chair in the room and prepared to suffer the amateurs.

Instead, he heard an exceptionally talented harpist and a decently accomplished musician at the clavichord attack a Mozart sonata someone had arranged for the two instruments.

"Very nice, indeed, Juliet. And you as well, Mr. Wyllard. Although there is one passage I rather like to hear thus." And Alexander walked to the clavichord to render a section of the music perfectly, thankful that this was one piece he had learned.

Juliet immediately rang for tea, and the three of them sat discussing music and roses until Mr. Wyllard reluctantly decided that he really had to leave.

When he had gone, she rounded on Alexander like a spitting cat. "Did you really have to do that? Did you have to be so superior to poor Mr. Wyllard with your knowledge of roses and music?"

He shrugged, aware he walked a fine line here. "My dear *wife,* I desired your local friend to know that I am not only his superior, but that I am capable of assisting you, joining you in any activity you may desire, and that I will brook no poaching on my territory."

"Dear heaven, I would hate to cross you," she muttered.

"But dearest, you already have," he replied with equally devastating quiet.

"Do you actually play the clavichord, or was that a smattering of music you happened to know?" she demanded.

"Oh, I truly do play. Not that particular piece by memory, but most anything if I have the music. I must say, dear little *wife,* my grandmother would dote on you to hear you play as you do." Then he dropped his mockery and added, "You amaze me, for you play incredibly well."

"Thank you," Juliet replied, clearly bemused by this turn of events. She cleared her throat, then suggested, "You would like to hazard a duet with me?"

"Where is your music?" he countered, not about to agree to a duet unless he knew what he was getting into. They hunted through the assortment of music contained in the canterbury to find a simple sonata both knew somewhat.

Thus it was that when Mrs. Bassett paused by the drawing room door, thinking that the nice Mr. Wyllard had remained, she discovered Lord and Lady Hawkswood in a lovely duet. Juliet at the harp delighted the ear with lush arpeggios while his lordship at the clavichord produced chords and harmonious accompaniment.

Mrs. Bassett went to the kitchen to tell Cook, "I have never in my life heard anything so wonderful as the music those two make."

"That is a lovely sonata," Juliet said when she dropped her hands into her lap to study her most remarkable "husband." "Do you have any more surprises up your sleeve?"

"I believe I shall just continue to astonish you. If I were to give you advance warning, it would spoil all the fun. Now, allow me to go over the accounts with Mrs. Bassett and consider what may need doing—that you have not already handled," he added with a gallant bow.

They had a truce of sorts the rest of the afternoon until it came time to leave for the Tackley dinner party.

Juliet was almost dressed, needing only a necklace, her shawl, and gloves to complete her ensemble, when the door to the adjacent room opened and Alexander strode into the center of the bedroom. She gestured to Pansy to leave, which the maid did most reluctantly. Juliet picked up her pearls and clasped them about her neck while watching Alexander.

"I assume there is good reason for this intrusion, my lord?" she questioned firmly. She had never seen a man in his shirtsleeves before and found it most unsettling—all that fine cambric through which muscles and skin could be seen.

Black stockinet breeches over black hose fit him far too well, and his black evening pumps would likely put the local gentlemen into a green melancholy. What seemed to be giving him a problem was his cravat. At least, he held a length of linen in his hand, a frustrated expression on his face.

"Randall had to press my coat, and I have no desire to try this myself. Can you tie a cravat?" He looked at her then, really looked. She felt his gaze as it traveled up her simple silk gown of palest green until he reached the scalloped sleeves edged with fine lace and then studied the ivory satin sash tied beneath her bosom, she felt sure with a connoisseur's eye.

"That is all wrong, my dear. Allow me." Placing his cravat

carefully on her bed, he pulled her close to him, undoing her sash with impatient fingers.

"You appear to have had much practice at undoing sashes, my lord," Juliet said evenly.

He glanced down at her and smiled, rather grimly, she thought.

"Do not try to tease me, Juliet. I can best you at every corner." He efficiently looped the satin, tying an exquisite little bow off to one side instead of the center as Pansy had done. When Juliet glanced in the looking glass, she could see it was far nicer.

"Another of your many talents? Perhaps I may be able to dispense with Pansy in that case," she shot at him without thinking what she said.

"If you mean that, I just may take you up on it." His eyes danced with mirth, and Juliet was quite mortified when she realized what she had uttered in annoyance.

"Of course I did not mean it, my lord," she snapped, vexed at the effect Alexander had on her.

"Pity, that. Well, if you cannot manage a simple bow, I scarcely think you can cope with a cravat." He touched her cheek lightly, then added, "You look very nice this evening, my Juliet. I trust all will go well and that we shall be able to convince these good people that we are indeed husband and wife, estranged but working at renewing our marriage."

Juliet found it difficult to reply with him standing so close to her. She managed a smile of sorts and stepped away from his disturbing presence to pick up her shawl and gloves. "Indeed. Our reputations may depend upon it."

"I fear my reputation may have preceded me, if what you told me is correct. Do you think you can redeem me, dear Juliet?"

"Do not mock me so, or no one will ever believe you desire to reconcile with me," Juliet scolded, draping the shawl about her shoulders.

She found him close once again, adjusting her shawl, his fingers brushing her tender skin with careless regard.

"They will believe what I wish them to believe, and *that* is that I do desire you. Make no mistake, my dear, when this evening is over, they will be convinced of it."

Juliet was a-twitter with nerves when they entered the Tackley residence. She wasn't sure if it was the touch of Alexander's fingers against her bare skin or his softly worded threat that affected her the more.

"Dear Lady Hawkswood, Lord Hawkswood. I declare, what a lovely surprise, your coming to Woodbury," Mrs. Tackley directed to his lordship. She and her dormouse of a husband stood in the over-decorated entry to greet their dinner guests. The lady's glance darted from Juliet to Alexander, no doubt in an effort to see how his lordship was received by their little friend.

Someway, without Juliet realizing how he did it, Alexander drew her close to his side, smiled down at her, then bestowed one of those devilishly handsome smiles—the sort that made Juliet's heart flutter—on their hostess, and she could see he had won the night.

Contrary to London custom, married couples were seated next to one another, so when Juliet removed her gloves to eat, Alexander could plainly see her hands.

"Wherever did you find that ring?" he asked in an undertone while the conversation was general about them.

"I found it in the library desk," she murmured in reply while sampling the soup.

He paused to give her hand with the ring on it another look, then said, "I believe it is my mother's. How appropriate." Which remark he was unable to amplify, causing Juliet to wonder why on earth was it appropriate for her of all people to be wearing his late mother's ring.

Perhaps it was the customary ring for the Viscountess Hawkswood to wear, in which case, why was it sitting in the desk at the manor instead of the vault at his abbey?

Juliet pretended to be somewhat in charity with Alexander, just as they had discussed. She hoped to give the impression of a woman who needs to be persuaded to love again, which was difficult when she hadn't loved in the first place.

"I knew your grandmother well, my lord, when she lived in

the manor house. I have not seen her these many years," Mrs. Tackley said between courses, signaling the footman to hand his lordship a sorbet.

"Indeed? She is still well, lives in London, and is the terror of Society," Alexander said with just the right amount of amusement, so that his hearers were not certain if he joked or it was the truth.

"You have met his grandmother, my lady?" Mrs. Tackley asked, pouncing on Juliet when she had just placed a spoonful of sorbet in her mouth.

Swallowing gave her time to think of an answer, which proved not to be necessary when Alexander answered on her behalf.

"Unfortunately, my wife enjoys country life and Grandmama loves the city. Perhaps I can persuade Juliet to join me in London so they may meet?" He turned to study Juliet as she sat in silence at his side.

She wondered if her smile was as strained as she felt. They were on thin ground here, and they both knew it.

Mercifully, it was time for the ladies to retreat to the drawing room. Juliet gave Alexander a warning glance before she left the table, then braved the cluster of women gathered, it seemed, to question her regarding her husband.

"My dear Lady Hawkswood, you must have been very surprised when your husband so gallantly arrived on your doorstep. I vow I think it vastly romantic, do you not, Fanny?" Mrs. Tackley concluded with a look at her friend.

"Indeed," Mrs. Ogleby agreed. "I am glad to see that he *has* returned to you, my dear. Anyone can see he is besotted with you, but then, why not? You are the prettiest of creatures."

Juliet doubted Alexander had truly looked besotted. She suspected Mrs. Ogleby saw what she wished to see. Uncomfortable with the conversation, she longed for the gentlemen to join them and perhaps survive the evening with Alexander to support her.

"I trust you will entertain us with a duet this evening? It was good of you to send over your harp. If only my girls were musical, but then they spend their time with needlework and improving books," Mrs. Tackley intoned.

Juliet gave her an uneasy smile, then sighed with relief when the gentlemen appeared in the doorway, two by two like so many creatures for the ark.

She rose and thought to ask Mr. Wyllard if he was ready to play when Alexander forestalled her, murmuring, "We had best do our duet. I have just endured a bit of heavy going with jests regarding your Mr. Wyllard. There will be no more of that, I assure you."

Juliet flashed him a furious look, then, realizing she had to be most proper, took a seat by the harp. Once absorbed in her music, she forgot her ire. At the conclusion of the duet, the gathering applauded enthusiastically, as well they might, Juliet thought. Alexander and she had gone quite nicely.

But she would still see Mr. Wyllard. Alexander was not going to stop their friendship.

Chapter 5

The week after the Tackley dinner went by faster than Juliet would have believed. As well, her firm demand that Alexander stay out of her room had been honored, somewhat to her surprise. She had thought his a piecrust promise, the sort made to be broken.

Given his background and the gossip she had gleaned about him, she had fully expected to end up pushing a chest in front of the connecting door so she might retain her privacy and whatever else a young woman was supposed to keep to herself. For reasons she did not understand she was loathe to put up such a barrier. Perhaps it revealed a distrust of him, and oddly enough she wanted to trust him, or at least allow him to think she did.

She was startled when he sauntered from the house to join her in the garden. A quick search of his face revealed nothing to her. The gray eyes were as inscrutable as ever.

"Our truce goes well," Alexander said quietly. "Mrs. Bassett seems to have the impression that we are settling our differences. I believe she fancies there might eventually be the patter of little feet around the house. She just asked me if I wished to have the furniture in the nursery replaced; it appears it is a trifle shabby. The heir to a viscountcy ought not begin life in an inferior crib, it seems." His grin mocked her.

"Good heavens!" Juliet cried softly in dismay. "I'd not thought we were *that* convincing. Perhaps I am destined for a life on the stage in that event."

"So you realize you cannot go back to being Miss Winterton of Winterton Hall when you leave here?" he inquired quietly, taking her arm to guide her along a garden path and away from the house.

"I would say that there are a great number of things preferable to being Lady Taunton! A life on the stage could be one of them," Juliet snapped. She did not add that even being married to Alexander was better than Taunton, but the thought hung in the air between them.

"I asked Randall if he was acquainted with your Lord Taunton and amazingly enough he had heard of the chap. I apologize if ever I seemed to question your aversion to the man. Randall informed me that Taunton is a thoroughly bad fellow. He's not the sort of man your father would wish to marry his daughter."

Juliet paused, turning to face him. "My instincts were right, then. It was a good thing I ran away from a marriage with him."

"I believe the common phrase is out of the frying pan and into the fire," Alexander responded dryly. "I cannot imagine what you'd confront were you to attempt to convince your brother that a marriage to Taunton is displeasing. Worse come to worst, you should be prepared to make this marriage of ours a reality."

"But surely you do not want such a thing," Juliet countered. "Neither of us wished to wed," she reminded. Although the man she thought existed behind the facade of Lord Hawkswood was not quite the same as she was finding to be true. He had been charming company—but of course a rake would be—and he had honored his word—but perhaps he thought her so unappealing it was no difficulty to keep away from her. That thought was so distressing that she resolved to be a trifle more amiable to him.

"How do you feel about that possibility?" he countered.

"I haven't the faintest idea," Juliet replied in kind, but somewhere deep inside the idea that marriage to Alexander would be vastly different, perhaps more agreeable, than to anyone else she had ever met took root and began to grow.

They strolled along the graveled path in reasonable harmony, giving rise to hopes that they might make it through a day without an argument. Their accord ended when Mr. Wyllard rounded the distant corner, a potted plant in hand.

"Ah, I see your country swain has arrived," Alexander said in an undertone.

"He is not my swain, and why do you call him that simply because he carries a plant for the garden?" Juliet quibbled.

"He is much taken with you, and make no mistake on that score. Were I not here, he would be making genteel love to you." Alexander drew to a halt, turning her to face him.

"Alexander!" Juliet whispered, utterly scandalized at his words, glaring at him with furious eyes.

"Lovely," Alexander said, his eyes crinkling up with barely concealed mirth. He bent to kiss her, quickly and most efficiently. "There, let the chap see who is lord and master here."

"You are not my lord and master," Juliet declared softly, quite forgetting her resolve to improve relations with Alexander.

"*He* thinks so," Alexander reminded her. "I merely wished to remind him where he stands. And that, my dear *wife,* is on the outside, looking in, so to speak. As I mentioned before, I allow no poaching on this particular property."

"I am not your property, you know—any more than you are my lord and master." She stamped a slippered foot, then wished she hadn't, for the feel of the gravel was not kind to her feet.

"Tell that to a judge," Alexander murmured with a chuckle.

"Oh, you are impossible."

"Good morning, Wyllard," Alexander said in a pleasant voice, quite unlike the nasty, insinuating whisper that had reached her ears moments ago.

"G . . . good morning, my lord," Mr. Wyllard replied, looking most uncomfortable. Doubtless he was one of the many who felt a husband and wife ought not be demonstrative in public—even if this was their private garden. He was here, and they both knew it.

He came closer, and Alexander observed that the chap's gaze settled on Juliet's hand where it rested against Alexander's chest—in protest, if Wyllard but knew it. Alexander glanced down to note the absence of any betrothal ring. Juliet wore the simple gold band his mother had worn until she'd died—here. He decided that had best be remedied, but he'd say nothing to her about it now when Wyllard was within hearing.

"I promised you an autumn anemone, my lady," Wyllard said, holding up a plant that had nice green leaves and not a hint of a bud. "As the name implies, it blooms late in the summer until the frost. The flower is a fiery red," he concluded, faltering somewhat under Alexander's sardonic stare.

"Most appropriate," Alexander murmured wickedly.

"How thoughtful you are, sir," Juliet said more warmly than she otherwise might. She gave Alexander an admonishing look, then went forward to greet her guest.

"I suppose you have already heard the news," Mr. Wyllard offered hesitantly.

"That depends on the news," Alexander replied, languidly strolling over to lean against a statue that graced one side of the path.

"Old Mr. Taunton died. I imagine his nephew will come to look over his inheritance one of these days."

Fortunately, Mr. Wyllard was in the act of placing the autumn anemone in the flower bed where it was intended to go and did not see the look of alarm that flashed across Juliet's face before she might compose herself.

Alexander, however, had seen that expression of horror compounded with fear, and rapidly put things together. "His nephew is young Lord Taunton, lately of London, I believe?" Alexander inquired just to make certain his suspicions were correct.

"So I understand," Mr. Wyllard replied, a bit more comfortable now that Lord Hawkswood had moved away from Juliet. He began to explain about the plant he had brought, how high it could be expected to grow and a little about the charm of the flowers when in bloom.

Alexander wandered off to the house, knowing full well that the chap was far too timid to do anything untoward while Alexander was in residence. He didn't know why he felt so fiercely possessive regarding Juliet, but he did. Perhaps it was because he knew there was likely but one conclusion to this farce, regardless of Juliet's talk of going on the stage or any other proffered solution.

He settled on a chair, prepared to wait for Juliet to come back to the house, as he suspected she would before long. They needed to discuss what was to be done regarding the possibility of Taunton's appearance in the little village. There would be slight chance that Taunton would not see Juliet.

What the likelihood might be of convincing Taunton that there was a marriage was something else. Alexander would have to persuade Juliet that drastic measures might be necessary.

He found he was proven right about Juliet within twenty minutes.

"There you are; I have been searching for you," she said brightly when she paused in the doorway. She glanced back in the hall, gave an order to Mrs. Bassett, then walked close to where Alexander sat. "We had best find someplace to talk where we cannot easily be overheard," she murmured.

"Whatever you think," Alexander replied, rising swiftly from his chair. "This room is obviously not good—the library, perhaps?"

"The maid is cleaning the windows. Perhaps upstairs? My bedroom?" she asked casually while blushing a delightful pink.

For an answer, he took her arm to guide her to where the stairs curved upward. The entry was devoid of activity, and chances were they could reach Juliet's room without detection if they hurried. He led a brisk pace up the steps, then along the hall to her room. It was empty.

"Mr. Taunton's death presents complications," Juliet began once the door was safely shut behind them. "If there is any money involved, I feel sure that Robert Taunton will be here as soon as may be."

"No doubt you have the right of it," Alexander replied slowly. "Can you convince him you have married in such a rush, without your brother's permission, or your father's for that matter?"

"With Papa in Russia, that is a moot point, but surely he would think a viscount preferable to a mere baron?" Juliet said with a decided twinkle in her eyes. "Besides, I am one and twenty, so I am my own mistress, so to speak. Marius had thought to see me wed before then, and he missed."

"You had a birthday after you came here?"

She looked self-conscious and nodded. "Indeed, it was the day after you arrived. We never have made much of birthdays, particularly after Mama died. With Papa gone, it was just Miss Pritchard and I to eat a piece of cake. Since she is not here, it scarcely seemed worth mentioning. Indeed, I quite forgot about it."

"I see." Alexander took a turn about the room, not believing that last bit. He'd not known birthday parties or the like, but he thought a pretty little thing such as Juliet should have had more than her governess and a cake. And that she would forget the date also seemed unlikely. Women were always more sentimental about such things, he'd found.

"I shall do my best to convince Lord Taunton, you may be sure," she continued. "Although . . . I do not know what he could do about it even if he doesn't believe me. He can scarcely cart me off like a lost parcel, or could he?" Juliet's eyes looked worried, and Alexander crossed to give her a comforting pat on her shoulder.

"You appear to have satisfied everyone so far. Indeed, there are moments—such as over the dinner table—that I am almost persuaded myself." He grinned down at her earnest face, then added, "I find I must go to Salisbury, and the sooner I go the better. I shall return shortly, you may rest certain on that score."

"Contrary to what you may think, I am resigned to your company, for I see it is necessary now." Juliet avoided meeting his gaze, crossing over to the window seat, where she settled before looking at him.

Alexander gave her a most thoughtful stare, then went through to his bedroom to prepare for a fast drive to Salisbury. He wished he had his stallion here, but the lack of a speedy horse could not be helped. His curricle would have to do for the trip. He made certain he had enough money and the letter of credit Mr. Small had given him should it prove desirable, then he soon ran down the stairs and out to the stables. Within thirty minutes he was gone.

Juliet watched the dust slowly settle back to the lane after the curricle had disappeared. The tension slowly ebbed from her shoulders, and she relaxed against the window surround to contemplate what was to be done.

That Lord Taunton would show in Woodbury she had little doubt. However, she had great confidence that she, together with Lord Hawkswood, could manage to convince the man that they were indeed wed. As to the details, she had meant to ask Alexander when and where they had been "married," for she hadn't a clue what to say to that question should anyone ask. When he returned from Salisbury, she would tax him with that little matter, and then perhaps she could rest easier.

But Alexander did not return to Woodbury that evening. Juliet wandered distractedly about the drawing room, plucking halfheartedly at the harp, picking out a melody on the clavichord. She requested dinner be delayed until Mrs. Bassett kindly suggested that it would be spoilt if she did not eat it. It was a lonely meal. She wondered what he might be about in that city and tried to picture him there, for she had paused in Salisbury on her flight for her freedom from Marius and Lord Taunton.

He would be at the finest inn, she suspected, dining well and enjoying fine wines. Perhaps he sought to replenish the cellar at Hawkswood Manor? Or maybe he had another reason? Like a woman? A sharp pang shot through her at the very notion of Alexander with another woman. She'd be beautiful, no doubt. He'd not tolerate mediocrity in anything. Why this idea should upset her so very much she chose not to examine too closely.

Then again, he may have encountered a friend or two and remained to enjoy their company. She and Alexander had been a trifle confined here, and she could understand his pleasure in other company. She resolved to do something about that.

In Salisbury Alexander checked the list he had made, worriedly rubbing his chin as he considered what remained to be done. He ought to have thought to tell Juliet he would be gone overnight, but he was not accustomed to giving an account of his time to anyone, never mind that he had become used to her company. And truth to tell, he had hoped to complete his business in the town much more quickly than he had. It was frustrating to deal with strangers who did not know his tastes.

The ring had proven the most difficult. At last he had found a setting that pleased him, and a yellow diamond that had the proper brilliance and perfect cut. He felt it would complement Juliet's unusual coloring. Otherwise, he had bought wines, a pretty fan he wanted as a belated birthday gift for her, and a few other necessities for himself.

He missed her. He turned in early, determined to pick up the ring as soon as it was ready, then head back to Woodbury at a goodly clip. Not that he would tell her he'd missed her. Oddly enough, he, who had the admiration of a good many women in Society, was unsure of precisely where he stood with his pretend wife.

Juliet woke feeling that something was wrong. She stared up at the golden fabric over her head until she remembered. Alexander had not come home last evening. He had stayed in Salisbury for unknown reasons, and she had missed him dreadfully, going to bed at an early hour, right after her dinner. A dreary evening alone was not to be contemplated. Alexander was most amusing, and she had enjoyed their music making very much. His playing was improving, what with a bit of practice. Juliet had guessed he was not given to playing much while in London.

Pansy brought in chocolate and rolls, her thoughts plain on her face.

"Good morning," Juliet offered. "I believe I'll wear my yellow dress this morning." Juliet hoped that Alexander was not as tired of her gowns as she was. But then none of the few men she had known had ever paid the least attention to what she wore, and there was little reason to think Alexander was otherwise.

"Indeed, my lady," Pansy said with a sniff.

For the first time Juliet eyed her maid with less than charity.

"I understand there is a very capable young woman in Woodbury who is aching to become a lady's maid."

Pansy's head shot round, and she gave her mistress an uncertain look. "Indeed?" the maid replied carefully.

"Remember that, if you please, should you contemplate expressing any thoughts likely to be displeasing to me."

Juliet dressed slowly, then allowed a very subdued Pansy to dress her hair, placing a wisp of a cap atop her chestnut curls when done.

Leaving her maid to consider what had been implied, Juliet went down to a lonely breakfast. Odd, how one could become accustomed to a voice, a face, a person.

Following her light meal, she settled herself with a piece of needlepoint until she realized that she was short a particular color. "Oh, bother," she exclaimed, thinking she had best go to the village to see if she might find more of the same yarn.

It took but a few minutes to don a pretty little chip straw bonnet, tie its ribands under her chin, then take off in the direction of the village shop that sold practically everything one would want in basic necessities.

She was delighted to find yarn to precisely match the snippet she'd brought with her. After exchanging pleasantries with the shopkeeper, she left to begin her walk back to Hawkswood Manor when she caught sight of a traveling coach entering the village. No coward she, she remained where she stood, waiting to see if the worst proved true.

The children of the village came tumbling forth from various cottages, agog at the sight of a grand traveling carriage with a crest on the door panels. Dogs barked, women paused in their activities, and the innkeeper came to the door of his establishment to see what all the fuss was about.

The coach drew to a halt, and when the door opened, Juliet was dismayed to see not Lord Taunton, but Marius! He stepped down, then said something to another person within. In moments Lord Taunton joined Marius to stand looking about the village with scornful gazes.

Juliet wished she had prudently ignored the lack of yarn, that she'd not paused to chat with the shopkeeper, and that she was at home in her garden. Marius, of all people, and with Alexander gone to Salisbury!

She might as well get the worst over with and greet Marius, thus perhaps securing an advantage over her stepbrother, at least for the nonce. Juliet courageously advanced.

"What a surprise, Marius. I scarcely expected to see you in Woodbury." Her words had the effect of a quiet bomb.

He whirled about and stared openmouthed at his stepsister.

"I daresay when you journeyed with Lord Taunton to survey his inheritance, you didn't think to see me."

"What are you doing here?" he demanded, taking several threatening steps toward her before realizing a great many of the village inhabitants were his audience.

"Once you have located the Taunton home, perhaps you will wish to visit with me at mine?" she said with a demure smile, holding her small package before her like a shield.

"What do you mean—yours?" he inquired nastily. "We never owned any property in this godforsaken village."

"I know," she agreed sweetly while edging away from him and his friend. "My husband does. Ask anyone how to reach Hawkswood Manor when you are ready to see me," Juliet said, then hurried off in the direction of her home without seeming to speed in the slightest.

Marius was so astounded at her last remark that he likely couldn't have chased after her had he thought of it.

As Juliet rounded the first of the turns in the lane, she heard Lord Taunton demanding to know what the devil was going on. Juliet grimly smiled as she considered how Marius would explain this to Lord Taunton.

Fairly running to the house, she dashed up the stairs to her room, and once safely there, tossed her small parcel on her bed, then followed it with her bonnet. "Drat! Double drat! and blast!" she cried. "Lord Taunton, I expected, but not Marius!"

Knowing that she had little time in which to prepare her welcome for the two most unwelcome guests, she informed Mrs. Bassett that it was most likely her stepbrother and his friend would be putting up at the house for a day or so.

"Do not give them the best chambers, nor ones close to

mine," she instructed. "Ah, Marius snores dreadfully," she temporized.

Mrs. Bassett, being nobody's fool, rightly guessed her mistress did not welcome these guests and set about arranging two guest rooms to suit her ladyship. On one of her trips through the kitchen while carrying fresh linens, she paused to inform Cook to expect company.

"And let us hope that his lordship returns in time, for her ladyship looks almost frightened."

Cook picked up an iron skillet and hefted it. "We shan't allow any harm to our lady!"

"No, indeed," Mrs. Bassett agreed and went on her way.

It was about two hours later that Juliet's stepbrother and Lord Taunton appeared at the front door of Hawkswood Manor, having inspected the Taunton house. She composed her features, clasped her hands together, and instructed Mrs. Bassett to show the gentlemen to the drawing room.

"My lady, Lords Winterton and Taunton to see you."

"What, Marius, taking Papa's title already? I, for one, am not convinced he is departed from us forever." Juliet stood by the fireplace, taking comfort from the proximity of the iron poker.

Not expecting his stepsister to challenge him on this, Marius looked taken aback. He quickly recovered. "Never mind that, Juliet. What are you doing here, and what is this nonsense about you being married? You are to wed Lord Taunton."

"But I cannot," Juliet replied in a sugar-coated voice. "I am already married, you see." She held up her left hand to show him her simple gold band. "This is the ring that once belonged to the previous Lady Hawkswood. *I* wear it now."

"I do not believe it!" Marius exclaimed loudly. "Any fool can find a gold band and put it on," he sneered.

"This is an exceedingly lovely ring and has Lord Hawkswood's initials inside. Not that I will remove the ring to show them to you. Knowing you, I'd not have the ring returned to me." She gestured to two chairs by the windows. "Sit down, please."

She joined them and listened to her stepbrother continue his spate of words, arguing that he did not believe her, demanding to know when and how had she married without any notice to him, or his permission for that matter.

She seized the latter point. "I had my birthday some time ago. I did not need your permission, nor Papa's, for that matter, even were he here. You must release my dowry now, Marius. It would be unseemly for you to disgrace our family name before such an important man as Lord Hawkswood."

"That don't make sense," he snarled in return. "Hawkswood to marry my stepsister? What a laugh. He's seen with none but the cream of the *ton*, which you ain't."

"On the contrary, Mr. Winterton," Alexander, who had been warned by Mrs. Bassett of the visitors, said from the doorway, where he stood in all his refined splendor. His bottle green coat was one of Weston's finest, the nankeen breeches he wore fit him superbly, and his waistcoat was a miracle of understated elegance, its stripes in the best of taste. His cravat was quite enough to strike awe in the heart of one who aspired to be accepted into the *ton*. "As my wife, Juliet will be welcome anywhere from Carlton House to Almack's."

Juliet bit back a smile at this, knowing her stepbrother had never managed to achieve an entrée to either place. "Welcome home, Alexander." She smiled as she rose from her chair and quickly crossed to his side, touching his arm in an intimate manner. "It seems as though you have been away for an age instead of hours."

Alexander, taking note of the two men who had risen and by their very stance looked threatening, clasped Juliet to him and proceeded to kiss her very nearly senseless. When he released her, he was pleased to see her cheeks were becomingly pink and her eyes held stars in them rather than fear. His own gaze warned her that drastic measures had been necessary, hence the kiss.

"Oh, my," she whispered, the pink fading a trifle.

"You will be pleased to know that the jeweler in Salisbury was able to size your betrothal ring for you. It ought to fit you now." He glanced over to Marius to add, "Juliet has such dainty fingers, the family ring needed altering."

"I can't accept that she is truly married. I've arranged for her to wed Taunton here."

The heretofore silent Lord Taunton made a few strangled noises that Juliet and Alexander accepted as words, even if not understood.

"He was counting on the marriage to my fair stepsister," Marius declared.

"Indeed?" Alexander said with a shrug of indifference. "Pity, that. Juliet is mine, and I would never let her go."

"She don't look very married to me," Marius muttered.

"But, Marius," Juliet inserted at this point, "I would never permit a man who is not my husband to kiss me as Alexander just did. Would I?" she inquired archly. She took a step closer to Alexander, admiring the ring he had placed on her hand while wondering how he had obtained it. Was that the reason for his hasty trip to Salisbury? She glowed at the very thought, turning to give him a beatific smile.

"The ring is truly lovely, Alexander. I will take great care of it." Juliet gazed up at him, not at the ring as he expected.

Looking down at her happy face, Alexander felt something within him that he couldn't identify at all, but whatever it was it felt good. "I am pleased you like it. I know my grandmother would be delighted." This last he directed at the two men, who stood glowering at the pair of lovers from the other side of the drawing room.

"I expect you have had rooms prepared for them, Juliet?" He looked down at her, adding, "She is an excellent mistress of this house."

"Mistress!" Marius seized upon the word like a hungry dog upon a bone. "That is what she is, my lord, your doxy!"

"I shall forget you said that, sirrah," Alexander said in the coldest voice imaginable. "I'll thank you to keep a civil tongue in your head, even if you are my wife's stepbrother."

He crossed to tug at the bellpull, and within moments Mrs. Bassett arrived in the doorway. "Show these gentlemen to their rooms, will you?" he said with courtesy.

When the two men were gone, Juliet impulsively hugged Alexander and whispered, "Thank you, my lord." Then she added, "There are still things to be ironed out . . . like when and where we were married. Marius demanded to know, and I managed to avoid a reply, but we must think of something to tell him."

"Come up to your room, and we shall talk."

Chapter 6

Relieved now that she had someone to share her worries, Juliet hurried up the stairs to her room, closely followed by Alexander.

He wondered if she gave any thought to the impropriety of their meeting thus. He doubted it. She revealed a single-minded intensity when she had an objective in mind—witness her flight from her home.

Once in her room, Juliet crossed to the far side, perching on the edge of a dainty Hepplewhite fruitwood chair, its seat covered in a gold and cream satin stripe that contrasted nicely with her yellow morning gown. Once settled, she surveyed Alexander where he had taken a position leaning against the fireplace surround.

She touched the betrothal ring with a hesitant finger. "It was enormously thoughtful of you to think of this. Such a beautiful ring. Marius hatefully insisted that anyone could find a plain gold band, but to have you put this elegant ring on my finger, declaring it to have been a family ring properly altered to fit me, well! That put him in his place."

Alexander gave her a wry look. She was such an odd combination of practicality and feminine logic, all overlaid with an innocence he found touching. What a pity she had been pushed to such a situation.

"I am pleased my efforts meet with your approval," he began. "Now, as to our supposed marriage . . . when did you leave your home?"

She gave him the precise date, and he rubbed his chin while

he considered the matter. "Is there a calendar around here? I should like to study it."

Juliet dug around in the dainty desk by the window and ultimately found a small one, promptly offering it to him.

He studied it, then pointed out that it would be possible for them to have been wed on the twentieth of February after a meeting on the eighth, then separated immediately, whereupon she traveled south, ultimately concluding her trip in Woodbury.

"And where were we married?"

"Gretna. 'Tis the only answer we can give, for it would be too easy to check any other place. You can say you traveled north with your former governess and I met you there, persuading you to flee to Gretna with me."

"I suppose," she inserted cautiously, "Marius will have no difficulty in believing you swept me off to marry me at once. You have a most commanding way about you, my lord."

"Do I, indeed?" Alexander said somewhat austerely. He paced back and forth for a few minutes, thinking about what they might possibly meet with, then spun about to face her. "There must be no more friendly calls from Mr. Wyllard. No more exchanging plants and seeds, receiving pretty little nosegays, wistful looks—at least on his part. And above all, no duets with him." Alexander waited for her to explode and was not disappointed for long.

She flew at him, coming to a halt close to where he had waited for her. "I cannot believe my ears. Mr. Wyllard is as harmless as a butterfly. He means no wrong and respects you greatly."

"Think what construction Marius will place on his attendance. Do you wish to give your stepbrother the impression that ours is *not* a love-match?" Alexander placed his hands on his hips, watching her struggle with her warring feelings.

"After that kiss you gave me, I do not see how he could fail to believe we are not madly in love," she said at last. Then she gave him a curious look. "Tell me, Alexander, do you often kiss like that?"

"What?" he sputtered with laughter and a wonder at her innocence.

"I have received few kisses, it is true, but that seemed most extraordinary to me. I doubt you could repeat it." She watched him from slightly narrowed eyes as though wondering what he might do at her words.

Without pausing to consider what he was doing, Alexander pulled her into his arms and kissed her again.

"Amazing," she whispered when released. "I had not thought that kiss could be duplicated." She turned away as though to compose herself, glancing back at him with a hint of mischief in her eyes that Alexander immediately caught.

"Minx! What a blessing that you were never given a Season in Town. You would have had the place upside down in no time."

"I believe I am becoming a shameless flirt!" she said with an odd expression, then continued. "You realize Marius may believe it was heartless of you to leave me alone and spend time in London whilst I lived in this remote village. He has said nothing so far, but it will take a bit of time for the thought to filter through his brain. If we are so in love, why were we living apart? Did we quarrel?" she inquired. "Mind you, he does not know all this at the moment, but someone may inadvertently tell him, people loving to gossip as they do."

"Lovers do quarrel, it is true. Perhaps we disagreed on the attentions paid you by some gentleman who shall remain nameless?" Alexander searched her face for a clue to her thoughts; his words appeared to upset her.

"I doubt he would believe anyone would take offense at that," she said forlornly. "My stepbrother has forever criticized my looks, my conduct, my dress. Nothing I did ever seemed to please him." She glanced at the pretty clock on the mantel. "It will shortly be dinnertime. I had best change, although I suppose you need not. You look very splendid," she concluded naively.

"But I wish to impress that nasty stepbrother of yours," Alexander said with a smile. "Randall shall do his best to make me look imposing."

Juliet gave him a considering look, then said, "I believe you would look imposing in your dressing gown—or indeed, in nothing at all." Then she realized what she had said and blushed furiously. "Oh, do go away before you make me say something else highly improper."

Chuckling to himself, Alexander went through the connecting door to his room, shutting the door most firmly behind him. He had a motive for his action; he desired Marius Winterton to believe that the marriage was very real, that the connecting door between Alexander's room and Juliet's was often used. That it was a bit like putting a noose about his neck he considered, then discarded the thought. He was far beyond the point of return now.

Juliet heard the door click shut, then took her hands from her burning face. How *could* she have uttered such words? Would she never learn to think before she spoke? She had meant to tell him that his clothes had nothing to do with his imposing manner, and look how it had come out! *Stupid, stupid girl.* And she had said a thought would take time to filter through Marius's brain. She doubted *she* possessed one!

Pansy scratched on her door, then hesitantly entered the room, carrying a pretty periwinkle silk dinner gown. It was simply cut with a shirred panel across the bosom and a neckline edged in white. Once dressed, Juliet hunted though her belongings for something that would go well with it.

A rap on the connecting door brought her head up from the drawer she searched. Alexander entered, one hand held behind him.

"I forgot—happy birthday. It's a trifle late, but better that than not at all." He crossed the room to hand her a small, neat box.

"The ring and now this?" she inquired in a wondering tone. Upon opening the box, she found the lovely fan, white with a painted scene on it, and ivory sticks that were prettily carved. "Oh!" she cried with delight. "I have never had such a pretty fan, and it is just the thing to set off my gown. Thank you, dear Alexander." She brushed a kiss on his cheek, mindful of the watching Pansy, then flicked open the fan to hold it before her. "Very nice, indeed. You spoil me, my lord."

"I believe you could do with a bit of spoiling if you think that extravagant," he replied, then abruptly returned to his room, the door clicking loudly behind him.

Although Juliet said nothing to her maid, she wondered if she had not been properly appreciative, or perhaps she had not thanked him correctly. He had seemed remote, almost bitter. Doubtless, Miss Pritchard could have told her, but Juliet was on her own now, and she would have to take greater heed of her words, not to mention actions.

Upon leaving her room to go downstairs, she encountered her stepbrother. She gave him a questioning look as he barred her way.

"I wish to talk with you before we go down, and not with Lord Hawkswood around." He gestured to the door behind Juliet, indicating they should enter.

Pansy took one look at Marius and left the room at once. Juliet knew her maid detested him, but felt abandoned by one she thought she could trust to assist her.

"Well?" she asked unhelpfully, standing in the center of the lovely room, while refusing to take a seat so he might tower over her.

"When did you meet your *husband*?" Marius demanded nastily. "And where?"

"I met him while with Miss Pritchard. He swept me off my feet, which you can readily believe now you have met him. He is a most persuasive man, indeed." She summoned what she hoped was a reflective smile to her lips.

The connecting door opened. "Juliet, will you help me with—" Alexander paused in the doorway, then entered her room as though he did it often. "Sorry, I did not know your stepbrother sought time with you. I shall see you later." But Alexander didn't move, looking to Juliet for a clue, she suspected.

"Do not leave, Alexander. I can help you in a moment. I was merely telling Marius how we met. He wants to know about when we married." Turning to her stepbrother, she continued, "It was most romantic. He whisked me off to Gretna Green, where we were married by the local parson."

"A parson, you say?" Marius said with a frown.

"It would not do for a viscount to wed over an anvil, would it?" Juliet countered.

Marius shook his head. "There is something distinctly fishy about this entire thing. It stinks to high heaven."

"Indeed?" Juliet snapped. "Then perhaps you will want to leave immediately. I would not wish to think you found our company or our home objectionable."

"Can't until Taunton finishes with the estate business. His uncle left him a tidy sum." Marius gave Juliet a superior look as though to make her think she chose the worst of two bargains.

"Which Lord Taunton will promptly lose at the gambling tables," Juliet charged.

"No, no," Marius insisted. "His luck has turned now. Can't help but make a fortune. Likely to reform and all that, you know."

"Give me leave to doubt your words," Juliet replied, turning to Alexander as though to dismiss her stepbrother and his unwelcome inferences.

"I wish to speak with Juliet," Alexander said quietly but with unmistakable authority. "Be so good as to meet us downstairs in a few minutes."

There was little Marius could do but agree and leave the room at once.

"Thank you, Alexander. It was difficult, talking with him."

"When Pansy informed me that Marius had confronted you, I decided I had better intervene. You are a tigress, my pet, but not up to his weight, I think."

Juliet was delighted that Pansy had not forgotten her as she first believed. Then she considered Alexander's words. "I doubt I am your pet, but 'tis true I have never been able to face him down. He was ever the bully."

"And I doubt he will change. And you are my pet, dear girl." With those words he returned to his room, not bothering to close the door behind him.

Juliet stood frozen in place while she listened to the soft conversation between Alexander and Randall. Was she Alexander's dear girl? She doubted that just as she doubted her stepbrother would leave here willingly if he thought he might cause trouble.

"Still here? Come, we will go down together, present a united front so to speak." Alexander took her hand to place on his arm, then led her from her room. "You must not permit Marius to intimidate you."

"I believe I can withstand him now that I have your protection," Juliet said simply, trembling a little at the thought that one day she would no longer have that protection.

"My dear girl, you unnerve me."

Juliet chuckled. "Now that I refuse to believe."

Her eyes were still lit with amusement when they entered the drawing room to find Marius and Lord Taunton awaiting them.

"Dashed good of you to put us up for a bit," Lord Taunton ventured to say in a burst of speech quite unlike his usual taciturn self. "Uncle left me a packet."

"I suspect the house will bring a goodly sum as well, should you want to sell it," Alexander said with suave politeness.

"Know anyone who'd buy it?" Taunton inquired eagerly.

"I may," Alexander replied thoughtfully. "I shall tell you when I find out more." And with that Taunton had to be content, for Alexander had spoken with finality.

Dinner was a constrained event. Marius tried to bait Juliet and Alexander at every turn, endeavoring to trick them about the date of their marriage, the manner of their meeting.

Juliet was thankful that she and Alexander had agreed upon most things earlier. Any minor detail Marius dreamed up, she subtly referred to Alexander, deciding he had a more inventive mind than hers.

At the meal's conclusion she left the men to their port, thinking that Marius would find it tough going if he thought to best Lord Hawkswood.

She seated herself at the harp, idly playing a melody she had tried the day before. A glance out the window revealed storm clouds rolling up from the south. It would likely be a wet and wild night, for the storms could be fierce. She shivered, for she had ever been afraid of thunderstorms, and now there was no Miss Pritchard to comfort her. Pansy was little help, for the maid was apt to cower beneath the covers the moment she heard a distant boom, and as for lightning, it was hard to say who was the more afraid of it—Pansy or Juliet.

"Shall we play a duet for our guests?" Alexander asked upon entering the drawing room, bringing Juliet's gloomy thoughts to an end. He turned to Marius, adding, "That is another bond Juliet and I have—we are both musically inclined. It is most delightful to have such a talented wife."

Marius gave him a disbelieving look, then crossed to lean against a window surround to stare moodily, first at one, then the other of the pair of musicians.

Unprepared for such a request from Alexander, Juliet fussed with the music for a few moments, then settled on the one piece she felt they both could manage without problems. She gave him a nod, then began her introduction with him easily following her a few bars later.

Lord Taunton settled on the settee, a polite expression on his face, while Marius looked disgusted. The piece of music Juliet had selected was mercifully short. When she had played the last note, Marius promptly shifted his position, walking across to Alexander.

"How about some cards?" he said, obviously not caring how rude he sounded.

Alexander looked to Juliet, who nodded slightly. "If you would enjoy a game, I am willing. My love, do you go upstairs?" he asked in an aside to Juliet.

"Yes, dearest. I shall see you later?" she said with what she hoped was an implication in her voice. It might offer him an excuse for leaving a game he had no liking for.

Alexander hastily stifled a grin and nodded. "Later, my dear."

As she swiftly left the room, Juliet could hear Marius making offensive remarks regarding the hasty marriage and probable outcome. While she climbed the stairs, she hoped Alexander would have more patience than she would show to her lout of a stepbrother. What a comfort to know they were only related by her father's marriage.

Papa's first wife had died shortly after her son's birth. Her own mama had died of putrid sore throat when Juliet was a small girl, thus leaving Lord Winterton widowed a second time. Small wonder that he had taken himself off on a long journey to Russia on behalf of his majesty's government. Juliet refused to believe that he was dead. He couldn't be.

She closed the door behind her, leaning against it with relief when she could no longer hear Marius' voice. She crossed to her desk, placing her pretty fan atop it, tracing the design on one of the sticks. How thoughtful of Alexander to buy her a present. She'd not have expected it of him. Certainly he was not what she had anticipated. She had thought a rake such as he had been described would be uncaring, conniving, and manipulative. Rather, he was considerate of her, seeming a friend, and mindful of the proprieties involved.

She might argue with him over Mr. Wyllard, but inwardly she had to agree with his reasoning. If Marius thought there was the slightest flaw in their "marriage," he would do all he would to destroy it and her. The more she considered a marriage to Lord Taunton, the more she was convinced she had done what was necessary, even if it did involve her in a predicament beyond belief.

"There be a storm brewing," Pansy said as she entered the room, bearing a pitcher of hot water so Juliet might wash before bed.

"I know. I saw the clouds forming off to the south of here. I suppose there will be thunder," Juliet added in a quavering voice. "You are free to console yourself belowstairs, Pansy."

"A bit of wine would not come amiss. And that Randall, he is an agreeable chap who is willing to chat for a bit. I'd as soon postpone bed if you know what I mean."

"As you wish," Juliet murmured, then said, "Thank you for seeking his lordship's interference on my behalf before dinner. You well know how my stepbrother can be at times."

"Aye, more times than I could count," the maid replied while pouring the water into a basin after helping Juliet from her gown.

Juliet bathed her face and washed off the rest of her body as best she might, given that she had no tub. She had no desire to demand a bath, knowing the servants had far too much to do with guests in the house.

Donning a fine lawn nightgown edged with pretty lace and properly buttoned up to her neck, Juliet crawled beneath the covers, pulling them over her head when she heard the first rumble of thunder approach. Pansy lit a candle, placing it on the bedside stand before leaving the room.

The storm was slow in coming. Juliet had hoped she might fall asleep before it struck, but that was not to be. What a pity Marius was not likewise afflicted; he would take to his room and leave Alexander free to do as he pleased.

Curling up into a little ball, she whimpered as the first lightning, followed by a crash of thunder, hit close by. Another streak of lightning brought an even greater boom of thunder that brought a faint scream to her lips; it seemed far too near.

"Juliet? Marius mentioned you are afraid of storms." When Alexander saw the miserable little heap huddled at the top of the bed, frightened eyes peering at him from over the covers, he strode to her side, dropping to the bed to gather her into his arms.

"Afraid? Not I," Juliet declared, creeping closer to him, seeking his warmth and comfort. "I am utterly terrified of thunder and lightning. I am such a coward, hiding in my bed."

"At least you are alive."

"True, but terrified," she retorted, leaning back to look at him, dark and forbidding in the dim light of the lone candle. A flash struck again, and she tensed, waiting for the thunder to follow.

"Lightning in particular can be fascinating but deadly," Alexander said, tightening his hold on Juliet.

She stilled at his words, sensing there was more to them than revealed. "What happened?"

"My mother, unlike you, found storms bewitching. She would go out on the terrace and watch the flashes of light, revel in the crash of thunder, unheedful of the rain."

"What happened?" Juliet persisted, wishing she might drive the ache from his voice, from him.

"She was killed by a lightning strike."

Juliet could hear the bleakness in his voice, the pain that still haunted him. She tried to picture the boy who had cared deeply for his mother, that beautiful boy whose portrait hung above the mantel. "How dreadful," she whispered, snuggling closer to him in an effort to comfort him. "Poor boy. Were you here?"

"Yes, I was here. I found her."

Juliet considered the implications of those few words. He had come upon his dead mother, probably in tears, devastated at her death, not knowing what to do for her. "The ring," she wondered aloud.

"I removed it from her finger, placing it in the desk where you chanced upon it. I thought perhaps one day I would want it."

"Your father?" Juliet ventured to ask, deciding it was best to avoid the subject of the ring for now.

"He had gone out and was late returning home. He was too late to help when he arrived. I'd managed to bring her inside with the aid of one of the servants. I don't think he ever recovered from her death. She was a very beautiful woman, and he loved her deeply."

"That is why you are so beautiful," Juliet said, thinking of the portrait again.

He drew away from her a little. She could sense he was looking down at her, likely with puzzlement at her words.

"You are handsome now, but as a boy you were a beautiful child. I expect you'll have beautiful children unless you marry some antidote."

"There is no chance of that," he said with an odd little chuckle.

She wrapped her arms about him more tightly, wishing she could have been there when it happened, that she could have taken that poor little boy into her arms and comforted him as he needed comfort. Perhaps that was why he was now so self-contained and at times aloof; he'd had to learn to be alone, just as Juliet had learned.

The thunder crashed again, and she buried her face against him, shaking with fright. She'd not pulled all the draperies in her room, wanting to know the worst of the storm even as she feared it. Alexander made a move to rise, but she clung to him.

"Do not leave, I beg you," she cried softly.

"I thought to close the draperies," he explained.

"I far prefer to have you at my side. I can close my eyes," and then winced as a flash of light struck the ground outside her window. "How lucky you do not fear the storm . . . you'd have reason to, you know."

Alexander gathered her even closer than before, settling down upon her bed and leaning against the headboard to be more comfortable.

"Tell me more about your father," she demanded, knowing the sound of his voice would keep her fears at bay while the lightning and thunder crashed outside.

"He was a fine man, but seemed to lose heart after my mother died. The men in my family appear to love but once and then with devotion. He never married again and died relatively young."

"How sad. You lived alone? No brothers or sisters?" she asked hesitantly, unwilling to cause more grief, but wanting to know as much as she could about him.

"Alone," he said, wrapping his arms about her more tightly as a flash of light warned of another roll of thunder.

"Oh," she cried as the thunder crashed over the house, seeming to shake its very foundations.

"I'm here, Juliet. I'll take care of you."

"I know." She nestled against him, feeling more cherished than she had in many years. In gratitude she stretched up to bestow a kiss on his neck, welcoming the warmth of his skin revealed by his open shirt.

"Juliet," he said, and it sounded like a warning.

"What, Alexander? What do you want?"

For an answer he buried his face in her tumbled curls, holding her so close she felt that her bones might break. Yet it was a wonderful feeling, cherished and wanted.

It was a time before the lightning came again, and when it followed, it seemed like the thunder was not directly overhead.

"Alexander, I think it is waning. The storm, that is," she

added when she looked up in his face to see a look she couldn't interpret.

He didn't respond, but rather bent to touch her lips with his. It was not a fiery kiss as she had been given before, but instead seemed to be one of promise, a gentle soul-enriching kiss. Juliet responded as a flower to the rain, wrapping her arms about him, wanting to be close to him to comfort, to love, to cherish him as he deserved.

He released her just a little, and looking into his eyes, she thought perhaps he had been just as affected by their kiss as she. "Alexander," she began.

"Hush, do not say anything now. Try to sleep if you can." He shifted on her pillows, making himself more comfortable.

She placed her head contentedly against his chest, listening to the even beat of his heart, and did as he suggested.

Outside, the lightning faded to the distant horizon, taking the thunder with it, the rumbles ebbing to faint growls. Within the house peace came and eventually, sleep to everyone, even Alexander.

In the morning Juliet awakened feeling as though something was missing. Then she recalled the storm. And she recalled Alexander as well, all he had done for her.

What was she to do now? How could she think of any other man, *ever*, after all he had done for her? Once they were compelled to part, she would retreat to a hideaway, raise flowers, and have a cat. No other man could possibly compare to Alexander, nor did she want a substitute.

Pansy entered the room, set a pitcher of hot water on the stand, then crossed to gaze out of the window. " 'Tis a fine morning, my lady."

"Indeed," Juliet responded, looking at the morning sun beaming in the window, hearing the sound of birds outside. "How different it is this morning after the storm."

"Ye managed?"

"I managed, Pansy," Juliet said with a sigh, wondering how last night would change things, for change them it must.

She dressed and went downstairs with a cautious step. Her stepbrother greeted her when she entered the breakfast room.

"I suppose you sniveled in your bed last night? You always were afraid of storms as I recall."

"I have Alexander now, Marius. I'm not afraid anymore."

He gave her a searching look, but said nothing else as Lord Taunton entered the room, oblivious to any tension between Marius and Juliet.

Alexander followed on his heels and crossed to where Juliet had seated herself, content with a cup of tea before her.

"All right?" he queried softly.

She gave him a gentle nod. "Fine." She searched his face for a clue to his feelings and was none the wiser.

"You must have more than that," he said after a glance at her teacup.

"Whatever you say, my lord," Juliet said with a giggle, smiling up at him.

Marius gave the pair of them a thoughtful look, then took himself off, claiming he wanted to check his horse.

Chapter 7

The sky had cleared beautifully following the storm, and a soft, gentle breeze stirred the many-hued flowers in Juliet's garden. She studied the aquilegia, deciding to cut the tops back to new growth, dead-heading all blooms. Otherwise, she would have little plants springing up everywhere next spring from the abundant seed. Juliet preferred an orderly arrangement of plants. She liked flowers to grow precisely where she wanted them.

Then she sank down on a convenient stone bench when she realized next spring she would most likely not be here. It did not make any difference what she did, for the house would probably sit vacant in the coming year. Once Marius and Lord Taunton went on their way, she and Alexander could devise a means of separation, and that would be that.

Unless she could persuade him to permit her to remain here. Of course, that might make things a bit difficult for him when he returned to the city, particularly if he wished to marry and Marius or Lord Taunton made claims regarding his supposed marriage to Juliet.

"Surely, it cannot be that bad?" Alexander said quietly. "Actually, those flowers look rather nice there. Or do you have something else in mind?" He studied the effect of the various colored perennials Juliet had planted in the flower bed, his head tilted to one side.

"It does not make a farthing of difference," she said with a sigh. "I shan't be here next year to see them in bloom. I'll do what must be done, but not make plans. Unless . . ." She gave him an appraising look.

"Unless what?" he queried, looking a trifle uneasy as he sat down beside her on the cold stone.

"Unless you would permit me to remain on here after Marius and Lord Taunton have gone and we have made our arrangements," she said frankly.

"What arrangements?" he asked, clearly puzzled.

"Well, I do not know why you look at me like that," she cried softly, unsure as to how far their voices might carry in the morning air. "You must know that you will go your way and I shall go mine."

"And where will you go?" he inquired in a rather odd voice.

"I do not know. That is why I asked if I might remain here. I love the house, and everyone in Woodbury has been so kind to me. Even Mrs. Tackley is agreeable, and I suspect she can be rather patronizing if she pleases." Juliet gave him a hopeful look, then continued. "I could work new covers for the dining room chairs, and the linens would all be mended or replaced. Mrs. Bassett and I have devised a scheme to redo the morning room, bit by bit. There is a great deal I might do to improve the property for you—if you would allow me to remain."

"You do not wish to marry?" Alexander inquired with a sharp look at Juliet's troubled face.

She turned away from him to gaze off into the near distance, uncertain how to reply to that searching question. Once she had thought to remain single all her life. Now, after finding such comfort in Alexander's arms, she was not so positive about the benefits of single blessedness.

"Juliet? Have you altered your opinion of marriage?"

"I don't know," she admitted. "I can see where there are distinct advantages."

"Particularly during storms?" he asked gently.

"That," she conceded, "and the ability of a gentleman to cope with unsavory characters. For example, you are quite splendid with Marius. I confess I should not have had the success with him that you did."

"You have never been in love, of course," Alexander suggested.

Caught off guard, Juliet agreed with him before she thought

better of it. "But then," she added, "I have met very few gentlemen. I do not consider Lord Taunton eligible in any way—
even with his inheritance, which Marius seems to think will
change Taunton's life. Most likely it will make him more welcome at the gaming tables for a time."

"You have a rather jaundiced view of life for a young
woman."

"Perhaps. Rather say I am a realist. I cannot afford to build
on air dreams. *That* is why I must ask, no, beg you to allow me
to remain here when the others have gone."

"I will give it some thought, Juliet," he said, then was silent
for a few minutes before asking, "Are you so eager to be rid of
me, then?"

"Of course not," she denied. "You have probably been kinder
to me than anyone in the world save Miss Pritchard, and she
was paid to be so. Although in fairness, I would guess it is part
of her nature to be kind. She was forever finding lost dogs and
cats, caring for injured birds and that sort of thing. But you, my
lord, have nothing to gain by showing me kindness, and I do
appreciate it, believe me."

"You suspect no ulterior motive in my behavior?" he probed.

"None in the least," she said, giving him a direct look. "For
what could it be? I have but a modest dowry that Marius must
release to me. He has told me often enough that I am barely
passable in looks. And as to deportment, I fear I am sadly lacking in manners."

She reached out to pat Alexander's arm, then withdrew her
hand with haste. "I never imagined you to be so sympathetic
and of such admirable character. I must admit you have totally
revised my estimation of a rake's integrity."

"I suppose you realize that not all . . . ah, rakes are the
same?" he said with what sounded suspiciously like laughter in
his voice.

Juliet gave him a cross look, then said, "I gather one cannot
place everyone in the same mold, as much as one might like to,
that is. I may have lived a restricted life, but I am not stupid, my
lord."

"I never for a minute thought you were," he replied with a hint of a smile. "Aggravating, perhaps, but never stupid."

She sighed, bent over to tug a weed from the flower bed, then looked at him, her eyes troubled again. "I imagine I have given you nothing but aggravation since you arrived to seek your own refuge. Poor man. I am sorry."

"Never say that!" he said, laughing outright at her words. "To tell the truth, I have not enjoyed myself so well in a long time."

She gave a gusty sigh of relief at his words. "Well, that is a blessing, at any rate."

At that precise moment Marius rounded the far corner of the flower garden, and once he'd caught sight of them, they were both trapped.

"Oh, dear," Juliet murmured. "He looks up to his old tricks."

Before Alexander might question what those tricks were apt to be, Marius was upon them.

"Very dull life you two lead here, staring at some silly plants," he said, a faint sneer in his voice.

"We were talking, if you must know," Juliet was stung to reply.

"And other things," Alexander added, giving Marius a knowing look with a raise of his brow.

Marius frowned, something he seemed to have done a great deal since arriving, and said, "Well, city life is the life for me, thank you very much."

"We are not *keeping* you here, I trust," Juliet said, much tried with her stepbrother and his stupid remarks.

"Taunton still has a few details to iron out," Marius said.

"Such as how soon he can lay his hands on the money, I'll be bound. Has he discovered a buyer for the property as yet?" Juliet wanted to know, figuring that if Lord Taunton severed all ties with Woodbury, he'd never return.

Alexander rose from the bench, placing a cautioning hand on Juliet's shoulder as he did. At Marius's questioning look, Alexander said to Juliet, "Sorry, my love, lost my balance for a moment there." Then to Marius, he said, "Rumor has it that one of the local people wishes to buy that bit of property."

"I hope so," Juliet said fervently, wondering what it was that Alexander cautioned her about. "An absentee landlord is never a good prospect, or so I've been told," she amended when she recalled Lord Hawkswood's vast number of estates. Undoubtedly, he would be the best of landlords.

"Depends on the sort of chap the landlord is, my dearest," Alexander replied in the silkiest of tones.

Juliet decided she did not like to be called "love" and "dearest" in that fashion. If she were truly his love, it would be a different matter entirely. And that brought her far too close to the subject she preferred to ignore, namely her feelings for Alexander Barr, Lord Hawkswood.

She rose in a flurry of skirts, mumbling something indistinct about a matter in the house that needed her attention.

"I'll join you, my dear. There is a little problem we need to solve first, you may recall." He touched her arm lightly, guiding her along in such a way she knew she'd not escape him.

"Indeed," she agreed loud enough so Marius could hear. Alexander had yet to give her permission to remain at the house once he departed.

As soon as Marius was beyond hearing, Juliet resumed her attack. "I do believe it would be to your advantage to have someone in residence here. And I do not mean the housekeeper. She'd not have your interests at heart as I might," Juliet let slip, then hoped he hadn't caught her last words.

They had entered the house while she spoke, and Alexander pulled her into the library, shut the door, and proceeded to stare at her in a perplexing manner that quite put her on her guard. "What are you thinking?" she wondered aloud, backing away from him.

"Why you would have my interests at heart more than my housekeeper who is paid to keep my property in order?" He folded his arms before him, looking as though he was prepared to wait forever for her answer.

Juliet thought wildly. She hadn't expected him to put her on the spot like this. What could she tell him? One thing she couldn't admit was that she had tumbled into love with the dratted man, no matter how wonderful and caring he might be. She would undoubtedly be the last person on earth he would wish to wed.

"Well," she temporized, "I am your friend."

"Indeed, you are. Is that all?" He advanced on her with the stealth of a stalking cat.

"All I wish to say at the moment," she declared rashly, continuing to back away from him. What could he do? Shake the truth out of her? She'd always found it difficult to lie, even more so to him.

"Now we are coming to the heart of the matter. Do not worry so; I'll not press you for more—at the moment. But, my dear Juliet, unless you wish your stepbrother to renew his suspicions, we are going to have to behave more as a newly married couple might." He came to a halt before her when Juliet backed herself against the wall.

"I have never been around a newly married couple," Juliet declared. "I haven't a clue how they might act." She wondered if she might edge sideways and found she couldn't because he moved ever so slightly when she did. She would not evade him easily.

"But I have," he said with a smile.

Juliet wasn't sure she trusted that smile. Not that she didn't believe Alexander would behave with propriety, given the circumstances. It was the circumstances that bothered her.

"We must touch each other more often, and certainly not pull a hand away as though burned as you did while we were talking in the garden," Alexander declared.

"You noticed. I did not think you would," Juliet said dejectedly. If he thought she was going to hang on him, he was sadly mistaken, and so she told him.

"Not hang on me, my dear girl. Touch. Smile into my eyes. Exchange whispered words of love, that sort of thing. When two people are in love, they hate to be apart, long to be in each other's arms, and in general wish the rest of the world to be gone."

"Well, I can heartily agree with that last emotion," Juliet said, attempting a smile and finding she still could manage it. That she also agreed with him on the other points was something she would keep to herself. She missed Alexander the moment he left her, and when she had awakened alone in her bed this morning, she ached for his arms to hold her close once again. Pity violent storms were not that common.

"You wish them speedily gone?" he asked with a grin.

"Indeed." She gave a pointed look at the space between them, thinking he would realize she needed to be elsewhere. She was mistaken. He stepped closer.

"I suspect we need a bit of practice. If you've not observed a newly married couple, I could help you."

"I'll manage, I fancy," she said with a wary look at those broad shoulders she had buried her head against last night.

"Now, Juliet," he said with far too much persuasion in his rich voice.

"What?" she whispered, yielding to her curiosity.

He didn't bother to reply, but gathered her in his arms. "Now," he instructed, "touch my face—gently stroking as though you liked me more than lemon biscuits."

She repressed a grin, for he apparently observed her fondness for those sweets. "In the interest of keeping Marius at bay, I shall do as you say," she said, a hint of her amusement in her voice.

"Now call me your love in the same accents you admire a pretty flower," he persuaded.

"My love," Juliet said with no pretense in the slightest. Her gaze met his, and she faltered in her touch. This was becoming a dangerous game. Those eyes of his did not tease. She melted at his gaze, utterly quivered at the feel of his arms about her, and her knees had the solidity of a bowl of blancmange.

To her surprise, Alexander kissed her gently on her forehead and quickly released her, striding across to the door. "That's the ticket," he said when he paused, one hand on the doorknob. In a moment he had gone, leaving Juliet to grope for a chair so she might cope with her tumbled feelings.

"As a lesson, that was most instructive," she murmured to the kitchen cat, who had sneaked into the room, looking for a cozy place to nap. She scooped him up and stroked his fur. "Kitty, what am I to do now?"

"Meow," was her only reply, and she supposed that was all she deserved for being such a fool.

Alexander felt well satisfied for the moment, at any rate. Juliet was beautifully confused and on tenterhooks, which is where he hoped to keep her for a day or two.

Striding into the stables, he inspected his horses and then requested his carriage be brought around to the front of the house once the beasts were harnessed.

Leaving the grooms to get on with their job, he strolled beyond, looking about him with critical eyes. Things looked good here. His grandmother would be well pleased with the condition of the place. Which thought brought him to Juliet's request. He doubted matters would work as she wished. Indeed, he had his own desires. If they did not succeed, then he would allow her to remain at the house, for she needed a retreat from her brother.

Had she considered that she had placed Alexander in a bind with her actions? How could he return to London and even think about marriage to another woman as long as Winterton and Taunton were about? Even if they did not move among the *ton*, they would likely kick up a dust should Alexander attempt to wed another.

He sighed with the complexities he had yet to work out. Juliet did not make things easy for him, yet he was never bored in her company and found her a constant delight.

First of all, Alexander paid a visit to an elderly man who lived on the edge of the property. Mr. Smythe had been there since Alexander could remember and knew everything there was to know about the area, Alexander felt certain. A few well-placed questions gave Alexander all the information he needed.

It was an easy matter to jog into Woodbury and locate the solicitor who had come to the village in order to complete the transfer of the Taunton property. He welcomed Alexander into his temporary quarters at the local inn with a knowledgeable smile. He obviously knew who Alexander was and where he stood in Society. That made everything simpler.

"I wish to buy the Taunton property," Alexander declared

once the greetings were over. "Upon studying the maps and boundaries, I find that on one side the two properties march together."

"Indeed? In that case, it is most sensible." The solicitor went on a bit about the condition of the property, something Alexander had already learned, but listened to with great patience.

"What is the asking price?" Alexander said at last with the air of one who is familiar with the value of land and who will not be diddled out of a farthing.

The solicitor gave a figure Alexander considered fair, and he suggested the solicitor inform Taunton of the sale. "If he accepts that amount, the deal is set. One thing," Alexander said before leaving, "I do not wish him to know who buys the land."

The solicitor considered the request, then nodded. "Very wise, my lord. It has been my lot to see a number of deals queered when a man unfamiliar with the value of land attempts to demand far more than it is worth."

"Precisely," Alexander agreed.

Once he was quit of the inn, he strolled along the village walks, glancing into the shop windows, trying to picture Juliet living out her life in such a little place as Woodbury. He fancied she would do well enough. From what he had seen of her, she appeared to be a woman who could be content wherever she might settle.

"Lord Hawkswood," Mrs. Ogleby cried in fluting tones. "How is our dear Juliet today?" she inquired archly.

Alexander guessed that the older lady was inclined to believe he had appeared on the scene to attempt a reconciliation with his pretty wife.

"She seemed in good spirits this morning. Although I believe she finds the visit from her stepbrother a bit trying. You know how elder brothers can be, I feel sure."

"I know how my boys tease their younger sisters," Mrs. Ogleby declared. "I shall have a party, and perhaps that will cheer her. We are very gay here, you know. Perhaps not like London. But in our own way we have a most pleasant time of it. Tell your good wife that Mr. Ogleby and I would be pleased for your company on Friday next."

"I shall accept on her behalf, as well as my own," Alexander said with a tip of his hat. He bid her good day with the feeling that Mrs. Ogleby would do very well by Juliet—and himself, as well.

Juliet, when informed of the treat in store for her, gave Alexander a confused look. "A party? I ought to have had everyone here first, especially the Tackleys."

"In time. Allow the locals to entertain us, for we are supposed to be newly married. Soon enough you may invite them all here."

"Perhaps we could interest Mr. Taunton in the eldest Tackley girl," Juliet ventured. "She would keep him on a tight string, for she is as strong-willed as her mother. Of course he has been on his best behavior since he arrived—not as he behaved while at Winterton Hall."

"And are you not strong-willed?" Alexander said, leaning back against his chair in the drawing room, observing Juliet while she mended linen.

"Well, I know what Lord Taunton is, you see. She doesn't. Not that it makes things right, but we are such different creatures. She has money he wants, and he has a title her parents covet. I fancy her father would give control of the money in Lucy's capable hands were he to receive a hint as to Lord Taunton's true nature—in the event he did not see it for himself."

"I suppose you think I ought to dabble in this bit of matchmaking?"

"Only if you wish. On the other hand, it would bring the Tauntons back into Woodbury and that might not be desirable," she concluded with a frown.

"Why not let nature take its course?" Alexander countered. "You never know about these things."

"True." But she didn't sound convinced.

"I offered on the Taunton property," Alexander found himself confiding.

"Indeed?" Juliet said with a quick smile. "I *am* pleased. I shan't say anything until it is a certain thing. If I've taken Lord

Taunton's measure, he'd demand more money if he thought *you* wanted the land."

Alexander once again decided that while Juliet might be young and a woman to boot, she was no fool. He also found it was pleasant to discuss matters with her. He'd had not such a confidant before, and it was an agreeable change.

The party given by the Oglebys was a delight. Mrs. Ogleby had strung fairy lights in the rear garden, giving the place a festive air. The dinner was all that it should be, with Marius looking confused much of the time because the eldest Ogleby girl was flirting with him and he wasn't accustomed to such attention from a proper young lady.

"I told you we ought to let nature take its course," Alexander whispered to Juliet when she took note of the pair as well as where Lucy Tackley flirted with Lord Taunton in an ever so genteel manner. He appeared as bewildered as Marius at such regard from a young lady of means.

"Indeed, I confess you were right," she whispered back. She gave him a warm smile not missed by her hostess.

Rather than remain with the gentlemen and port, Alexander pushed back his chair, took Juliet's hand, then made a courtly bow to Mrs. Ogleby, saying, "You have created such a charming setting in the garden that my wife and I wish to enjoy it a little."

"But of course you do," she gushed. "I remember how it was when Ogleby and I were first wed." She made little shooing motions with her hands, then joined Mrs. Tackley, who had been watching her Lucy chat with Lord Taunton.

Juliet strolled along the Ogleby garden paths, her hand most properly placed on Alexander's arm. She could feel him very close to her side, and it made her nervous as well as slightly apprehensive.

"*Now* what are you thinking?" he demanded to know in a soft undertone. "I declare you are the most vexing creature alive, for I never can guess what will tease you next."

"I could say the same about you," she returned. "Must you walk so close to me?"

"Indeed, I must. And it might be well for you to touch my cheek just so, perhaps lean against me as though you enjoyed the feel of me against you."

"Good heavens," Juliet replied in mock horror that was not as faked as he might think. She did manage to touch his cheek; after all, her hands were gloved. But as to leaning against him, well, it brought vivid memories of being held snugly in his arms, wrapped in his concern during the storm. She recalled the feel of his lean form against hers all too well, and if he couldn't see her blush, it would be a miracle. She felt as though she could go up in flames any moment.

"How cozy," Marius taunted from behind them.

"Go away, Marius," Juliet demanded. "I wish to be alone with my husband."

"I could almost believe you two are truly wed," he said, a nasty insinuation in his voice.

"Oh, Lord Winterton," the Ogleby girl cried, scurrying to catch up with him. "Are the lanterns not the prettiest things?"

Marius turned from Juliet to contemplate the sweet young thing, arrayed in virginal white and looking like a pretty comfit, and looked confused again.

"One never knows, does one?" Juliet murmured.

"Indeed, one does not," Alexander agreed. He drew Juliet along the path until they were well away from Marius. Here he paused and looked back where a rosy tinted lantern shed its gay light upon Marius. "He still is not convinced. We shall have to try harder, my love."

"Well, I do not know what we might do that we have not already done."

"I have an idea or two up my sleeve."

Juliet took one look at those gray eyes alive with mischief and did not inquire what those ideas might be. She felt it better if she didn't know until it was too late to object, for he'd never change his mind anyway.

They all went back to Hawkswood Manor in a bemused state: Lord Taunton and Marius because they were unused to pretty young innocents flinging themselves at their heads, Juliet because she had not the slightest clue what scheme Alexander hatched in his head, and Alexander because he hoped his scheme would work.

Once at the manor, Alexander permitted no opportunity for Marius to speak with Juliet. He mounted guard on her as though he suspected Marius of foul play. Which was true, in a way.

At last they all went up to their respective rooms, supposedly intent upon sleep.

Marius stood at the top of the stairs, watching Juliet and Alexander enter their rooms, hearing Pansy greet her mistress with pleasure. He grimaced and turned to enter his own room, but deep in thought.

"My lady," Pansy said respectfully, not like her former familiar way. "I trust you had a pleasant evening?" she asked while she helped Juliet from her garments.

"Indeed, I did. Pansy, where is my nightgown? What have you there?" Juliet looked with alarm at the flimsy piece of muslin held by her maid. She was supposed to wear that scrap?

"Your other had a tear in it and needed a wash. This be an old one I found at the bottom of the drawer. Such a pretty thing it is, embroidered all over with rosebuds."

Juliet hadn't the heart to scold the maid, so she donned the trifle of muslin, thanking her stars there was no violent storm on the horizon tonight. Besides, Pansy looked so out-of-reason pleased. She bid the maid good night, then was about to crawl into bed when Alexander burst into her room. Juliet gave him an alarmed look and dived beneath the covers.

"What on earth is the matter?" she cried.

"Something in my eye," Alexander mumbled, holding one hand over his eye and looking as though he was much in pain. "Sent Randall down for fresh water, but hoped you might take pity on me."

Quite forgetting that she was not garbed in her usual sensible nightgown but a gossamer bit of muslin that offered about as much coverage as a cobweb, Juliet scrambled from her bed to hurry to Alexander's side.

She absently took note of his fine brocade dressing gown while she attempted to see what might be in his eye when the door to the hall flew open and Marius stood there, looking rather wild-eyed.

"Aha!" he cried, sounding sillier than an old maid who thinks she has found an intruder under her bed.

Alexander put a protective arm about Juliet, shielding her with his robe, then demanded, "What do you want here, Marius? My *wife* and I are about to retire—as you can see."

Marius stared at his stepsister as though he had never seen her before, then his shoulders slumped and he nodded. Without a word, he shut the door and could be heard walking down the hall to his room.

Alexander dropped his hand so it rested on Juliet's nearly bare hip and sighed with satisfaction. "I do believe he is at last convinced. That nightgown was a stroke of genius, if I do say so." He gave her an admiring look.

"You planned this?" Juliet demanded in a dangerously quiet voice.

"Brilliant, would you not agree?" He gazed down at her in such a way that Juliet was certain she blushed from head to toe.

"Get out of this room, my lord, before I do violence!"

Chapter 8

"I want you to take that nightgown, wash it, restore it to the chest where you found it, and never bring it out again. Is that clear, Pansy?"

"Indeed, ma'am," a subdued maid replied.

"And from now on I shall break my fast here in my room. Is that also clear?" Juliet turned from where she had been staring out of the window at the early morning mist that hung over the garden.

"Yes, ma'am" Pansy took the offending garment in her arms, prepared to gently swish it through suds, hang it to dry, then place it back in tissue.

"And I want you to scour the house—as I will—to see if we might find the key to the connecting door. Mind you, Marius must not know what is afoot. After the depths to which Lord Hawkswood descended to achieve our goal, I'd be a fool to change my stepbrother's opinion. Not a word. Is that also clear?"

"Yes, ma'am," Pansy replied with an audible sigh. She hastily slipped from the room as though afraid that Juliet would think of something else to add to her scold.

Alone, Juliet returned to her contemplation of the rising mist. It would be impossible to feel more mortified than she did at this point. How could he? Never mind it attained her objective. Scheming to dress her in that outrageous nightgown no more than a wisp of cobwebby fabric that offered not the slightest protection from his gaze was too much. She wanted to hide, bury herself where he could never see her again, never hear of her again, forget she ever existed, if such a thing were possible.

He had laughed at her!

She wrapped her arms about her as to ward off the memory of his amused laughter at her infuriated demand that he leave the room, else she'd do violence. Had she actually begun to believe he was a kind, gentle man? He was little better than Marius, and that was about the worst there was.

The door opened, and she swung around with alarm only to find that Pansy had returned with her morning meal.

"Your stepbrother is up, ma'am," Pansy offered while arranging the dishes on a small table Juliet had drawn up near the window.

"Is there any chance he might be leaving, do you think?" Juliet inquired with hope.

"I heard him ask Lord Taunton iffen he was about set to go back to London, and his lordship said he had papers to sign and besides, he liked it here."

"Good grief," Juliet said, seating herself on the Hepplewhite chair at the side of the table. "We can only hope that when Lucy Tackley makes her intentions known, Lord Taunton will flee to the city."

Amazingly enough, she could eat, and she made a good breakfast. Hot tea went a long way to easing anger, even if it crossed her mind that a pot of the substance dumped over his lordship in the adjoining room might persuade him to keep to himself.

She wouldn't remain in her bedroom, she decided once she'd drained the last of the tea from the pot. It was far too lovely a day to be stuck indoors. She'd potter in the garden for a time. Goodness knew the weeds flourished and required pulling daily, not to mention the dead flowers that needed to be cut. Old Mr. Lumpkin was fine at rough gardening, but delicate things like snipping off flower heads were beyond his ken.

Poking her head around her half-opened door, she could see no one about. Slipping down the stairs and out to her flowers proved child's play. She concentrated on the main flower bed, tugging weeds, dead-heading flowers, and making the bed tidy when she heard the crunch of steps on pea gravel behind her. Someone approached.

"Good morning, Juliet." There was a faint question in Lord Hawkswood's voice.

It was childish not to reply, so she said curtly, "Good morning."

"Am I to be unforgiven, then?"

She could hear that wretched hint of laughter in his voice, and it firmed her resolve as nothing else might have.

"If you refer to the contemptible incident that occurred last evening, you are correct." Juliet might speak to him, but she'd not look at the dratted man. That might weaken her determination to remain aloof from him and *that* would never do.

He crossed to stand at her side. She could see her reflection in the high polish of his boots and took a moment to brush her wayward curls from her face. "Go away."

"Juliet, I am sorry if you are upset, but my stratagem worked. Marius now believes we are truly married. That *is* what you wished, is it not?" he inquired in the silky voice she'd not trust again.

"There ought to have been something else, some other way," she blurted out in barely repressed rage.

"I gather it is too soon for you to see reason," he said with a sigh to the top of her gardening hat. "Very well, then. But he is not the only one you must convince."

Juliet paused, a weed in hand, then made the mistake of glancing up at him. "Who else?"

"The good folk of Woodbury, of course." He stood there as fresh as a daisy, smiling at her quite as though he hadn't made a fool of her last evening. She tore her gaze from him with difficulty.

"Why of course?" she countered, staring down at the aquilegia as though it were the most fascinating thing in the world.

"Mrs. Tackley knows my grandmother. She mentioned it to me the other evening. Were my grandmother to learn something havey-cavey was going on in this house, she would be down here in a trice."

"And you'd not want that, I gather?" Juliet asked dryly.

"You have not met her." What a wealth of insinuation lurked in that remark.

"I do not wish to talk with you. Go away. If any of the women come to call, I shall do my best to look the part you assigned me—a silly, besotted fool." Juliet resumed her digging, utterly destroying one plant Mr. Wyllard had given her in the process. She was in such a blind passion she didn't notice the destruction until after Alexander had gone, and then she sighed with vexation.

Eventually the garden was tidy, weeds pulled from the beds to be burned, dead flowers and trimmings wheeled off to the compost pile. Juliet sank back on her heels, surveying the results with satisfaction.

"Beggin' you pardon, ma'am," Pansy said hesitantly, "a glass of fine lemonade?"

"Ah, just the thing," Juliet declared fervently and drained the glass with appreciation.

"His lordship said as how you'd be mighty thirsty after bein' in the garden all this time."

"Lord Taunton?" Juliet inquired, knowing the answer before she asked.

"No, ma'am," Pansy replied, backing away from her mistress. "It was Lord Hawkswood." If she expected Juliet to hurl the glass at her, she was proven wrong.

"Thank you, Pansy. The lemonade was most welcome," Juliet said, her temper well in hand by now. "I should like a bath, please. I am all dirty and perspiring. I'll be up to my room shortly."

The maid scurried off, looking thankful no fireworks had exploded.

It took but a few moments to put away her gardening tools. Juliet had a short talk with Mr. Lumpkin regarding an area she wished to be spaded for more kitchen garden plots, then hurried up the back way to the first floor and her room, not wishing to see anyone in all her dirt.

Pansy was in the act of pouring water into the copper slipper bath. Juliet pulled off her drab gardening dress, hose, and shoes before pausing to stare at the connecting door. She looked around the bedroom to see what might be pushed in front of it. She hadn't taken time to hunt for the key.

"Did you ask about the key? Or find it?" she inquired as she tugged a low chest in front of the door.

"No key has been seen in many years, ma'am," Pansy said, coming to aid her mistress. "Besides, his lordship has taken the others and gone to Salisbury for the day."

Juliet stopped, looked at her maid, and smiled wryly. "Lovely. I can bathe in peace."

And it did prove peaceful. She relaxed in the tub, mulling over what had occurred in the past week, culminating in the scene last evening. Mortifying, true, but Alexander had done it—convinced Marius she and Alexander were really wed. Now Marius would go and leave her be, forget about marrying her to Lord Taunton. However, Alexander thought she still needed to placate the ladies of Woodbury. Perhaps it would be necessary for a time, until all danger was past.

Then she sat bolt up. Had there not only been danger for her, but for Alexander as well? How could she have forgotten the woman who aspired to marry him? Then Juliet relaxed once again. Just because Marius had stumbled upon her in this remote village did not mean that woman would uncover Alexander. What was her name? she wondered. More important, what did she look like—slender, blond, blue-eyed, and beautiful? Or perhaps dark-haired with flashing black eyes and a lush figure to tempt a man.

Juliet looked down at the body revealed through fading suds. Rather average, she supposed, as was her hair and face. As her stepbrother had so kindly pointed out, she was not much to look at. She rose from her tub to dry, then dress. She might be tired of her yellow morning gown, but she had little choice, so on it went with slippers to match.

With the men gone from the house, Juliet applied herself to tasks left undone when they were about. She checked sheets again, taking note of what must be replaced.

She was consulting with Cook regarding a dish Lord

Hawkswood had requested when Mrs. Bassett bustled into the kitchen to come to a halt by Juliet.

Juliet looked up with a question in her eyes. "Yes?"

"Mrs. Ogleby and Mrs. Tackley have come to call, my lady."

Juliet thought back to her words with Alexander this morning and nodded. "I shall see them at once. Bring a tea tray after a bit, will you?" She smoothed down her gown, patted her hair, then entered the drawing room with a genuine smile of greeting on her face.

"Lady Hawkswood, how well you look today," Mrs. Ogleby said, giving Juliet a searching inspection.

"Thank you. Indeed, once the mist cleared, it turned out to be a fine day and I have been in the garden. There is always much to do if one looks for it. And you? I trust both you ladies are fine?" Juliet sank down on a dainty Hepplewhite chair facing the two women.

"Indeed," Mrs. Tackley said with what passed for a smile on her somewhat dour face.

They proceeded to discuss the upcoming church fete, the coming marriage of the squire's daughter to the parson, and last, but most interesting, the manor house and its history.

"Did you know his lordship's mother?" Juliet dared to ask after a while. If they snubbed her question, she'd not take it amiss. Considering what had happened, it could be a touchy subject.

"I did, although never well," Mrs. Tackley admitted. "She kept herself aloof from the village when she and his lordship were in residence. They only came for a few weeks in summer, you see," she added in explanation in case Juliet didn't know this fact.

"She was not as gracious as you, my lady," Mrs. Ogleby inserted. "Had little to say to us. Of course we were young then," she added in a likely attempt to justify her late ladyship's behavior.

"It is a pity, for I believe she missed a great deal in not enjoying your company," Juliet replied truthfully. They might be curious, but their hearts were in the right place, and she had found them both a comfort in her lonely hours.

"It was a sad day for his lordship when she died," Mrs. Ogleby said, hesitating before saying anything more with a cautious look at Juliet to see, no doubt, if she knew something of that event.

"She was killed during a storm, I believe," Juliet offered.

"Aye," Mrs. Tackley said. "Struck by lightning, poor dear. It was terribly hard for the present Lord Hawkswood, boy that he was then. He must have had a lonely time of it after his mother's death."

Juliet wished she might halt the conversation. She didn't want to feel sorry for Alexander—no more than she already did, that is. "What a pity. I'm not fond of storms, myself. I'm a frightful coward, hiding beneath the covers until the thunder goes away." She ignored the comfort offered by Alexander. It was best to put that well behind her.

Mrs. Ogleby chuckled. "My girls are the same, shrieking and howling to wake the dead."

Mrs. Bassett entered at that point, pushing a cart laden with a teapot, cups, and a plate of dainty cucumber sandwiches, plus ginger and lemon biscuits.

Juliet poured out the tea, offering sugar and milk, biscuits and sandwiches, continuing to chat about anything other than Alexander.

The squire's wife and daughter came to call at that moment, and Juliet greeted Mrs. Otterly and daughter Mary politely, inviting them to partake of the tea.

Within minutes Mrs. Bassett returned with a fresh pot of tea and more sandwiches and biscuits. She bore a proud smile, happy to see her mistress entertaining.

The squire's wife echoed that thought when she said, "It is so good to see this house occupied again after all these years. We are very pleased you joined our little village society, my lady."

Mary nodded shyly, but said nothing, and Juliet wondered if she was truly shy or merely tongue-tied at being in the manor with the viscountess.

A noise in the hall indicated others had arrived, and shortly Alexander entered the room, followed by Lord Taunton and Marius.

Juliet turned to face the door, tensing for what was to follow. She pasted what she hoped was a loving smile on her face and greeted them all with equal charm.

"How agreeable, to be in such delightful company, eh, Winterton?" Alexander said pleasantly but with an edge to his voice that told Juliet he must have had a difficult day. "Ran into Mr. Wyllard, my dear. He sent his greetings and a plant for you," Alexander added. "I gave it to Lumpkin to put in the north bed."

"How nice," Juliet said with well-concealed ire. How dare Alexander accept the plant, then send it off in the care of Lumpkin, who'd likely plant it all wrong and kill the thing!

Alexander crossed the room to stand by Juliet's side, placing a possessive hand on her shoulder. The ladies took note of that gesture and exchanged smiles.

The conversation became general until Alexander spoke up. "We have been meaning for some time to invite everyone here for a party."

"True, we discussed it just this morning," Juliet added, mindful what he had said earlier. "Quite definitely a party."

"A ball?" Mary inquired breathlessly.

"Indeed, why not?" Alexander said with another caressing gesture to Juliet's over-sensitive shoulder. "I cannot recall when last a ball was held here. You are all invited."

The ladies began to chatter at once while Juliet rose, ostensibly to arrange some cups on the cart. "I wish you would have spoken of this with me first," she said to Alexander in a mere undertone.

"But you doubtless would have agreed with me, my dear. Smile, or they will think you do not wish the ball, and Mary will be crushed."

"By all means, Mary must not be crushed." But Juliet knew what he meant, and she smiled until her jaw ached.

Once the callers had left, full of the news to spread throughout Woodbury, Juliet retreated to her bedroom. What a good thing she had shoved the chest in front of that connecting door. Alexander could not tease her now.

She was wrong.

She had settled at her desk and was drawing up a list of all who must be invited when the door to the hall opened and Alexander walked in. Of course he immediately noticed the chest and gave Juliet a mocking look.

"I insist upon some privacy, my lord," she said chillingly. "It is not proper for you to come charging in here any time of the day or night without so much as a by-your-leave."

"Marius was in the hall. I dared not knock."

"I recall my father knocking on my mother's door, and they were truly married!"

"That is neither here nor there. Have you a list for our ball?" He bent over her shoulder to examine the names she had put down so far and nodded. "Do not forget the parson. He's to marry the squire's daughter, you know."

"I do, but I'm surprised you know anything about it."

"Common gossip, my dear."

Juliet leaned back in her chair, nibbling the end of her pen, a pretty carved bit of wood. At length she said, "I had not expected to find life so busy when I took refuge here. Nor you here, for that matter."

"Thank Camilla Shelford for that. Had that insufferable chit left me in peace, I'd have remained in London." Alexander paced to the window, where he stood gazing out across the gardens, hands behind his back. He looked over to where Juliet sat, waiting for her reaction.

She returned that look. "And be none the wiser for my having trespassed in your home."

"Or used my name," he added with a curious expression on his face.

"You do feel that we shall muddle through this with no great difficulty, do you not?" Juliet asked anxiously.

"Of course, of course," he said, leaving the window to contemplate the chest Juliet had tugged before the connecting door. "What if I need to talk with you in private?" he queried.

"Knock," was the terse reply.

"What if there is another summer storm?" he inquired, a canny expression momentarily crossing his face.

"I shall bury my head beneath the covers, stop my ears with

my fingers, and sing to myself," Juliet said, firmly repressing the desire to add, "so there."

"What if Marius comes to speak with you? And what of Mrs. Bassett? She is bound to talk."

Juliet shrugged and gave up the fight. "Very well. Put it back. But I still want my privacy!"

"As much as you please, my dear." He gave the chest a push. "And now for the ball. You will need a new gown—order one from Salisbury, a green satin, I think. Give Mrs. Bassett the menu as soon as you have one so she can order the foods. And I shall obtain the musicians."

"I have never given a ball before," Juliet warned.

"Neither have I, so we shall fumble our way along and hope for the best." He gave the chest a final shove and opened the connecting door. "This is much better. I prefer coming and going through here rather than the hall."

"So I gathered," Juliet said dryly. The man was hopeless. He simply could not get it through his head that she wanted to be left alone.

The following days were busy ones. She ordered a gown from the mantua-maker in Salisbury said by Mrs. Ogleby to be the best. Along with Juliet's measurements and a page torn from a recent copy of *The Lady's Magazine* went a request for ivory moire to be trimmed with pearl beads. She would pay for the gown herself. Alexander had said green satin, but she was not going to yield on everything. It was quite enough he had his way about the chest.

Not that he had intruded upon her privacy since then. To her surprise, he'd been amazingly good about knocking the few times he had a question for her, or wanted her opinion on something. Otherwise, he left her alone as she preferred. And Juliet insisted she was happy that way. Indeed, she had nearly convinced herself such was the case.

The musicians had been hired, and Mrs. Bassett consulted not only about the menu but opening the rooms to increase the space available for dancing.

"There are sliding doors over here, my lady. A stout footman, such as his lordship has hired for the occasion, will make short work of opening them."

Juliet was relieved to note that there would be ample space for refreshments, then worried about the decorations, flowers being what they were.

"Temperamental?" Alexander asked in bewilderment. "Flowers have tempers?"

"The weather affects them. Too hot and they fade rapidly. Too cool and the buds delay their opening."

He shrugged, gave her a strange look, then left the drawing room, where she had spread out her papers.

"His lordship will come through for you, madam," Mrs. Bassett said comfortably. "Just like his father, he is."

Which thought intrigued Juliet for hours.

The next crisis came when her gown was delivered. The mantua-maker arrived in her own modest carriage to make a final fitting for so impressive a customer as the Viscountess Hawkswood.

Juliet put on the gown, enormously pleased with the results of her order. It was undoubtedly the loveliest thing she had ever owned. The neckline was probably a trifle low, but she had sufficient bosom to do it justice. She puffed out the tiny sleeves, then turned before her looking glass to admire the pretty design done in pearl beads around the hem. It was even more elegant than the illustration.

Then Alexander knocked, entering without waiting for her to reply. "Mrs. Bassett said your gown had come." He halted just inside the door, staring at Juliet as though he couldn't believe his eyes. "Ivory? Trimmed with pearls?"

Juliet met his gaze, tilted her chin, then said, "I am a trifle tired of green, my dearest. Do you not agree that this will be a most satisfactory gown for the coming ball?"

"Beautiful, my love."

But Juliet knew there would be words to follow and wondered if real husbands and wives had these arguments regarding such trifling matters as a dress. Of course she had ordered what she wished; he'd had no right to tell her what she should have, and so she would tell him as soon as might be.

It was not easy.

"See how well the pretty fan you gave me goes with the gown?" she queried once the mantua-maker had made a few adjustments and gone on her way.

"Why did you order ivory moire instead of green satin?" Alexander demanded. He had wanted to see her in green satin. He could well envision the effect of the lush satin combined with her hair and that incredible skin, not to mention her beautiful eyes. Whenever he had made a suggestion to his former mistress, she had complied with eager willingness. But then, he was forced to admit, he paid the bills, and she wore the gown merely to please him.

But why couldn't Juliet have seen how well she would look in such a gown?

"What is the matter with this gown?" she demanded. "Is the style not the very latest? The fabric lovely? I know what it is— you like to give orders and expected me to obey your wishes instantly. You are a spoiled, pampered boy, my lord. Well, hear this," she said quietly, "I am not your wife, no matter that everyone thinks I am, nor can you command me as you would a servant. I have paid the bill from my own funds. The dress is mine, and as such I hope you will not be displeased by my appearance in it. But I *will* wear it."

Alexander watched the flash of her eyes, thinking passion brought out golden lights in them. What a lovely creature she was. He studied the effect of the ivory moire against her skin and hair and decided it looked nice—but not to be compared with green satin. Next time he would go to the mantua-maker himself to order Juliet's gown, and next time it would definitely be green satin—trimmed in ivory lace.

"There was no need for you to pay the bill," Alexander remembered to tell her. "When I set up the ball, I intended to pay for your gown. And I am *not* spoiled or pampered," he finished, for those words had stung badly. True, people were inclined to let him have his way, but after all, he was a very sensible man with sensible proposals.

"Indeed?" she said while crossing to place her lovely fan gently upon her desk. "If you say so."

Her words made him feel foolish, and he stalked from her room in high dudgeon.

Dinner was an ordeal that evening. Marius and Lord Taunton discussed a horse race they had attended, debating the merits of the horses with Alexander. Juliet sat in self-imposed silence at the foot of the table, biding her time until she might escape.

Just before she left the room, Marius spoke up. "If I'd thought you two were not married, this evening has convinced me. The pair of you are acting like an old married couple. Had a tiff, did you?" He guffawed, nudging his friend, who managed a mild chuckle and looked uncomfortable.

"I shan't bother to answer that remark," Juliet snapped, "other than to say that if Alexander and I have a difference of opinion, it is not cause for discussion with you."

Feeling as though she had put her stepbrother nicely in his place, she swept from the room only to come to a halt beyond the closed door when she heard the men break forth in laughter.

Believing herself greatly put upon, she charged up the stairs to her room, slammed the door behind her, shoved the chest back in place before the connecting door, and threw herself on her bed to burst into tears.

"He is a heartless beast," she sniffed when Pansy entered later to help her from her dinner gown.

"He helped you with your stepbrother, my lady."

"At the moment I do not wish to hear how good he is. I am angry, most put-upon, and if I wish to have a good cry, I will."

Pansy, knowing when to make herself scarce, did what she must and hurried away.

Thinking over the evening and that hateful laughter following dinner brought a fresh spate of tears. When a knock came on the door, Juliet muttered, "Who is it?"

"Alexander."

Wonder of wonders, he didn't barge in as was his custom. "Go away."

The door cracked open, and Alexander stuck his head around it to be greeted by a pillow tossed at him.

"I said, go away."

"I am sorry if your feelings are hurt. I'll buy you the green satin next time."

"There won't be any next time. Just go away!"

He went, and Juliet cried all the harder.

Chapter 9

Things always look better in the morning sun, and so Juliet found upon arising. In the small hours of the night she had decided upon her course of action, and all that remained was to see it through, not that she particularly relished the prospect of what she determined necessary.

There was much to be done for the coming ball; she whisked herself from bed with alacrity. This was not the day to be mooning about, regardless of her inner feelings.

She studied a somewhat wan face in her looking glass and decided that with a dusting of rice powder over a hint of rouge she would pass. There was little point in reflecting on what had happened last evening. Most likely Miss Pritchard would tell her she was being a silly goose to fuss so over the green satin gown and to get on with what had to be done.

"Remember, you foolish girl, all this is in aid of freeing you from a man you detest and providing Lord Hawkswood with a haven until that Miss Shelford looks elsewhere," she scolded the image in her looking glass. Juliet wondered how long it would take. If the girl were truly in love with Alexander, it might take time. Juliet knew that it would take a great deal of time for her to forget the viscount.

When Pansy entered the room, she had a hesitant look on her face, Juliet was amused to see. "Morning, my lady."

"I suppose the others are up and gone?" Juliet asked with seeming casualness, fiddling with her linen napkin before consuming the dainty breakfast Pansy had brought.

"Indeed. His lordship went off to Salisbury again, and Lord

Taunton and your stepbrother took themselves off some-wheres," Pansy said.

"A quiet day, in other words. Good—there is much to be done."

Pansy gave Juliet a curious look, then took the yellow morning gown from the wardrobe. "The yellow again. You need some new gowns, my lady," the maid ventured to say.

Juliet was becoming heartily sick of the dress, but she had never owned an extensive wardrobe while at Winterton Hall, and now her lack of suitable clothing was even more vexing.

"Indeed, I do. Perhaps when the ball is over and Lord Hawkswood is off to wherever he intends to go, I can order a few." Maid and mistress exchanged a look of complete accord.

"Think you your stepbrother will release your funds, then?" Pansy dared to inquire.

"I devoutly hope so." Juliet tossed her napkin aside after swallowing the last of her morning tea. Then she slipped on the yellow morning gown, tied an apron over the dress, and prepared to go to work.

There was an additional maid and a footman to instruct, Cook to soothe, and Mrs. Bassett to consult. The ball would be held on the morrow, and there was not a moment to lose in preparation, not that the ball would be all that grand. Fifteen couples had accepted her invitation, but they would be a select group of local gentry. Besides, it was Juliet's first attempt at giving anything so important, and she was terrified she would fail.

What a pity she did not have the comfort of Miss Pritchard and her intelligent advice. When she passed the looking glass in the lower hall, she glanced in it, scolding herself, "You will have to rely on what common sense you have, dear girl."

Her thoughts dwelt briefly on Alexander, wondering what he found to occupy himself in Salisbury all day, then realized he would not know of her feelings and likely hoped to avoid a tongue lashing.

Well, he would be relieved, she felt certain, once he knew the decision she had made during the night.

*   *   *

Alexander relaxed in the dim recesses of the Rose and Crown, wondering when he could return to the manor. Fine thing, a man driven from his own home just because he had teased the woman who pretended to be his wife. All this in aid of avoiding a disagreeable marriage, only to find himself tangled in a plot not of his making. Yet he had adjusted to it, he decided, thinking of Juliet and the charms she'd revealed while in the rosebud nightgown.

He drained his ale, then made to leave the inn, only to duck back into the shade of its door once again. *It couldn't be.* His eyes must have played tricks on him. There was no possible way in which Camilla Shelford could have tracked him to Salisbury. He inched out once again and could see nothing of the woman he thought he had glimpsed. An overactive imagination, that's what it was.

However, he prudently decided to head back to Woodbury and say nothing of his suspicions. After all, even if by some remote chance Camilla was in Salisbury, there was nothing and no one to lead her to Woodbury.

When he rode through the village, he noted that the little shop in the village center was overflowing with customers and rightly figured that the main interest of the calls was gossip. Yet, each woman would purchase something while she probed for news. At least he and Juliet had served some purpose—an increase in custom for the village shop!

The house smelled deliciously of flowers and baking, beeswax and the heliotrope scent that Juliet preferred. He hunted through the various rooms only to find Mrs. Bassett at work, polishing silver.

"Your wife is in the garden, my lord," she said, unconsciously echoing the very words she had used the day Alexander had arrived at the manor some weeks ago.

At the sound of footsteps on the gravel, Juliet looked up from where she contemplated the flowers she intended to use on the morrow. Wiping her hands on the apron she had put over her yellow morning gown, she rose, squared her shoulders, and prepared to say what she must.

She couldn't blame him for his wary look as he approached. Poor man, the last time he had seen her she had tossed a pillow at him, behaving like a silly goose.

"How does everything proceed?" he asked hesitantly.

"Well, I believe. Although I am pleased you are home so early. I should like the benefit of your experience, for I feel certain you have attended any number of balls, even small ones like this, and I could use a bit of help."

"Certainly." He took a step toward her.

She crumpled the apron in her hands, suddenly shy and unsure of what she intended to say. Was she correct? Yet she must clear the air and free him from any feeling of guilt in the matter.

"There is a problem?" he prompted, coming a step closer and removing his hat only to thrust a hand through his hair in what seemed to her a gesture of frustration or possibly annoyance.

"Alexander, there is something I must say, and I beg you not to interrupt until I am finished," she began, ignoring his startled exclamation of surprise.

"I *must* apologize for my behavior last evening. I was a silly little fool to react so to your words about my gown. Could we be friends again?"

She was staring at the graveled walk, a pity, for she quite missed the sudden gleam that lit his eyes, which had disappeared by the time she looked up to search his face for a reaction to her words.

"Of course," he said in a manner guaranteed to soothe her nerves. "I am relieved you feel that way, but I must confess my own guilt in the matter. I am sorry that I behaved so when I should have suspected you were not accustomed to such conduct. Forgive me, Juliet?"

"Indeed, I do." She dropped the badly treated apron, smoothing it down with nervous fingers while trying to think of something else to say. He took another step to her side, looking down at her with kindly regard.

"I went to Salisbury to find something to atone for my behavior."

"There was no need," she began to protest, and he silenced

her by tossing his hat on the stone bench, then placing a finger across her mouth.

"There was every need." He reached into an inside pocket to take out a little packet that he held in his hand, teasing her with its possible contents. "That ivory gown is lovely on you, and if I hadn't been so desirous of seeing you in green satin, I would have praised it at once. In a way it is your own fault, for I do believe green satin would be most elegant on you. However, as a gown for your first ball ivory moire is most suitable."

"And?" Juliet urged, curiosity consuming her.

"I found what I think is a finishing touch for your gown tomorrow evening. I trust you will find it an acceptable expression of contrition." He extended his hand, offering his gift with a watchful gaze.

Juliet accepted the packet with trembling hands, then tore open the wrapping to find an exquisite little pearl brooch, precisely the sort to dress up the neck of her ivory gown without being ostentatious. "It is quite perfect, my lord," she said, feeling breathless, her heart fluttering. Other than her pearl necklace and ear bobs and the betrothal ring Alexander had loaned her, she had no jewelry. This was quite splendid.

He looked beyond where they stood to note that Marius Winterton was observing the little scene. "Your stepbrother watches us. Perhaps we ought to convince him that we have truly reconciled our differences?" Alexander's voice was lazy and his manner deceptively casual.

"Just so," Juliet said at once, before considering what Alexander might deem an acceptable way of convincing Marius.

She discovered immediately as she was swept into Alexander's arms to be soundly kissed in a manner she had not experienced heretofore, even in the other kisses Alexander had bestowed. This kiss was lingering and most stirring, although it turned her knees to blancmange again and her pulse tripled. She clutched at his fine Bath cloth coat with desperation lest she swoon as virgins in those silly novels were wont to do. Perhaps they weren't so silly after all, she thought.

Once released, Juliet leaned against him, thankful for the

strength of his arms about her, for she was quite unable to support herself. Taking a deep breath, she summoned a voice that proved less shaken than she'd have expected.

"If that did not convince him, he is beyond hope," she whispered.

"Good," Alexander said quietly. "Now, perhaps we can go inside, and you can tell me all these things you wish to discuss."

"Discuss?" she echoed, thinking her brain had turned to fried mush again.

"For the ball?" he said, twinkling a gentle smile down at her while leading her into the house.

"Oh, the ball," she replied, recalling the event that had totally absorbed her attention only minutes before.

"Decorations?" he prompted. "Perhaps the punch? Or do you worry about the time to serve the supper?"

"All of the mentioned," Juliet said with a quavering laugh, accepting his company to the morning room, where her plans were spread out for his approval. They spent a most agreeable hour going over the final arrangements, with Alexander soothing Juliet's nerves considerably on all points.

Marius had little to say at dinner. He studied his younger stepsister as though greatly puzzled by her.

Lord Taunton nattered on about the satisfactory sale of his unwanted property and the unexpected charm offered by Miss Lucy Tackley.

"The young lady is not only pretty, but I understand her father has provided a most acceptable dowry," Alexander tossed out as Juliet closed the dining room door following a pleasant dinner.

She left them to their port and a discussion of the finer points of negotiating a marriage settlement. Would Alexander suggest to Marius that the time had come for Juliet's funds to be released? She sighed at the complications she envisioned. The money would doubtlessly be handed to Alexander, and she would have to tax him with giving it to her.

Men considered women far too lacking in intelligence to

handle money of their own. Never mind that she had done very well in administering the manor before Alexander's arrival. He most likely would insist upon some arrangement for her whereupon some man controlled the sum of money, doling it out to her in bits and snippets. A banker in Salisbury, no doubt. Unless Alexander decided she could not remain in this house once their charade was over. She hadn't considered this possibility lately, for he had seemed quite the friend.

She sat down at the harp, plucking out a melody while she wondered where she might go. Perhaps Miss Pritchard might agree to join her in a little village like Woodbury? They could set up a modest household and live quietly. The thought of never seeing Alexander again was so depressing she began to play a melancholy piece of music that had Alexander frowning when he entered the room.

"Come now, something more lively than that!" he exclaimed. Seating himself at the clavichord, he commenced to play the lively sonata they had worked on the past days, a Mozart piece Juliet thought her favorite.

She joined in at once, and when Marius and Lord Taunton peered in on their way to play a game of billiards, they found a congenial, smiling couple who looked for all the world as though they had been married for ages.

"Lovebirds, bah," Marius said with a sour expression.

Juliet heard him, but dared not take her eyes from the music. If he but knew the whole of it!

The ball, small as it might be, appeared to be accounted a great success right from the start. In Woodbury the notion of arriving fashionably late to a gathering had never taken hold, so that early in the evening all thirty guests had arrived and the musicians were playing a gay tune softly in the background until such time that Juliet and Alexander led the dancers in the minuet.

Juliet had never felt quite so self-assured. Earlier, Alexander had knocked, waiting politely until she invited him inside. He admired her gown, pinned on the brooch in precisely the right place, then escorted her to the ground floor with all evidence of pride in her appearance. Juliet glowed. From that moment on, nothing could or would go wrong.

Nor had it. The punch was just right, neither too sweet nor too sour. The flowers were obligingly lovely, arranged in every vase to be found in the house.

"My dear Lady Hawkswood," Mrs. Ogleby said with a pleased smile as she inspected the decor of the ground-floor rooms, "you have exceeded all expectations. This ball will be talked about for years to come."

"Thank you, Mrs. Ogleby. Mrs. Bassett has been an enormous help. She showed me how to open up the rooms so we could have a great deal more space. I am most fortunate in my assistance." Juliet looked about her with an air of contentment; the house had never looked better in her eyes.

"And your husband, if I make no mistake," Mrs. Ogleby said archly. "We are all pleased you have reconciled with him. A handsome gentleman like his lordship ought not be left on his own for long. There are too many unscrupulous women who will take advantage of such a situation, if you know what I mean."

Juliet didn't, but murmured a soft agreement, resolved to ask Alexander about what had been said when she had the chance. What a shock poor Mrs. Ogleby would have if she knew the truth of the situation. Juliet would be sunk far beyond the pale, declared no better than she should be.

As for Lord Hawkswood, Juliet suspected nothing but a touch of scandal—soon to be forgotten—would mar his life. Life was different for men; they had their own standards to live by. In a way Juliet envied his independence, quite forgetting the muddle she had drawn him into, one he declared was difficult to extricate himself from without the greatest difficulty.

Alexander claimed her hand for the minuet, leading her out to be followed by the Oglebys, the squire and his wife, the Tackleys, and the parson with Mary Otterly, then the others of lesser degree as was proper in a minuet.

"You have found excellent musicians, my lord," Juliet whispered from behind the lovely birthday fan Alexander had given her, a fan that went so perfectly with the ivory gown.

"They are good, aren't they," he replied, pleased for her, but also impressed with the talent to be found in such a remote area as Salisbury and its environs.

"I understand they play for the assemblies during the Season. How fortunate they were free this evening."

"As to that, I have found a title commands a certain edge when obtaining what I want. Usually," he added, not at all certain where he stood with the elusive Juliet. She might have melted in his arms, but he had not forgotten her claim that she hated him. It was possible to experience both emotions at the same time.

However, he thought while executing a neat turn, then keeping eye contact as dictated during the dance, she showed promise. Her apology was well done, and it revealed a maturity of character he'd not expected. Not that he had been without blame; he'd had no business to be at her about the green satin gown. Even were she his wife in truth, she would have the right to select her clothes as she pleased. That would not prevent him from choosing one for her as a gift, however. And *that* would be green satin.

He held her hand at her shoulder level, taking notice of the graceful line of her arms, the contour of her bodice, where the brooch he had given her sat so nicely. Life with Juliet would have its positive aspect, he was sure.

Juliet sank in a elegant curtsy at the conclusion to the dance, wondering what Alexander was thinking to give him such an expression. He looked enormously satisfied with something. She hoped it was with their modest ball.

Mrs. Tackley brought Lucy over to chat, commenting with caution on the attention her daughter received from Lord Taunton. Here was one mother not completely overwhelmed by a title. Juliet gave her high marks for common sense.

When Mr. Wyllard requested Lucy's hand for the next country dance, Mrs. Tackley watched them walk away to join the others and said, "I intend to write to the dowager Lady Hawkswood to learn more about Lord Taunton. She may live a secluded life, but she knows all that goes on in Society."

Juliet felt a sudden chill hit her. "Is that so? I do not think my husband is on close terms with his grandmother. At least," Juliet amended, "he never speaks of her to me."

"You must have met her, surely?" Mrs. Tackley probed with circumspection.

Forgetting that she had revealed very little of their past to the local gentry, Juliet said, "My husband and I most romantically eloped to Gretna. I had not had a Season in London because my mother died and then my father went off to Russia. There was no opportunity for me to have met the lady."

Mrs. Tackley appeared to digest this bit of information, then moved off to join Mrs. Ogleby where she shared the tidbit.

The squire's daughter, Mary, joined Juliet by the punch bowl, eyeing the single men in attendance with an assessing eye.

"When do you marry Parson Richards, Mary?

The girl blushed and said, "Come September. I am to go to Salisbury for my wedding trousseau. Mrs. Ogleby said we had best go to the same mantua-maker you used. Your gown is very lovely, my lady."

Juliet thought of green satin and smiled. "Thank you, Mary. I think she did very well for me. I feel certain that she will make you a lovely wedding gown."

"Did you have a wedding gown when you married Lord Hawkswood? Or did you wear something you brought along?" Then Mary blushed again, realizing the impropriety of her question.

"A simple gown," Juliet replied, not wanting to snub the girl, yet unable to think of a suitable fiction.

Juliet wished she might know the comfort of a friend in whom she could confide and seek advice. For the moment she dare not think of such a thing. But Mary seemed such a sensible girl, and for the moment Juliet forgot she was supposedly a married woman. She merely wanted a friend.

"I believe I shall want something simple as well. If I am not extravagant on my wedding dress, I shall have more to spend on other things," Mary said wisely.

"True, true," Juliet agreed, wishing the parson would come to claim Mary and whisk her away from here.

Instead of the parson, Alexander joined them, thus effectively silencing the shy Mary. When the parson actually claimed his bride-to-be, Juliet turned urgently to Alexander.

"Mrs. Tackley said she intends to write your grandmother to inquire about Lord Taunton—his background and prospects, most likely."

"Good," Alexander said absently, then looked to Juliet. "Not good," he said in reversal.

"Most assuredly not good. Mrs. Tackley was certain I had met the dowager, and I fear I mentioned our flit to Gretna—most romantic, you know—as well as my mother's death and Father's trip to Russia being the cause of my not having a Season. As soon as I had said the words, I knew I ought to have kept silent."

"Well," Alexander said with a touch of philosophy in his voice, "what has been said cannot be unsaid. The trouble with not telling the truth is that you have to remember the lies that have been told and keep them straight."

"Do I see Marius pouring something into the punch?" Juliet asked with alarm.

"I'll have the footman exchange it for another bowl. Mrs. Bassett has one in the kitchen, I trust?"

"Indeed, she has. But why? Does he wish our guests to be tipsy? That would be a scandal."

Alexander murmured agreement, then went off to inform the footman to make the exchange before confronting his supposed relative.

Juliet watched worriedly as the two men spoke, plying her fan with more energy than she had expected to have at this point in the evening. Whatever Alexander said to Marius had a strange effect on her stepbrother. He grew rather red in the face—had it been a woman, Juliet would have called it a blush—and appeared to offer an apology. Alexander uttered a few more words, then returned to Juliet's side.

"He seemed to think things needed to be livened up a trifle. I explained."

"Thank you, Alexander. What else can go wrong?" she said softly. "I do hope Mrs. Tackley writes nothing about us to your grandmother."

"As do I," he agreed, clearly thinking it impossible Mrs. Tackley would do otherwise.

But the remainder of the evening went well. The supper was enjoyed by all, and if Marius thought it a bit dull, he knew better than to attempt again to add spirits to the punch.

They were about to leave the supper room when the footman approached Alexander, drawing him to one side and murmuring discreetly to him.

Juliet wondered what might cause Alexander's look of alarm, rapidly followed by an expression of dismay. He excused himself at once to hurry after the footman.

Alexander entered the library and stared at the person who awaited him, his expression something between horror and astonishment.

"Harry Riggs! Dare I hope this is not what I fear it to be?" He crossed over to a narrow table to pour a glass of claret for his friend, then one for himself.

"I dislike to be the bearer of bad news, Alexander. I caught wind of a tidbit regarding the beautiful Camilla and managed to follow her to Salisbury. How she has tracked you this far is beyond me. *I've* not said a word," Harry asserted, then took a long swallow of the excellent claret. "I do *not* think she has seen me, nor does she know she has been pursued. She is hot on your trail; a more determined woman I have yet to see. I trust your clever mind can think up an excellent reason to fob her off?"

"The best, my friend," Alexander replied dryly. "I am already married. She can hardly insist I commit bigamy."

"Oh, I say, that is good. Who will play the part?" Harry asked with a chuckle.

A tap on the door halted the exchange, and Alexander invited the person in, having a fair idea as to whom it might be.

Juliet entered, then stopped when she saw the stranger.

As for Harry, his eyes nearly popped when he beheld the lovely woman who crossed the room to stand intimately by his friend's side.

"Alexander? Introduce me," she commanded nicely with a demure sparkle in her fine amber eyes.

"Juliet, this is my oldest friend, Harry Riggs, down from

London. Harry, may I present my wife?" Alexander tucked her hand close to his side and waited.

"You *really* have a wife? It's not a ruse? That's a bit extreme, is it not?" Then Harry appeared to realize what he'd said, for he turned a deep red and blustered, "That is to say, charmed to make your acquaintance, my lady."

"We are giving a ball this evening," Juliet informed Harry with a smile. "The others are having supper at present, but they will be filtering back to most likely dance once again. Will you join us?"

"Harry will be staying with us. I expect his man has already unpacked his gear, and Harry will happily change, to return in a trice. Am I not correct, Harry?"

"Yes. Yes, indeed. I won't be but a moment."

Alexander rang for Mrs. Bassett, who took Harry away with her, not revealing by so much as a frown that he upset her evening in any way.

"You did not seem greatly pleased to learn your friend had arrived," Juliet said, a question in her voice.

"He was only to come in the event he knew something regarding Camilla and any danger she might present to me."

"And?" Juliet asked, looking at Alexander with dawning consternation in her eyes.

"Camilla is in Salisbury. There is every possibility she will come here."

"What a disgustingly persistent female, my lord," Juliet said, that sparkle returning to her eyes. "What a pity she has gone to so much trouble, only to find that you are already married." Whereupon Juliet drew her supposed husband along with her to rejoin their guests, an odd little smile tilting her lips.

Chapter 10

Alexander met Harry Riggs at the breakfast table before Marius Winterton and Lord Taunton came downstairs.

Harry helped himself to buttered eggs, a thick slab of ham, a stack of toast, then nodded to the maid to fill his cup with steaming coffee before he taxed his friend for the truth.

"Where did you find that enchanting creature you introduced as your wife?" he asked around a mouthful of ham. "You haven't been here long enough to have wooed and won so fair a young maiden as she."

"It is a long and complicated tale." Alexander filled his plate, poured a cup of coffee, then toyed with the food while he considered how much to reveal.

Harry forked another bit of ham in his mouth, then leaned back in his chair, chewing thoughtfully as he surveyed his companion. "Well?" he inquired as the silence went on too long. "Never say there is something questionable here?"

Alexander rubbed his chin, still unsure, then decided his best friend, who had pursued Camilla and come to warn him of her proximity, deserved nothing less than the truth or nearly all the truth. So he explained as best he could about discovering Juliet in residence when he arrived, that she had captured the hearts of the local gentry, and that she had needed him quite as much as he would need her assistance. He avoided details of any marriage.

"Didn't care for that brother of hers in the least," Harry mumbled. "Something not quite right about him. Don't look the least bit alike."

"Stepbrother—and he'd taken it upon himself to find Juliet a husband. Only she didn't want a fellow just like Marius," Alexander said dryly.

"Can't say I blame her for that, old fellow," Harry said quietly, mindful that others in the house might be coming down for a meal. "But did you have to marry the girl? I thought you wanted to avoid that situation?"

"Now, if you walked into a house to find that lovely woman capably handling all affairs, talented, charming, everything you might like in a wife—and claiming to be your wife—what would you do?" Alexander had spoken softly, but he rose to check the hall to make certain no one was about. The house was almost too silent.

Harry stared at his plate a moment, then looked up at Alexander. "I see what you mean. I'd likely do the same thing. So what happens now?"

"You really think Camilla will come here?" Alexander countered, avoiding a discussion of the future with Juliet for the moment.

"I should think so. Girl must have a nose like a bloodhound. If she tracked you to Salisbury, she will most likely find Woodbury. Amazing woman, Camilla. Can't think why she is so set upon having you—not that you aren't a fine chap and all that, but to go to such lengths is not normal, is it?" Harry leaned back in his chair to contemplate the last of his toast.

"Not in my book," Alexander agreed.

"I wonder what she will do when she arrives to find you already married?" Harry mused before sipping his cooling coffee.

"Juliet called her a disgustingly persistent female," Alexander said, remembering the concise evaluation from his wife. "I have no doubt but what we will be saddled with another guest until she is convinced of the marriage."

"I'd give a pony to see her face when she hears the news," Harry concluded with a chuckle.

"You are on," Alexander said, pushing aside his scarcely touched plate of food. "All you have to do is remain with me for the day." He rose from the table, gestured to the rear of the house, and inquired if his friend would like a brisk canter, seeing the morning was so fine.

"Juliet?" Harry asked with a glance up the stairway.

"My wife has her chocolate in her room while she plans her day. We will see her later. I believer she is supposed to call on one of the neighbors this afternoon." Alexander was not sure why he made a point of calling Juliet his wife in every reference to her, even to Harry, but he found he could do no less. Considering what he knew would be their fate, it was the least he could do.

"Well, she did a dashed fine job with your ball."

"She did, didn't she?" Alexander agreed. "I am fortunate to discover a woman not only beautiful but capable as well."

They strode from the house and off to the stables in perfect harmony, ready to face the day and what it brought with equanimity.

At the top of the stairs Juliet remained in her doorway, quite shaken at what she had inadvertently overheard. Alexander thought her beautiful and capable? He was pleased with her efforts on the ball? Well, if he truly feared this Camilla creature, she, stalwart Juliet, would do all she could to help the gentleman who had assisted her.

And he was a gentleman, no doubt about that. She ignored the episode with the rosebud nightgown; *that* scandalous event she preferred to forget if possible. In every other instance, however, he had been the courteous *preux chevalier.* It remained to be seen if he could turn out to be her knight in shining armor in actuality, but Juliet was content as things stood now—more or less.

One of these fine days Alexander would discover that he loved her—as she had found she loved him. Surely it could not be so great a step from thinking her beautiful and capable to lovable and loved?

She returned to her room to dress for the day, sighing as Pansy took the white muslin dress from the wardrobe. How tired she was of the same dresses over and over again. There was nothing for it but to go into Salisbury and order several new gowns. Particularly now that this Camilla creature loomed on the horizon. Juliet could have the bill sent to Lord

Hawkswood and then reimburse him from the money that was bound to come from Marius.

Knowing she had best depart promptly were she to spend much of the day with the mantua-maker, Juliet requested Pansy to don her bonnet and prepare to accompany her.

"Yes, ma'am," Pansy said with enthusiasm. "Your gowns are going to fall apart before long iffen you don't order some new ones." The maid happily took herself off to her room, then joined Juliet at the front of the house when the groom drew up with the small carriage that had been in the stables. It was old, but the leather had been kept oiled and softened, the rest maintained in decent repair, and it certainly would do for the short drive to Salisbury.

"What will his lordship say, you taking yourself off to Salisbury like this, ma'am?" Pansy inquired with the sort of boldness she'd shown before coming to Woodbury.

"I left him a note with Randall. I fancy his lordship is as weary of my old gowns as we are." With that, Juliet settled back in the carriage, admiring the view of the countryside and thinking it was about time she visited town for a bit of shopping.

She was almost to the edge of Salisbury when she was passed by an imposing traveling coach lumbering in the direction of Woodbury. The driver and groom were dressed in fine livery, and in the coach window Juliet caught a glimpse of a pretty face framed with golden curls, sporting a jockey hat of the latest design.

"Now that is a fine way to travel," Juliet murmured to her maid.

"Beats a post chaise, it does," Pansy agreed. "Slow, though, I expect."

Juliet ignored this comment as they entered town, and she directed her groom to deposit her at the mantua-maker's establishment and to return some hours later.

Once inside, she renewed her acquaintance with the pleasant, respectful seamstress and then prepared to spend all the time necessary in pursuit of her desire. She wanted clothes that would appeal to Alexander. Above all, she wanted a green satin gown. She didn't know where she would wear the thing, or quite why he wanted to see her in it, but have it she would.

All went as she hoped. She selected fabric for several muslin gowns in various colors and prints, then chose a primrose sarcenet gown with tulip-shaped sleeves that would look well when she was at the harp, and would be splendid for evenings at home. Nothing would do but she would have a new riding habit in rust trimmed with smart jet beading and black embroidery. And then she brought up the matter of the green satin gown.

The mantua-maker frowned, then excused herself to go to the workroom area, returning with a gorgeous length of leaf green satin over her arms.

"How lovely," Juliet said, but gave the woman a questioning look.

"I just finished this for a lady who then had a death in the family and must go into blacks at once. It is a loss to me—unless you might find it pleasing?"

Juliet jumped to her feet, "I shall try it on at once. The color is excellent, and if it does not require much alteration, I can take it home with me." She wasn't certain why, but all at once it had become important to have that green gown, thus pleasing Alexander. It would atone for her earlier behavior. Which brought something else to mind she'd do before returning to Woodbury.

The gown proved better than she had hoped. Tiny sleeves extended from the low-cut bodice, which had an elegant French style to its cut. Around the lower skirt were very nice ruffled loops of the same satin in the centers of which were delicate embroidered panels. It needed little alteration.

"It is splendid and will do quite nicely. How fortunate for me that the dress is available just when I have need of it." Juliet took off the lovely garment, then said, "Are there perchance any other dresses such as this one that have been rejected for one reason or another? I truly have need for several additional day dresses."

The delighted mantua-maker had three such day dresses in

pretty muslins, all requiring little alteration for Juliet's slender figure. Eyes agleam, Juliet bought all three.

"I have a few errands to do. Could they be altered within an hour?" Juliet discovered being a viscountess had distinct advantages. Whereas a mantua-maker might have put off an ordinary lady, one with a title rated far better treatment.

"They shall be ready, I promise, my lady."

Juliet left the shop, thinking it would be difficult to go back to being plain Miss Winterton from Winterton Hall.

It took hunting through several shops before Juliet found what she wanted next. It was an exquisite oval gold snuff box, the top and side inlaid with lapis lazuli. It was the size to fit perfectly in the palm of a man's hand. Although Juliet hadn't seen Alexander use snuff, she wanted something special for him to remember her by just in case worse came to worst and they parted.

After that happy find, she prowled through the delightful shops to locate two parasols, three pretty bonnets, some hose Pansy reminded her she needed, a dozen handkerchiefs to embroider, and several pairs of gloves in delicate cream.

The green satin gown and the three muslins awaited her when she returned to the mantua-maker's. The groom presented himself with the carriage in front of the shop, and Juliet entered the vehicle with a contented sigh—and a great number of parcels.

Pansy gathered the parcels around her while Juliet managed two hatboxes and her reticule with the neat package inside containing the snuff box.

The morning had gone well for Alexander. He and Harry had returned from their ride to learn Juliet had traveled to Salisbury on a shopping expedition. It gave them a chance to stroll about the modest property, explore the tidy little estate lately belonging to Mr. Taunton, and enjoy a hearty repast at noon.

Marius and Lord Taunton joined Harry and Alexander. Alexander figuring the more the better, insisted upon their dubious company. They had settled in the cool of the library with glasses of claret when they heard the sound of a coach and four coming up the drive to the house.

"Expecting company?" Marius inquired lazily. It was quite evident he was in no hurry to leave the charming manor house.

"It is always possible friends come to pay a visit when one is living in the country," Alexander countered, not revealing the possibility of Camilla's arrival on the scene. "Your stepsister went to Salisbury this morning, but I doubt she returns so soon."

"Juliet? Shopping? Suppose she might take some time. Spend your money, too," Marius concluded with a snide little laugh.

"But not for long," Alexander replied. "You will release her dowry to me soon, I feel certain. My solicitor will see to it." There was a hint of steel in Alexander's voice that even Marius could detect.

"Oh, yes, to be sure," Marius replied, somewhat abashed the others had to hear that bit. "Immediately I return."

Mrs. Bassett, looking harried and displeased, entered the room, pausing just inside the door to say, "You have more guests, my lord. A young lady and her mother." She might have added the maids and other servants, but didn't. Servants did not count as guests, never mind they had to be housed and fed.

Alexander took his time about going to the entryway to greet his unwanted visitors. He wasn't looking forward to the meeting in the slightest.

"Lord Hawkswood, how providential we found you in this little village," Mrs. Shelford boomed, the feathers on her bonnet trembling as she spoke. A massive-bosomed, well-corseted, and highly rouged lady, she was probably one of the most irritating woman Alexander had ever met.

"Indeed?" Alexander said in reply, looking politely curious, but certainly not welcoming.

"Hello, my lord," Camilla gushed, the brim of her jockey bonnet tilting dangerously to one side as she dashed to greet him with a dainty kiss on his cheek.

"My, my, what a surprise. I hadn't expected to see you *here*," Alexander said with a distinct lack of enthusiasm, stepping away from her as though she might be contagious. Any other woman with even a modicum of intelligence would immediately have known her presence was not wished. Camilla was not so blessed.

Marius, Lord Taunton, and Harry Riggs sauntered out to join Alexander and his new guests with varied reactions, none of which were agreeable.

"Hullo, Miss Shelford. Fancy meeting you here, of all places," Harry said in dulcet tones.

"I thought I left *you* in town," she snapped with not quite the sweetness of voice and manner displayed when greeting his lordship.

"Alexander needed something, and I brought it to him. Friends do that sort of thing, you know," Harry said, not the least put out by her reception. Camilla Shelford might be a beautiful girl; she was not known for her many friends.

"Allow me to present these gentlemen, Miss Shelford. Marius Winterton—a relative of mine—and Robert, Lord Taunton, come to claim an inheritance. His late uncle was a neighbor."

The men bowed politely and stood shifting from foot to foot while looking uneasy.

"I am sorry my wife is not here to greet you; she went to Salisbury to shop today." Alexander waited while his little bomb dropped into the following silence. It took but moments for a reaction.

"Wife? But you are not married! You could not be married!" Camilla vowed. "You were not married when you left London . . . there has been nothing in the papers, no news of you. How could you possibly have married in so little time?" Camilla gabbled. "I was worried; I wondered if you were ill and thought to offer comfort. Mama recalled this little estate that once belonged to your grandmama, so . . ." She halted in her wild speech, her gaze darting from one impassive gentleman to the next.

"Mr. Riggs, it is a joke, is it not? A good joke," Camilla cried gaily, somewhat desperately.

"I have met the lady," Harry said with a pleased smile. "She is a charming creature."

"You are lying to me," Camilla snapped, her voice a trifle shrill. "There is no wife. It is a nasty little plot to tease me."

"Look here," Marius inserted, "that's my stepsister being nattered about. Nothing havey-cavey about it. She is married to his lordship, and that is that. They are as any married couple right down to the rings."

"When!" Camilla demanded, sounding more shrewish by the minute.

"Why do we not all go into the drawing room and have a cup of Mrs. Bassett's excellent tea?" Alexander inquired suavely. How he was enjoying this tempest in a teapot; it quite made his entire day.

The formidable Mrs. Shelford firmly grasped her daughter by the arm to propel her along to the drawing room of the interesting old manor house.

"I do not see how it happened," Camilla grumbled in an audible aside to her mother.

Mrs. Shelford pushed her daughter down on the sofa, looking about her all the while. The room was spotless, with carefully arranged bouquets of summer flowers gracing several tables. Music sat on the stand by the harp, witness to recent usage. Everywhere one looked feminine touches could be seen. The final blow was the charming workbasket, a piece of needlework in progress dangling from beneath the cover.

"I do not know if you indeed have a wife, my lord," Mrs. Shelford intoned majestically, "but it is evident there is a woman here. Somewhere," she added a moment later after realizing she didn't see said wife.

Tea was duly brought and drunk by all. The room was remarkably silent, considering Camilla and her mother sat therein.

"Miss Tackley said there is a village fete coming up," Lord Taunton at last offered.

"Indeed," Alexander said. "I believe my wife agreed to open the thing. Parson Richards has asked her to do a special bit of needlepoint for the altar, you know."

The four men discussed the coming fete for a bit.

"Nonsense," Camilla murmured. "All nonsense. I shan't be-

lieve you are married until I see your wife, and I may not believe it then." She took a long sip of her tea, then hungrily bit
into one of Mrs. Bassett's excellent lemon biscuits.

Alexander raised his brow at this bit of impertinence, but he
was relieved to hear the sound of a carriage in the drive. It was
too soon for Juliet to return, unless she had hurried.

"Mrs. Ogleby and Mrs. Tackley, my lord," Mrs. Bassett said
with a smile, for the ladies were admired by all.

"Good day, ladies." Alexander made the introductions, then
sat back to wait and watch.

"You have traveled far?" Mrs. Tackley politely wanted to
know of the visitor.

"Salisbury," Camilla snapped, while at the same moment her
mother said, "London."

"All the way from London with a stop in Salisbury," Mrs.
Ogleby said, sounding impressed. "My, I doubt I could manage
such a trip in a brief time," she added, taking note of the
strained atmosphere in the room.

"We have come," Mrs. Tackley said to Alexander, "to ask
dear Lady Hawkswood about the fete. We are so pleased that
someone from the manor will be there this year. It has been a
long time . . ." Her voice faded off as she took note of the expression on Camilla's face. "Are you well, Miss Shelford?"
Mrs. Tackley inquired. "You do not look at all well, I think."

"He said he is married," Camilla blurted, unmindful of the
scene she created.

"And so the dear man is," Mrs. Ogleby said comfortably in
reply. "You have not had the pleasure of meeting his wife,
then?" She gave the two women on the sofa a penetrating look.

"Such a dear creature," Mrs. Tackley gushed. "She is so talented, so lovely, so fine in every way, quite the most proper
lady to be the viscountess."

Those words could not be pleasing to Camilla. She looked
about to explode when Alexander rose. "I believe I hear her carriage now." At least he hoped that was her carriage he heard. He
walked to the door, fancying that he resembled an anxious,
lovesick, newly married husband without half trying. Naturally

he was anxious—he needed Juliet to fend off this man-eating tigress.

Mrs. Bassett bustled to the front door, and soft voices were
soon heard. Within minutes Juliet rushed into the room and
threw herself at Alexander. Delighted, Alexander held her close
in his arms and bestowed a lingering kiss on those delectable
lips.

"Oh, dearest, the morning was far too long without you at my
side. I missed you very much," Juliet purred charmingly. "But
just wait until you see what I have brought home with me."
Then she gave a pretty start, seeming to take note of the callers
for the first time.

"Mrs. Ogleby and Mrs. Tackley, how very nice to see you. I
trust you are well?" Juliet said pleasantly.

The ladies murmured greetings and preened a little, pleased
with being noticed before the strangers.

Turning to Alexander, Juliet linked her arm with his, drawing
him toward the sofa. "I do believe this is that young lady you
mentioned—the one with the yellow hair? And her mama, no
doubt. I can see a resemblance," Juliet said with patent satisfaction. At this Alexander interrupted her flow of speech to
make a proper introduction.

"How kind of you to visit us in our dear little honeymoon
home," Juliet gushed. "We have not been married so very long,
I suppose, but it seems as though dearest Alexander has been
mine forever."

Alexander looked down, utterly bemused as Juliet bestowed
a beaming smile on him, meeting his gaze with twinkling eyes.
"We are unfashionably in love, I know, but the moment we met
we knew we were destined to spend the rest of our lives together. He is such a romantic, Miss Shelford. Perhaps you
guessed that of him?"

"No," Camilla said baldly. "I would not have thought Lord
Hawkswood to be a romantic." She shifted uneasily.

"We both adore music, you see, and play sonatas together,"
Juliet bubbled. "Alexander reads me poetry, as well. And he is
such enormous comfort to me when it storms. I vow, a

thunderstorm isn't half as bad when I am nestled in Alexander's arms."

Alexander wondered how she managed to blush so convincingly, then decided the blush was not pretense. It was not easy for Juliet to portray this role; she was far more private in her personal life, scarcely revealing anything to others. He patted her hand in appreciation.

"But you must be exhausted traveling all the way from London," Juliet said prettily while implying both women looked like hags. "I insist you have a rest in your rooms before dinner. It will do you a world of good. There is something about country air that quite revives one."

Juliet summoned Mrs. Bassett, who had already had the sense to prepare rooms for the new guests. With majestic calm, Mrs. Shelford, followed by an angry Camilla, sailed from the drawing room in Mrs. Bassett's wake.

The other men stated an intention to saunter off to the village inn to sample the home brewed and abruptly left.

Mrs. Ogleby and Mrs. Tackley rose to clasp Juliet's hands, their faces alive with curiosity.

"Dear girl," Mrs. Ogleby began, then recalled to whom she was speaking. "My lady, if there is anything at all we might do for you, do not hesitate to let us know."

Mrs. Tackley nodded a firm agreement to this offer and drew a confused Mrs. Ogleby with her from the room, leaving Juliet alone with Alexander.

When he was certain all had gone, Alexander picked up Juliet in his arms and swung her about in a circle. "My dearest girl, you were magnificent!" He bussed her on the cheek, chuckling at the memory of Camilla's face when Juliet, his beautiful, talented Juliet, waltzed into the room and into his arms.

"Well, I do think she is an odious creature," Juliet said, her cheeks tinted peach and her eyes a flashing amber. "Mrs. Bassett informed me as to what had been going on. I gather Miss Shelford could be heard from one end of the house to the other. She insisted you could *not* be married. If she but knew," Juliet ended, looking lost and sad for a moment.

"Juliet," Alexander began, knowing that sometime he would have to explain to her precisely what their future would be. He was cut off by a tug on his hand and her excited little giggle.

"Come with me to my room—oh, dear, that does sound compromising, doesn't it?—I want to show you what I brought home," Juliet said, looking more cheerful.

Alexander gave up for the moment, deciding the time was not right for a serious discussion with his wife. He followed Juliet up the stairs, hoping Camilla would poke her beautiful yellow head out to see him enter his wife's room.

Juliet pulled him inside, shut the door, then pointed out a chair. "Now sit."

He did as commanded and accepted the little parcel she gave him with a quick frown. Upon opening, he was amazed to discover an incredible gold and lapis lazuli snuff box. "I don't know what to say, Juliet," he murmured without his usual aplomb. "This is overwhelming."

"Good—that means you are truly pleased and impressed. Now close your eyes. I have something to show you." Juliet paused until he obeyed, then went behind a screen where Pansy waited with the leaf green satin gown. It didn't take long for Juliet to remove her simple muslin and replace it with the elegant satin. She signaled for Pansy to go away, waited until the maid had left, then slowly went around the screen to face Alexander.

"Open your eyes now, my lord," Juliet whispered. She swallowed, hoping Alexander would see her and perhaps fall a little in love with her.

"A green satin gown, my dear?" Alexander said, utterly astonished. Then he knew a disappointment because he had planned to buy her just such a gown, perhaps a trifle more elegant, but clinging to her slender form just as this one did, with her looking beautiful and his. Then he caught sight of her face and rose to his feet at once.

"You are quite beautiful, my dear—as is the dress. Dare I add you would look quite beautiful no matter you had nothing on as someone else I know said once?" He walked around her, admiring the cut, the low neckline that revealed just so much of that perfectly proportioned bosom.

"You do like it, do you not?" Juliet said softly. "I wished to please you, and the mantua-maker had this one ready. I think it might be just the thing to wear to dinner, perhaps?" She gave him a cautious smile.

"With that gown, your diamond betrothal ring, that look of having just been kissed on your lips, I cannot see how Camilla will refuse to accept our marriage as bona fide."

"What if she insists upon seeing the marriage lines?" Juliet queried hesitantly. "My stupid stepbrother never asked, but I suspect Miss Shelford is a different matter altogether." Juliet ignored the business about looking well-kissed. Those were just so many words.

"Should she be so rude, I shall put her in her place, you may be assured. No one is going to hurt you while I am around." Alexander sounded very much the Viscount Hawkswood.

It was scarcely a loverlike declaration, but it sounded rather good to a worried Juliet.

"Thank you, Alexander. I shall keep up my part, you may rest assured. That odious woman, stalking you as though you were prime game," Juliet said indignantly.

"To her, I *am* prime game," Alexander replied. "Now I had best dress for dinner, acquire a little elegance to match yours. And do not think I've forgotten the kiss."

Juliet stood stock-still while he went though to his room. Life was not going to be easy the next few days, but she'd cope, especially if Alexander kissed her from time to time.

Chapter 11

When Alexander joined Juliet prior to dinner, she had to admit they made a fine pair. He looked splendid in a green vest that picked up the color of her gown; his elegant dark gray coat and breeches offered a pleasing contrast.

She fumbled with the clasp of her pearls, grimacing when it proved obstinate.

Glancing up at him, she said, "How splendid you look, my lord. Some of your London attire?"

"Yes," he murmured in agreement, then walked to her side. "Allow me. Where is your maid?"

"I suggested she assist Mrs. Bassett with the extra work our latest guests have brought. Miss Shelford does *not* realize this is a small household. Even with the extra footman and two maids someone like her makes things difficult; calling for a bath, demanding tea, insisting upon fresh flowers in her room."

"I'll ask Randall to help as well. He'll not wish to be bested by Pansy, you know."

Juliet stiffened slightly as Alexander's hands brushed her neck while he fastened the necklace. "I had no idea they were competitive," she managed to say in a somewhat strangled voice.

Alexander turned her about to study the effect of the pearls with the green satin and shook his head. "I would rather you wear mother's emeralds, but they are in the London vault."

"But I feel better wearing my own jewelry," she countered. "As it is, I worry about this diamond every time I put it on. It is very grand."

"Camilla Shelford would think it very odd were you not to

have a fine diamond and excellent pearls. She'll likely make some remark about the family emeralds, so be prepared with one of your clever answers." He stood looking down at Juliet, a peculiar expression on his face.

"I am sorry if the remark about reading poetry bothered you," Juliet said, wondering if that had annoyed him. "My father used to read poetry to Mother, and I always thought it so admirable." Juliet looked off into space, adding, "Mother would sit in the arbor, working at her embroidery, while Papa read. I can't recall the poems, but I do remember a few lines. 'Paradise is sweeter there than the flowers and roses here; here's a glimpse, and then away, There 'twill be forever day; where thou ever in heaven's spring shalt with saints and angels sing.' I don't know who wrote it, but it seemed to be a favorite of Mother's."

"My nurse was apt to read me stuff like, 'How doth the little busy bee improve each shining hour, and gather honey all the day from every opening flower'—I believe with the hope I might ultimately give a good account of myself."

Juliet chuckled. "So did mine, along with 'Be you to others kind and true, as you'd have others be to you.' "

"It might be rather clever of me to fetch a book of poetry and read to you while you sew seated in the arbor."

"We do not have an arbor, Alexander," she reminded him.

"I'll have Lumpkin build one," he said, laughing at her disbelieving look. "I'm partial to Herrick, myself—'Gather ye rosebuds while ye may, old time is still a-flying.' " The look he gave Juliet was positively impish.

She frowned at him, then glanced at the clock. "Which serves to remind me that the hour flies now as well. If we are to greet our guests beforehand, we'd best go now. I sent a message earlier to the Tackleys' asking Lucy—to make the numbers even—and she graciously agreed."

"That ought to dampen Camilla's fire. You forgot something," Alexander said quietly.

"I do not think so," she said, glancing in the looking glass to see if all was as it should be. The green satin glowed softly in the dim light.

"Your splendid performance is much appreciated. I can think of one way to show my gratitude."

Juliet paused to look at him, her hand on the doorknob.

Instead of explaining, Alexander leaned down to give Juliet a very sweet kiss, the sort that a girl might build her dreams on when once abed.

"There now, with stars firmly in place in your amber eyes, you are ready to greet the odious Camilla and her even more repellent mother." Alexander placed his hand over Juliet's and opened the door. Her hand had ceased to obey her commands some minutes ago.

Camilla met them near the top of the stairs. Alexander observed her gaze dart to the slightly open door of Juliet's room. There was little doubt in his mind that she had put two and two together and made six. He tucked Juliet's hand in the crook of his arm and gave Camilla a pleased smile. "Lovely evening," he drawled.

"It is going to rain, maybe thunder. I hate storms," she retorted with an angry pout.

"So do I," Juliet agreed fervently. "How comforting it is to have Alexander to take my mind off it all."

He patted her hand and grinned at the thought of a thunderstorm. "I do not mind in the least. Quite happy to oblige, my dear."

Juliet blushed a delightful ripe peach at his words, and Alexander barely kept himself from laughing.

Once in the drawing room with the others gathered about them, Camilla became a trifle more subdued. For one thing, Lucy Tackley proved to be extremely pretty and fresh. Her artless ways and shy, dimpled smiles could not but please the men, in particular, Lord Taunton. This gentleman now revealed vastly improved manners and had eyes for none but Lucy.

Juliet suspected that even if Camilla was not convinced the marriage was real, she knew better than to create another scene with unmarried gentlemen and an unknown young woman around. Camilla ignored Harry Riggs—oddly enough—probably because he knew her too well to be taken in by her artifice. Neither Marius nor Lord Taunton were acquainted with her, and she could try her wiles on them—provided Lucy didn't attach Taunton—at the same time showing Alexander what he was missing. Camilla's face was easy for another woman to read.

She did manage one barb. Juliet and Alexander played a short duet before dinner while the others sipped the fine wine Alexander had found in Salisbury. When the music ceased, Camilla drifted over to Juliet to study her.

"I am surprised you do not wear the Hawkswood emeralds, my dear," she said in a cold, patronizing taunt.

Juliet, having been alerted by Alexander, smiled and said, "The emeralds are in London. This is our honeymoon house, you know. Pearls and diamonds are quite acceptable for a simple country setting." She'd removed her gloves to play the harp, and now when she touched the pearls at her neck, the diamond in her ring flashed and sparkled in the fading daylight augmented by braces of candles. There was no comment from Juliet regarding the ostentatious display of rubies on Miss Shelford's ample bosom.

"I do *not* believe you are married," Camilla hissed for Juliet's ears alone, although a note of doubt crept into her voice as she surveyed the magnificent diamond ring. "He belongs to me."

"I doubt Alexander will ever *belong* to anyone. He is very much his own man. However, he shares his life with me—to the fullest degree, dear Miss Shelford." Juliet bestowed a kindly smile on her enemy, then floated off to join Alexander.

"She struck, I suppose? Were her mother not a gossip who has the ears of every other gossip in Town, I'd tell those two to be out of here at first light. We must convince them. Are you game, Juliet?"

She glanced over to where Camilla graciously bestowed her charms on Marius and Harry since Lord Taunton danced attendance on Lucy Tackley. "Indeed, I am, sir."

"Good girl. I knew you'd not fail me."

Randall appeared in the doorway, looking like a very superior butler. "Dinner is served."

Giving the valet an approving look, Juliet accepted Lord Taunton's escort while Alexander led in Mrs. Shelford. Harry Riggs followed with an irate Camilla, while Marius chatted amiably with Lucy. The table was set with sparkling crystal and the best china, a pretty Wedgwood pattern.

"I must say, you and your blushing bride—if she is indeed your bride—have done well with the house," Mrs. Shelford admitted, examining the lovely dining room with a critical eye.

Marius might not be of the highest *ton,* but even he knew one didn't make statements like that about one's host while at the dinner table. He glared at the pompous old bat and said, "I'll thank you to keep a civil tongue in your head, madam. My stepsister has always been most proper."

"Well!" Mrs. Shelford gasped indignantly.

It was a good thing that Juliet had not yet taken a sip of her cream soup or she'd likely have choked. "Thank you, Marius. I appreciate your defense of my character." She shared a look with Alexander, then concentrated on the gentlemen at either side of her. Lord Taunton was lost to Lucy. Harry Riggs was an unknown quantity.

"You do well with the lovely vixen," he said quietly when the clatter of cutlery on dishes and the hum of conversation made excellent cover.

"Thank you. She does not make me pine for London. I believe I far prefer Woodbury society if she is an example of what the City has to offer."

"Surely you would not deny us the pleasure of your company next Season, my lady."

Juliet gave him a speculative look, wondering precisely how much Alexander had revealed to him of their situation.

He said nothing more on that score, and the dinner proceeded nicely. After Marius's spirited defense of Juliet, Mrs. Shelford remained fairly quiet. Camilla said little, either. When it came time for the women to leave the table, the two Shelford women went eagerly. Camilla conversed about nothing in a polite manner Juliet had not thought possible from her.

It was as Camilla predicted. Rain began later in the evening, sending Lucy Tackley hurrying home before the roads became impassable. The rumble of thunder grew ominously closer. Camilla dropped little hints about requiring comforting, but no one took pity on her, least of all Juliet. Mrs. Shelford could take care of her daughter's alarums; that was her duty.

Juliet wrapped a shawl about herself with trembling hands, not happy at the thought of facing the night alone. She'd not expect Alexander to comfort her foolish fears again. Besides, had she not told him the next time she would bury her head beneath the covers, poke her fingers in her ears, and sing to herself? As though that would actually help!

The storm was mild as storms go, thunder crashing now and again, but not so fiercely as last time. The lightning seemed not to threaten the house as before. Still, Juliet wished she could remain with others all night, and with reluctance she watched them go to their rooms.

"Time for bed, Juliet," Alexander said, his voice brisk.

"I know," she replied nervously. "I am such a little fool, to be so bothered by a little noise. Pay not the least attention to me, Alexander. I shall crawl under the covers and make the best of it."

He put an arm around her shoulders and led her up the stairs to her room. Inside, candles flickered in the draft from the windows, threatening to plunge the room into darkness at any moment.

They both entered, just in case there was someone about to take notice. Juliet turned to Alexander and said, "Go now, for I intend to go to bed with all speed. The sooner I sleep, the better."

She was sorry to see him leave, but quickly turned her attention to preparing for bed, donning her all-covering nightgown after hastily removing the satin gown, Pansy having been dismissed after her hard day's work. Juliet tucked her auburn curls beneath an elegant wisp of a nightcap, then made for her bed.

The connecting door opened.

Alexander entered carrying a small oil lamp, nicely lit, and a book.

Juliet gave him an indignant look. "I didn't hear a knock."

"Hands were full," he answered. "I heard you moving about and decided you must be near ready for bed by now." He wore a fine brocade banyan over his breeches and shirt. The neck of his shirt fell open to reveal hints of dark hair. Juliet looked else-where with effort.

"I want you to crawl into bed while I read to you. After all, you told the group I did precisely that. Now it will not be a lie."

"Alexander . . ." she began, then dove when lightning struck not far away and a clap of thunder vibrated throughout the house.

"Good girl," Alexander said with approval. He turned up the flame and began to read passages from Shakespeare, having explained it was the closest thing to poetry he could find on the library shelves.

Juliet closed her eyes to escape the lightning. His voice soothed and drowned out the thunder. How comforting he was, and who would have thought a man termed a rake could be so caring, so considerate of her foolish fears.

He had begun, "Under the Greenwood tree who loves to lie with me," when a sharp tap came. Before Juliet could leave her bed, Alexander crossed to see who dared to knock at this hour. Juliet slowly followed, curious as to who might disturb the night of a supposedly newly married couple.

"The storm," Camilla began, then realized that Alexander was not alone, that Juliet—in her nightwear—was at his side. "Oh, you are together." Camilla looked at Alexander, seeing his banyan wrapped and tied so that only his skin showed at the neck, and gulped.

"What did you expect, Miss Shelford?" Juliet asked in a firm, quiet voice, even though she trembled. "My husband is where he belongs—with me. I suggest you seek out your mother. She is the properest person to comfort you—a single woman." Juliet had grabbed her shawl, and now Alexander adjusted it with what must appear to Camilla a possessive touch. He let his hand rest on Juliet's shoulder in a gesture of intimacy.

"What will it take to convince you, Camilla?" he queried dryly. "Dare I suggest you and your mother depart tomorrow for London—or wherever you deem best? I know it must shock you, but Juliet and I would rather be alone—together." He looked down at Juliet, and she dared to meet his gaze, barely stifling a gasp at the heat she saw therein. "You interrupted us," Alexander said gently, then shut the door.

"Oh, my word," Juliet exclaimed softly, allowing a great sigh to escape. "What she must think."

"Precisely." He nudged Juliet back to her bed, then resumed his reading.

When she woke in the morning, Juliet couldn't remember what she last heard before she drifted off to sleep. She had a hazy recollection of someone—Alexander—kissing her on her forehead—at least she thought that's what had happened. She would not ask him.

Somewhere someone was pounding. She could hear voices beyond her window, and from within came the gentle sounds of the house wakening to another day.

"Morning, ma'am," Pansy said quietly as she entered the room. "Word has it that those two Shelford ladies leave today. Miss asked for her trunks."

"She certainly travels with a great deal of clothing."

"Never mind," the maid comforted, "you have one of the new muslins you brought from Salisbury to wear."

"There is nothing like a new dress to cheer one up." Juliet slipped from her bed, ready to be dressed.

"The fete is today, ma'am," Pansy said after doing up the back of the pretty morning gown. Juliet admired the hemline, which featured a double row of gathered muslin held in place with bands of riband. The fabric was a pretty coral print and rather becoming, she thought.

"There is a great deal of pounding outside. Was there damage from the storm?" Juliet inquired on her way from the room, deciding it might be interesting to have breakfast downstairs today.

"Mr. Lumpkin is building an arbor, my lady." The maid busied herself about the room, putting it to rights.

Juliet ran lightly down the stairs and out to where Mr. Lumpkin and Alexander stood in debate.

"Good morning, Juliet, my dear. You are just in time to give us your opinion. Think you a simple trellis arbor will do for the vines? Or ought we erect something more substantial?" Alexander gave her his charming smile, extending a hand in greeting.

"I hardly know . . ." she began, then faltered under Mr. Lumpkin's amused stare. "A simple arbor will do nicely, I believe." Rather than look foolish, she accepted Alexander's hand and knew reassurance from its warmth.

"A garden seat of sturdy proportions to hold two is necessary, and trellis work without, I believe," Alexander said, looking around the spot he'd selected for the arbor. It was a pretty place, close to the garden wall with an excellent view of the perennial beds.

"Alexander—" she began, only to be cut off by him.

"I would like you to see the splendid arbor at the Abbey. It is a trellis sort, but lengthy and covered with pink climbing roses that offer delightful scent come June. Next June we shall be there, just so you may enjoy it."

"Have you eaten breakfast?" she inserted at last. "I would like to talk with you."

Alexander paused to give Mr. Lumpkin a few instructions, then left him to his job. Sauntering along with Juliet, Alexander placed his arm across her shoulders and whistled.

"Alexander," she hissed. He continued to whistle and tightened his hold on her.

Not knowing his reason, she smiled as though this were normal, and bided her time.

"Breakfast, my love?" he said when they entered the house.

There was activity everywhere; maids coming and going, Randall and Pansy up and down the stairs in a rush, Mrs. Bassett mumbling to herself as she bustled along the hall.

"Come with me. There is only one place I know where we can talk."

"This sounds serious," Alexander said as Juliet pulled him into the library, then shut the door on all the hubbub.

"It *is* serious. Once Mrs. Shelford and Camilla leave, I believe Marius and Lord Taunton will depart as well. Harry Riggs does not plan to remain long, does he?"

"Harry will leave the moment I give him a clue," Alexander said, looking wary.

"*Then* what are we to do? You go building arbors, and it is time either both or one of us must leave," Juliet said dejectedly.

"We cannot depart from here immediately," Alexander said quietly.

"Why not?" Juliet demanded with hope in her voice.

"Mrs. Tackley and my grandmother, for one. If I go and leave you alone here, my dear relative will be here in a trice with probing questions. I doubt you would want that."

"Er, no," Juliet agreed, frowning. "You believe we must remain here . . . together . . . for a time?"

"Most assuredly. I have promised Parson Richards to be at his wedding."

"Alexander, that is not until next month!" Juliet exclaimed.

"Hush. You do not want Camilla to hear you."

"Oh, bother Camilla," Juliet said with a sigh.

"Well, she is a great deal of bother, but she can also be a troublemaker. I'd not wish her to return to London bearing tales."

Juliet bit her lower lip in vexation. "Of course. I quite forgot you must return to Society. It would not do for that sort of gossip to circulate regarding you. Reputations are fragile things."

"I was thinking of you, my dear."

"Oh."

Alexander watched Juliet cross to stare out the window to where Lumpkin worked on the arbor. "I do not wish my wife to be the object of speculation and unkind gossip."

"But I am *not* your wife," Juliet replied in a little voice.

Alexander was about to explain their future when the library door opened and Harry Riggs along with Marius entered the room.

"Sorry," Harry said after a quick look at his friend's face and Juliet's back.

She turned, a bright smile on her face. "Only see what Alexander is having built for me—an arbor. I have long wished for an arbor where I might sit on fine days. Remember the arbor at the Hall, Marius?"

He looked confused, then nodded. "More or less. I don't spend much time at the Hall."

"You ought to, you know," she replied. "Excuse me, gentlemen. I have yet to breakfast." She slipped from the room followed by Alexander's frustrated gaze.

"The path not as smooth as you might wish?" Harry asked.

"Not at all. Everything is fine," Alexander said with a glance at Marius.

"I understand the Shelfords leave today," Harry offered quietly.

"Dashed good thing, if you ask me," Marius said. "That old bat questioned my stepsister's propriety. There isn't anyone more proper than Juliet. Wildest thing she ever did was run off with you," he said to Alexander. "Refused to marry Taunton because he was a rowdy good fellow, and look at him now—turning into a dull-wit who can't talk about anything except being leg-shackled to that Tackley girl."

"Is that so?" Alexander said. "I fancy he will want to linger here to do a bit of courting. By all means, stay. You are most welcome."

Marius looked astounded. "That is dashed good of you, my lord. I mean, the way Rob and I charged in here, accusing you of whatnot and now you are offering your hospitality?" He shook his head in amazement.

"The fete is due to begin shortly. I had best round up Juliet, bid the unwelcome guests farewell, and prepare for a busy day."

"Shall I follow Camilla to make certain she indeed returns to London or wherever she may hide out?" Harry inquired quietly. "She hinted to a good many that she intended to return as your bride."

"No, I care not where the dratted woman goes as long as she leaves here. Stay on if you like. The more the merrier, or so they say." Alexander ran a hand through his hair, a gesture of sheer frustration.

Harry gave Alexander a curious look, but said nothing beyond the thought to try the nearby river for trout.

"Not come to the fete?" Alexander demanded, crossing to the door, throwing it open to expose the view of trunks piled high in the entry. "We must celebrate," he said softly.

Mrs. Shelford made short work of their departure. She bid

Juliet a frosty good-bye, nodded severely to Alexander, ignored the other men, then entered her massive traveling coach without further ado. Camilla followed meekly behind her mother.

"Coach suits the old gel, don't it," Marius observed.

"Indeed," Alexander replied, bursting into laughter.

"Well," Juliet said, casting a reproving look at her errant stepbrother, "I am supposed to open that fete so I will leave you now."

"I believe I shall go with you," Alexander said promptly. "You chaps will join us?"

The three men, for Taunton had joined them to see the Shelfords off, all nodded with varying degrees of enthusiasm.

So it was that the five of them, Juliet and Alexander in one carriage, Harry, Marius, and Taunton in another, traveled the short distance to the village green.

It was a typical village celebration, with home-brewed ale flowing freely, fresh-baked cakes and biscuits a-plenty, and children and dogs running everywhere.

"We wish to thank his lordship for the repairs to the church roof," Parson Richards said with a nod toward Alexander. "And we are most grateful for the new baptismal font donated by Lady Hawkswood, the old one having succumbed to worms."

There was gentle laughter from a few; the others merely looked polite.

Juliet stepped forward, said her little bit, then retired to sit with Alexander.

"Are we supposed to stay here and not have any fun?" she murmured behind her fan.

"I rather think so. I fear if we join them, we might spoil the day," Alexander replied thoughtfully.

"Rubbish," Juliet said briskly. "I intend to buy a few ribands, perhaps a nosegay, certainly a few sweets."

"Then I shall come along and see what is to be found."

Alexander assisted her from the shallow platform and walked at her side through the milling crowd. Farmers had taken the day to come to town, bringing their families and workers with them. People from neighboring villages had joined in as well. It was a happy day for all.

"What a good thing Camilla has gone," Juliet said. "She would have had all the charm of a bucket of cold water, looking down her lovely nose at the locals. I suspect she would have managed to offend them all by the end of the day."

"I must celebrate my freedom from Camilla in a suitable way," Alexander teased, his dark eyes merry.

"Hm, let me see, perhaps a new watch fob, or an elegant cane? I see a very nice whip over there. One can never have too many whips, can one?" she asked pertly.

"Do not tempt me, minx. I shall think of something presently. Now for your ribands and frippery."

Alexander helped her select several ribands, insisting she must have at least one to match her eyes. Then he found a pretty nosegay for her. The sweets were easy, offered at every turn.

He paid for a sack of sweets, then popped a piece of toffee in her mouth. "That ought to keep you occupied for a time, my dear." With that, he strode off to join Harry Riggs, and the two men were in laughing conversation in no time.

"It was ever so, my lady," Mrs. Ogleby said at her side. "The gentlemen indulge us for a bit, then go off to enjoy themselves. I understand two of your guests have departed this morning?"

"Indeed. The house is far more peaceful with them gone. I cannot say I was pleased to have them."

"Perhaps I ought not say so, but I found them to be a very haughty sort."

Juliet smiled and replied, "My stepbrother gave Mrs. Shelford a rousing defense of me last evening. I doubt she will ever recover from being called *madam* in that manner."

"Goodness!" Mrs. Ogleby paused to contemplate the scene and chuckled. "Lucy Tackley enjoyed her evening at any rate. I doubt she will ever forget your kindness."

"How do you think Lord Taunton will fare? My stepbrother complains that he has become a dull dog. He is a far cry from the man I . . ." Juliet hesitated, then realized she could not reveal Marius's plans in that direction. "I first knew."

"Mrs. Tackley wrote and received a reply to the effect that while he has been a rather wild young man, the right sort of gel might well be the making of him. He's not poor, yet not rich, the sort of man who might ignore a lack of background if the chit had a proper dowry."

"And he is besotted with her," Juliet added when the pair in question came into view.

"That, as well. We shall see how it goes. 'Tis all well and good to talk, but what counts is the ring on the finger," Mrs. Ogleby concluded with a sage nod.

Juliet agreed a trifle stiffly, then made her excuses. There was no way she could remain in this dear village if Alexander left her. She'd not need to explain; they wouldn't expect such from her. But life would be extremely difficult. She would have to locate another village far from here.

"Come now, only smiling faces allowed today," Alexander teased. "See my purchase."

"A book?" she said with great surprise.

"Indeed—a book, my dear, of poetry."

Chapter 12

The fete was pronounced a great success by one and all. The villagers particularly enjoyed seeing those from London enter into the spirit of the day. It pleased everyone—especially the gratified Tackleys—to see Lord Taunton show such marked attentions to Lucy, who was a great favorite among the locals.

Marius and Harry Riggs went back to the manor first, claiming they intended to do a bit of late-day fishing. Lord Taunton, dull dog that he'd become, escorted Lucy wherever she pleased to go and remained in the village.

"I suppose we are free to leave now," Juliet said wistfully. She hadn't had such fun in ages. Miss Pritchard had claimed it unladylike for Juliet to mingle with the villagers near Winterton Hall.

"I doubt anyone expects us to remain until the very last. Come, we can ride back now if you are tired. Besides, I would like to see how Lumpkin is faring with the arbor."

Juliet eyed the book of poetry tucked beneath Alexander's arm and nodded thoughtfully. She allowed him to hand her up into the carriage, waved farewell to those she had come to know, then sat in silence on the brief ride to the manor house.

Pounding could still be heard as they entered through the modest brick gates. "Lumpkin must still be at it," Alexander said with a quick frown. He guided his horses up the graveled drive, then halted before the house. While he assisted Juliet from the carriage, his groom came running from the stables, prepared to take over the carriage and horses.

Juliet admired the scene before her, wondering how long she could remain here. The brick house gave such a feeling of solidity and welcome. It was a friendly house, inside as well as out, with sparkling windows and fine trim. Now that she had restored the gardens to their prime glory, the charming old house had a setting worthy of its design.

"Come with me," Alexander said, interrupting her musings. "Shall we see what has been accomplished while we have been in Woodbury playing lord and lady of the manor?

"Playing, indeed," Juliet replied. "I fear I left poor Mrs. Bassett with a dreadful lot to do."

"Mrs. Bassett was likely thankful to have us all out of the way for the day."

"I am sorry she missed the fete, though. I will give her a day off later to compensate," Juliet said, allowing Alexander to take her hand, telling herself his help was quite necessary over the roughly scythed grass.

When they reached the garden, the arbor was found to be well along. Mr. Lumpkin pounded in a few more nails, then stood back to view the finished creation.

"Ye want it painted, or is it to weather?" the older man inquired with a frowning look from beneath his worn cap.

"I wish it painted green," Alexander said. "Leaf green." He turned to Juliet, a gleam in his eyes, "I am particularly fond of leaf green."

She couldn't help but smile at that bit of nonsense and walked back to the house in great charity with him.

Once inside, she left Alexander to his own devices, seeking out Mrs. Bassett to discover how things had gone while Juliet frittered her time away at the fete.

"Everything looks in fine shape," she told the housekeeper while inspecting the drawing room. It was as though they had not been subjected to the visit from the aggravating Shelford women, and no sign of the men could be noticed.

Upstairs, Juliet found all the guest rooms neat and ready for another round of company. She studied the room where Camilla had been housed and turned to Mrs. Bassett to comment, "I hope it will be a while before we have guests again. It might be pleasant, but wearing, assuredly for you, Mrs. Bassett."

"There are guests and there are guests. The men are no trouble at all. 'Tis the women who are a bother, most often. However, with the extra help it has gone smoothly, I believe." The housekeeper gave the last room they checked a satisfied smile when Juliet exclaimed over the pretty flowers on a small table near the window.

"I am glad I have you to run the house. What would become of the place were you not here, I cannot imagine."

"Well, enjoy the peace for the moment. When those men return from their fishing and Lord Taunton comes back from courting Miss Tackley, 'twill be busy again."

Juliet took her advice and returned to the drawing room to practice a piece on the harp. She was still there when she heard the sound of an approaching carriage.

She flew to the window, curious to see who it might be. She doubted Mrs. Ogleby or Mrs. Tackley would come this late in the afternoon. Perhaps Lord Taunton, finished with squiring Lucy about, returned to the house?

Instead of a familiar carriage, a large traveling coach lumbered into view. The four matched chestnuts looked worn to a flinder, and the coach was covered in dust, telling Juliet it had come some distance. *Now* who descended upon them? she wondered.

The coach drew to a halt before the doors, and when Mrs. Bassett went to great the personage arriving, Juliet was stunned to see the coach door open to reveal an older woman stepping down—an older woman who looked remarkably like Alexander.

While her hair appeared to be laced with white, she was slim, regal, and dressed in the very latest fashion. From the respectful curtsy bestowed by Mrs. Bassett, Juliet feared the worst. The dowager had come to visit. She prayed Alexander would have heard the arrival of the coach and come to investigate.

"Grandmother," he said from where he paused in the doorway. "Best come and try not to look too overwhelmed. If she thinks you are afraid of her, she will turn into a terror. Rather, shower her with affection; she won't know what to make of you."

Juliet gave him a nervous smile. It was all well and good for him to talk about showering that formidable-looking woman with affection—he was her grandson. It was quite another matter to pass inspection as the wife of said grandson, especially when they were not really married! How could they manage to pretend to be wed under such scrutiny?

She went to the entryway, intent upon greeting their most unwelcome guest. Nervous and apprehensive, she smoothed down her dress, patted her wisp of a cap into place, and wondered what Cook could whip up for a special dinner. Then a horrible thought struck like lightning.

"What if she asked to see the marriage lines?" Was it possible to fake a Gretna license? Juliet had never seen one, hadn't the slightest idea of what one looked like, and furthermore didn't know if her ladyship knew about them, either. "Oh, bother," she whispered to herself.

One could only hope for the best. For the very first time, Juliet prayed for more company.

"Alexander, my dear boy, when I had the news I decided not to wait for you to come to me for a visit. I elected to please myself and come here first. How lovely of you to prefer my gift to you for your little honeymoon house," the dowager said as she entered the manor that was anything but little in Juliet's estimation.

The dowager's voice was pleasing, somewhat throaty and rich like treacle. Her dark eyes, so like Alexander's, pinned Juliet in her steps. "Your wife, Alexander? Introduce me."

"Grandmother, Juliet Barr, Viscountess Hawkswood, my wife," Alexander pronounced so proudly that Juliet felt a sting of tears in the back of her eyes. Would that it was true! Juliet dipped a court curtsy, then walked over to bestow a light kiss on the smooth cheek.

"Mrs. Tackley wrote that Juliet's father is Viscount Winterton. I understand he is off in Russia on some fool errand for the government. Is that correct, girl?"

"Indeed, my lady. I have missed him these years he has been gone," Which was nothing but the truth, at least.

"I daresay you have. And this grandson of mine came along to sweep you off your feet and to a Gretna wedding. Badly done, Alexander. This young lady deserved a wedding in Town at the very least, not some ramshackle dash to the border." The look of disdain she gave Alexander would have done in a lesser man.

Juliet didn't know what to say to the dowager other than to attempt to reply in some manner to at least part of those outrageous remarks. "He swept me off my feet, my lady, and continues to delight me with his thoughtfulness."

Her ladyship nodded regally as though that was only to be expected of the current Viscount Hawkswood.

The dowager strolled along through the entryway, looking every direction, then into the drawing room, again with a gaze that seemed to take in every detail.

"My harp!" she said with discovery. "You play the harp, Juliet?" The dowager inspected the music on the stand, looking to Juliet for confirmation with the most bland of expressions. There was no hint as to whether she was pleased or annoyed.

"I was just practicing when you arrived," Juliet said modestly.

"We play duets together, Grandmother. I felt certain you would approve." Alexander crossed the room to drape an arm about Juliet's shoulders, a source of comfort indeed.

The dowager turned to give him a searching look, but said nothing.

"Dinner will be shortly, but perhaps you would welcome a cup of tea," Juliet suggested, wondering how she might convey to Mrs. Bassett that dinner had to be more than special. Alexander's arm appeared to be pinning Juliet to his side, and it would raise eyebrows were she to wrest herself away to leave the room. After all, she was supposed to be a devoted new wife.

"If I know Grandmother, she will wish a cup of her special blend. Mrs. Bassett will have it here shortly."

Juliet, while thankful that Alexander had signaled for tea, felt inadequate as a hostess because of it. She trotted out all the little courtesies Miss Pritchard had drummed into her during the years at Winterton and was pleased to see the dowager give her a nod of approval.

Tea was an ordeal Juliet thought she weathered fairly well.

Precisely so much milk, then a small spoon of sugar, followed by steaming tea proved acceptable to the grand lady. Since Juliet had obeyed the dowager's request, it wasn't so remarkable, but it was a step in the right direction for agreeable relations.

"I should like to have the Rose Room, as Juliet no doubt properly has the one I occupied while I lived here," the dowager intoned in that rich, plummy voice.

"Indeed, she has made it her own," Alexander replied, referring to the little alterations Juliet had added—a screen, a comfortable chair, and changing the table that had been near the window for a larger size.

"I look forward to seeing it." She finished her tea, nibbled approvingly on one of Mrs. Bassett's lemon biscuits, then rose with queenly majesty.

"I shall go to my room for a rest before dinner. I fancy you wish to consult with Cook, Juliet. No rich sauces, if you please. They ruin my digestion." With that informative bit, the dowager rose from the sofa, walked to the stairs, and was gone.

"You did very well, Juliet," Alexander said quietly so that his words reached none but her.

"She is utterly terrifying," Juliet replied, giving him a smile of thanks for his encomium. "I always thought of a grandmother as being cozy and comfortable. She is neither. Yet I believe I rather admire her. She is much like you."

He grinned, then said, "Does that mean you like me as well?"

"Naturally," she replied with as much composure as she could gather. "Now, I had better do as your grandmama suggested—see Cook regarding dinner."

There were no rich sauces on the food that evening. Harry Riggs had brought back three fine trout, which Cook served to perfection following a delicate cream of mushroom soup that was heaven itself. The beef roast proved excellent, and the pureed carrots with a dish of new peas could not have been better. If the trifle was a bit lacking in sherry, it seemed to please the dowager.

"Nice little spot, that," Marius said, referring to the fishing hole Harry had found. "I've never been much of a fisherman, but Harry showed me a number of pointers. I may take it up," he concluded with a bite of the tender fish.

"It would be good if you did," Juliet said with the right amount of diffidence. If Marius took to fishing the bountiful streams of Winterton, he might see there were things that needed doing, that he ought to attend to while at the estate.

Lord Taunton seemed abstracted, polite to the dowager, civil to Juliet, absentminded to the men. He ate well, spoke little, and in general seemed barely with them. Marius gave him more than one disgusted look.

"I would like to invite several people over to dine, if it please your ladyship," Juliet said when she and the dowager left the table to the men and their port. "Perhaps in two or three days, depending upon how you feel. Travel can be so exhausting."

"I am never tired," the dowager claimed.

"How nice for you. I find I often become fatigued, especially when I have been in the garden. I thought to ask a number of people who have been friendly to us," Juliet said composedly. She was not going to let the old dragon get the best of her.

"The Tackleys, I imagine. Who else?"

"The Oglebys, for both have been very good to me—to us. Parson Richards and the squire's daughter, who is soon to be his wife—which also means Squire Otterly and his lady. And I must not forget Kate Ogleby—my stepbrother has paid her some attention. Lord Taunton is much taken with Lucy Tackley, and it would be a kindness to ask her as well."

"Is that why he was so preoccupied during dinner? He looks ready to propose. Is he?" The dowager led Juliet to the sofa, then seated her close so the dowager could watch her every move.

"I believe so, my lady." Juliet folded her hands neatly in her lap, wishing she had something to do with them.

"Are you in love with my grandson?" the dowager asked in an unexpected attack.

"Indeed, I am," Juliet answered truthfully.

"You like children as well?" her ladyship inquired with ruthless determination.

"I do. I always regretted that my mother died so young, else

I might have had a little sister or brother to love. Marius is so much older than I that I scarcely ever saw him." Juliet nervously pleated the skirt of her new coral print muslin, wishing the men would forget their stupid port and rescue her.

"You lived at Winterton Hall with a governess, I suppose?" darted the swift rejoinder.

"Miss Pritchard. Yes, she was as near a mother to me as anyone might have been."

"Likely better than a good many, from what I have seen," the dowager said half to herself. "You enjoy living here?" her ladyship continued with a searching look out the window at the trees beyond, now becoming indistinct in the fading twilight.

"Oh, yes, indeed," Juliet said warmly. "Who could not love this house and the pretty garden? Alexander is having an arbor constructed. Tomorrow you must see all that has been done."

"The garden must have been sadly overgrown when you came. After my foolish daughter-in-law died out in the rain, the place was abandoned, left to go to rack and ruin. It was a good thing when Alexander's man of business found Mrs. Bassett, I perceive. The house looks very fine."

Juliet nodded, thinking of the countless hours of polishing and mending she'd undertaken when first she had come. Even the furniture had needed the attention of a skilled needlewoman, something Mrs. Bassett was not, however good she was otherwise.

"You do needlework?" The inquiry followed the sighting of the workbasket with a telltale piece of needlepoint draped over the side.

"One of the upstairs chairs requires a new covering. I decided to replace it."

"There is no need to look at me for a sign of approval for what you plan. This house may have once been mine, but I have not lived here for many, many years."

"We were surprised to see you come," Juliet admitted. "Mrs. Tackley said as how you rarely leave London."

"I thought it advisable to see you before . . ." Her ladyship paused, sinking into a deep reverie. "Play for me. I would hear how well you do at the harp. It once offered me a great deal of consolation."

Thinking it was an odd way to phrase it, Juliet obeyed. Still, she had often found comfort in her music, and perhaps that is what her ladyship meant. She sat beside the harp and prepared to play for the most critical audience she'd ever had. "It needed but one string replaced and a good tuning. It is a fine instrument."

The delicate pieces she performed were well suited to the intimacy of the drawing room and a small audience. The dowager listened attentively; Juliet didn't know whether to be pleased or terrified.

She was in the middle of a Bachofen arrangement of one of Mozart's sonatas when the men entered the drawing room. Alexander immediately went to the pianoforte to join her in the music.

He played well, and she knew she excelled previous efforts. There was something about a critical listener that either brought out the best in one or routed one completely.

The dowager applauded with what seemed like pleasure when they finished. Juliet eased the harp away, then rose to ring for Mrs. Bassett and tea.

"I approve of your wife, Alexander. When Caroline Tackley wrote to tell me you were in residence with a charming young wife, I did not wish to believe it at first. Then I realized that you were being a dutiful grandson and doing what I have urged you to do for many years. At last—a granddaughter of whom I may be proud."

"Thank you, Grandmother."

"Caroline also wrote that Juliet lived here for a few months before you joined her. May I ask why?"

"No, I think not. That is private between Juliet and myself." Alexander gave his elderly relative a nice smile, but it was evident he was not going to tell her a thing unless he wanted to; she'd not bully him.

Juliet slowly expelled the breath she was unaware she had been holding. She was quite certain she had gone from a rosy pink to a parchment white within the span of seconds. Had her ladyship been in a position to observe, she might have wondered at that, especially the parchment hue.

"Humph," the dowager said before rising from the sofa. "Ask one of the maids to bring my tea to my room. I believe I shall retire now. I cannot stay up so late as I once did."

They all rose respectfully while the erect, quite magnificent old lady, her rose sarcenet gown swirling gracefully about her, left the room. The faint tap of her shoes on the stairs was followed by silence.

"I say," Marius said with a frown, "your grandmother is most unusual."

"That she is," Alexander said while he crossed the room to Juliet's side. "I see no damage. You appear to have survived in one piece."

"I think I will leave you gentlemen to a game of billiards or whatever you please. I intend to write out those dinner invitations at once. Sixteen for dinner. Can we manage?" she whispered to Alexander when he walked with her through to the entryway and the bottom of the stairs.

"After this evening I am convinced you could handle anything." He paused, then added, "In fact, I meant to tell you before—after your ball I knew you could handle an affair in London with no trouble at all. A dinner in Woodbury should be child's play."

"But your grandmother is here, Alexander," Juliet said without acknowledging his compliment. "You managed to avoid one question. There are others lurking that could prove most uncomfortable for us."

"Precisely what *did* she ask you?" Alexander said with a sharply perceptive look at Juliet's pale face.

She shot a cautioning look at the men, who now sauntered from the drawing room, intent upon enjoying a game of billiards.

"I'll be with you in a moment," Alexander said to them, his hand on Juliet's arm, showing his intent of going upstairs with her.

Harry Riggs grinned, Marius raised a brow, while Lord Taunton merely looked blank.

Once inside her bedroom, Alexander leaned against the door and fixed Juliet with a determined gaze. "What all did she say to you, ask you?"

"I told her I should like to have a dinner for her while she is here, and she inquired about the guests. She asked if I liked living here, about my upbringing, did I like children . . ." Juliet paused in her recital, turning away from Alexander so he could not see her face in the dim light.

"That is not all, I suspect. What else did my dear dragon want to know?"

"She asked if I love you," Juliet finished in a small voice. "Of course I told her I did," she continued in a rush. "After all, we are supposed to be a happy newly married couple."

Alexander sighed and pushed away from the door, crossing to enfold Juliet in a comforting embrace. "We will muddle through her visit somehow. Here you thought we were free of company."

"Not quite," she said in a muffled voice, her face buried against his waistcoat. She looked up at him and grinned. "We have Marius and Taunton, not to mention Harry Riggs. It is like a hotel, I think."

"I had best join them for billiards. You intend to write the invitations this evening?" He opened the door, prepared to leave.

"Indeed. I had not contemplated a dinner for sixteen so soon after having had a ball. Whoever said it was deadly quiet living in the country ought to come here for a bit."

"You will cope splendidly, I know. Do not be too late at it." He closed the door behind him, and Juliet was alone.

She glanced across her room as she went to the charming little desk that must have been the dowager's. The bed stood there in muted elegance. Never once did Alexander give it a look. That night of the storm, both storms, might not have happened. He had held her close, read poetry to her, comforted her, and what now? He treated her much as an old, comfortable shoe that has been around for ages.

It was a pity she could not ask the dowager for advice; she would likely have a great deal to offer.

*   *   *

The following morning Juliet sent off the invitations first thing. The groom, dressed in the splendid gold and black Hawkswood livery, would cause a stir in Woodbury. If her ladyship would bring servants, Juliet figured it could not hurt to make use of them.

Then she set to work in conference with Mrs. Bassett and Cook, concocting a menu to please the dowager as well as the local guests—who most likely did not care for rich sauces either.

It would be Cook's wonderful mushroom soup again, followed by trout—if Harry and Marius could manage to catch enough for dinner—with a delicious chicken dish Cook knew how to prepare. Various side dishes and removes were settled on with satisfaction all around.

"Thank goodness his lordship engaged those two maids and that footman," Mrs. Bassett said with a sigh. "Would Randall act as butler again?"

"I fancy that if Lord Hawkswood requests it, he will."

Later, Alexander found her in her room seated before the little desk with a pile of acceptances to peruse.

"All coming?" he inquired while lazily leaning against the connecting door frame.

"Need you ask? But of course. Speculation is high as to what her ladyship is doing here. Most seem to think she has come to inspect me as it were."

"Juliet, about our marriage," Alexander began. "We need to talk. It's no good going on as we are now."

She jumped up from the writing desk to hurry to the door leading to the hall. "No time for something so detailed now. I have a million things to do."

"You are avoiding what must be discussed," he said dryly. "So be it. But one day soon we *must* talk. It cannot be avoided!"

His words lingered in her mind as she went about her many duties the next two days. The dowager seemed content to let Juliet handle everything. Rather, she strolled in the garden, commenting acidly on the plants growing there.

For the dinner Juliet dressed with extra care, donning the ivory moire, her pearls, the pretty brooch Alexander had given her as well as taking her birthday fan to use as a defense against her ladyship's sharp eyes.

Conversation at the dinner table was charming, Juliet decided. All the guests seemed bent on outdoing the others in agreeable conduct. The meal progressed with no mishaps. They were being served dessert—a light castle pudding, an excellent fruit crumble, and sponge cake topped with whipped cream flavored with orange—when the dowager cleared her throat, no small sound with her voice.

"I wish to make a happy little announcement."

Everyone at the table paused, spoons or forks in hand, to stare at the dowager. Sensing it might be momentous, all utensils were lowered to respective plates. Silence reigned.

"I am very pleased with Alexander's marriage. He has chosen remarkably well, all things considered. I have therefore communicated to my solicitor my desire to give my grandson fifty thousand pounds upon the birth of their first child."

Not a sound was heard, not even a gasp.

Chapter 13

Juliet led the women to the drawing room, leaving the men to their customary port. Like the other women present, Juliet was in a state of shock. The possible ramifications of the offer, or bribe if looked at from another angle, whirled through her mind. She welcomed Mrs. Bassett and the tea tray, pouring Bohea tea into delicate Wedgwood cups with a not quite steady hand.

Mrs. Ogleby seemed to recover first and asked Juliet to play for them. "Something cheerful," she suggested, gesturing to the harp, her cup in hand.

Deciding conversation was utterly impossible at the moment, Juliet nodded agreement, sat by the harp, and commenced a gay little tune while her mind was elsewhere.

She glanced at the dowager viscountess, seated so regally in a bergère chair across the room. How pleased with herself she looked—smug, even—wearing a rich black velvet gown trimmed in gold cord that added to her regal look. Her black velvet turban was decorated with a large gold brooch set with a ruby such as to stir envy in Miss Shelford had she seen it.

How would Alexander feel about his grandmother's outrageous proposition? Obviously, the woman did not guess the marriage was nonexistent. Juliet and Alexander had fooled everyone—everyone but themselves. What would he wish to do? She felt confused and not a little worried.

The other women were recovering from the startling announcement and had begun to converse in soft undertones. Juliet concluded her little bit of music and offered more tea. She poured the dowager a second cup of tea, prepared it the way she preferred, while wondering how that woman would have felt had such a enticement been offered to her when newly married. There were times, Juliet suspected, when such a bribe could not have been fulfilled. What resentments might have occurred then!

"Lucy, favor us with a song," Mrs. Ogleby insisted. "You have such a pretty voice."

Juliet played a soft accompaniment while Lucy sang a country air in a sweet, clear voice.

During her simple song, the men came into the room to join the ladies, apparently having little to joke and talk about over the table. Most likely the sum of money offered had staggered them as much as it had the women. There would be a goodly number of speculative conversations this evening while preparing for bed. Juliet assumed most couples discussed the day's events such as she and Alexander did before sleeping—even if she and Alexander went to separate beds.

How embarrassing it would be were she truly a wife, to have everyone wondering were she in the family way as yet. Could the dowager not have made the offer in a more private manner? It would have been far more seemly, to Juliet's way of thinking.

Lord Taunton requested Lucy to sing again; they had missed part of the first number.

Juliet gladly played for her, thinking it preferable to attempting an intelligent conversation. Fortunately for all concerned, once Lucy had finished her song, Lord Taunton, with a look at Mr. Tackley, said he also had an announcement to make.

"Miss Tackley has done me the honor of accepting my suit. We shall be married shortly—I do not believe in long engagements," he said with a laugh.

The Dowager Viscountess Hawkswood did not appear pleased at the announcement that took some of the sensation from hers. However, the remainder of the guests were quite delighted, and much was made of the young couple.

To Alexander, Taunton said, "First, I shall go to my solicitor and have proper settlement papers drawn up, and see to preparing the country house as well. Parson Richards has agreed to marry us as soon as may be." He gave Lucy a fond look that surprised no one who had seen the couple at the fete.

Juliet suspected that Taunton thought to lodge with them prior to the wedding, and was surprised when Alexander offered Taunton's late uncle's home as a temporary residence until the wedding.

It was a chattering, happy group of people who departed from the manor that evening. The dowager, Juliet, and Alexander saw them on their way while Marius and Harry said something about leaving on the morrow along with Taunton.

Juliet did not urge them to remain, and Alexander was silent as well.

Once the guests had gone, those remaining went to their respective rooms, save for Alexander. As usual, he followed Juliet into hers, closing the door behind him with a feeling close to resignation.

"It is not quite what you might think," Alexander said. The dowager's announcement that had so stunned the little group still had Juliet in a mild state of shock.

"But such an enormous sum of money and to be given in *such* a manner," Juliet objected. She stood in the center of her room, wide-eyed and troubled.

Alexander firmly sat her on the comfortable chair, then drew up a Windsor armchair to face her. "My grandmother achieved an unusual degree of independence by her mother's will. She holds land in her own right and has refused to let it to be placed in trusts. When my father begged her to allow part of the trusts of *his* marriage to be placed on land she held in her own right, she replied that she had attained this independence and was determined to keep it. She forbid him to ever mention it again. I suspect that in part her decision was because of a strong dislike for my mother."

"But still—such a vast sum, a fortune!"

"That large sum of money is actually her income for two years," Alexander explained almost apologetically. "I know she has never been extravagant and can easily arrange for that sum to be paid."

"Oh," Juliet said in a small voice. While far from having to count her pounds, Juliet could not imagine such wealth. "Well," she concluded with a sigh, "it is a moot point, for we shan't have a child. She will wait in vain." She studied her hands, neatly folded in her lap, wishing she had settled in a simple cottage not belonging to anyone instead of this lovely manor house complete with a husband who was not a husband, nor did he wish ever to be her husband.

"In a sense we are married, you know." His words brought her head up to stare at him in astounded silence. "You wear my rings, you have taken my name, and everyone in this area views us as a wedded couple. Just because we have not consummated this sort of common-law union does not make it less effective. In Scotland we'd be legally wed if we simply stated we are man and wife. In Wales and Yorkshire they jump over the broom, or besom as it is known there, in a perfectly acceptable marriage ceremony. Shall we jump over a broom, Juliet?" He smiled at her as though joking, but his voice was quite serious.

Juliet sprang from the chair, staring at Alexander with confusion. "No,"—she shook her head in denial—"it cannot be. Surely you do not desire such a thing. When you came here, you said you had no wish to be married—to anyone. I felt the same. We must not allow pressures such as your grandmother has offered to change our original plans."

"The situation has altered during the time we have been here, Juliet. Surely you must see that." He had risen as well and with a worried gaze watched her pace about the room.

"I'll not agree to such an arrangement. I would never trap you into a marriage you have no liking for; it would be of all things detestable. I promised you that when we were free of the dangers of unwanted marriages, we could both go our own ways. I refuse to marry you, Alexander. I would not wed . . ." Juliet ceased her words, not wanting to admit to Alexander that she would gladly marry him if he loved her.

"Juliet—" Alexander began only to be interrupted by her.

"No, my mind is quite made up. Marius is convinced I am married. Camilla Shelford has gone, also persuaded that you are no longer free to wed her. Once the rest of our guests have left, we shall part. You may go your way; if anyone asks what became of me, say I disappeared—died—whatever you please."

"And you?" he asked, looking appalled.

"I intend to find a simple cottage somewhere as far away from London as possible. I shall change my name, pretend to be a widow perhaps, and see if Miss Pritchard will join me in my quiet life."

"Surely that cannot be what your father would wish for his only daughter."

"My father has been singularly absent for many years without so much as a letter. I find it difficult to believe that he would care one jot what happens to me."

Alexander took note of the stubborn tilt of Juliet's chin, the suspicious brightness in her eyes, and guessed she was fighting tears. The absence of her father hurt her more than Alexander had realized. He took a step toward her, then stopped. Perhaps now was not the moment to offer consolation.

"Very well, I shall leave it be, but only for now. You must come to see reason." Alexander crossed to the connecting door, opened it, then paused to say, "Good night, Juliet."

"Sleep well, Alexander," Juliet replied dryly, adopting the tone familiar to the dowager viscountess.

Marius and Lord Taunton, along with Harry Riggs, left directly after an early breakfast the following morning. Neither Alexander nor Juliet persuaded them to remain, simply smiling and wishing them Godspeed.

The dowager was another matter entirely. She appeared ready to remain until the birth of the new heir if necessary.

Juliet watched her strolling in the garden, issuing an occasional order to Mr. Lumpkin, who totally ignored it, much to her ire. Turning to Alexander, Juliet said, "I believe she intends to stay forever. What are we going to do?"

The problem was resolved, but hardly in the way they expected.

Three days later, Juliet was in the garden, enjoying the afternoon breeze, when she heard a carriage entering the drive. Curious, for it did not sound like a light vehicle, she walked around the corner of the house to see a dusty traveling coach. The crest on the side panel was coated with mud, but she gathered it had to be someone important.

Turning, she fled to the rear of the house, then hurried into the library to find Alexander. "We have company again," she announced a trifle out of breath.

He rose from his desk, joining her near the door where she stood wringing her hands.

"What now?" he murmured in a resigned voice. "Can you think of anyone else who might seek us out in this remote village?"

"Not a soul. All who might have had an interest but your grandmother have left."

Alexander placed a protective arm about Juliet while they took a position in the entryway. They stood quietly as Mrs. Bassett opened the large front door to reveal a tall, white-haired gentleman with a slim, middle-aged woman on his arm.

"Papa?" Juliet asked softly. "Can it be you?"

"So, I am still able to track my quarry even after all these years," the gentleman said in a genial way, crossing to envelop Juliet in a hug.

"And who are you, sir, if I may inquire?" Lord Winterton looked at Alexander with a piercing gaze that pinned him to the spot.

"Alexander Barr, Viscount Hawkswood at your service— your daughter's husband."

"You see, dear, it is all right; she is married to this handsome gentleman and quite settled. You worried for naught." The woman who had entered with his lordship joined the trio, then added, "I am Helena, your new stepmother, Juliet. I married your father while he was in Russia."

Juliet could not have spoken had her life depended upon it. She studied the attractive older woman, whose silvery blond hair was a pretty foil for blue eyes and a clear skin. She looked to be agreeable, but then, looks could be so deceiving.

"Come in, come in," Alexander said with feigned heartiness. To Mrs. Bassett he issued instructions regarding rooms, figuring Juliet would be in no condition to think in that direction.

They entered the drawing room, Alexander assisting Lady Winterton with her shawls and making certain she was comfortable.

Juliet stood by the bergère chair, her hand resting on the back while she studied her father. "Forgive me, Papa, but I have not seen you for so long, I scarcely recognized you. Your hair has turned white, although you are much the same otherwise," she admitted.

"And you have grown up to look just like your mother. I'd have known you anywhere," he replied, drawing her from her place by the chair to the window where he could see her better. "To think you are married."

"Yes, well, indeed we are," she said when she observed the dowager had entered the room and stood waiting to be introduced.

Alexander made the introductions smoothly.

"Did Marius arrange this marriage for you?" her father inquired after exchanging pleasantries with the dowager, not relinquishing the topic he wanted to explore.

"No," Juliet answered with a darted look of pleading to Alexander.

He joined her at once and attempted to ease her father's fears. "Juliet was visiting Miss Pritchard's family up north." Alexander bent his head to look down at Juliet with a warm smile. "We met, fell in love, and I persuaded her to fly to Gretna with me." If Alexander felt like a fool making such a dimwitted explanation, it didn't show on his face.

"And you fell in love with him, just like that?" Lord Winterton queried, giving his daughter a piercing look. "Not that I have anything against such an alliance. I'd be a fool to object," he concluded almost bitterly.

"I find Alexander very easy to love, Papa. He enjoys music as I do, reads poetry, indulges me in my gardening, and in general is a very good sort of husband," Juliet replied in all truthfulness, for Alexander would have made a splendid husband—had they been married.

"I see. Since you say that Marius had nothing to do with the arrangements and you eloped, I should like to know what manner of settlements have been drawn up." This was the father of the bride speaking, all business and suspicions in full arousal.

The dowager rose majestically from the sofa to join the trio. "I have arranged a settlement of fifty thousand pounds for their firstborn child."

Lord Winterton turned slightly to glance at his wife, then looked at the dowager. "Puts them rather on the spot, does it not?"

"Now, dear," the new Lady Winterton said quietly when she hurried from her chair to join the four confronting one another.

"I want you to know that Juliet has a sizable dowry," Lord Winterton said to Alexander, smiling, but having a frosty glint in his eyes.

"You need have no fears regarding the amount of her jointure—or her pin money," replied Alexander in a tone laced with steel.

Juliet, thinking the entire conversation utterly ridiculous in view of the lack of a wedding in the first place, suggested, "You both must be tired after traveling so far. Why do you not settle in your rooms, then return at your leisure in time for dinner. We dine at London hours here, about five-thirty. We can talk more then. I am anxious to learn all about your trip to Russia, how you met my new mama, and how you found me!"

The tension in the air abated considerably with this sensible suggestion. The newcomers followed Mrs. Bassett up the stairs. That good lady looked as though nothing and no one would ever again faze her as she showed the new guests to their rooms. Titles everywhere, far from the quiet job she'd been offered when hired.

"That was unexpected," the dowager said, returning to her preferred place on the bergère chair. "How lovely for you to not only be reunited with your father but to have a new mama as well."

"Indeed, ma'am. Lady Winterton appears to be a very pretty lady with kindly manners. I am sorry that it took so long for me to learn of her. It is apparent that Papa does not like to write letters."

Her lovely face composed, Juliet turned to Alexander and said, "I believe I shall change for dinner now. Do you join me?"

Taking the not so subtle hint, Alexander replied, "But of course. We shall see you later, Grandmother."

"Indeed so, Alexander. I quite look forward to the evening." The dowager looked off to the scene beyond the windows, a speculative expression on her face.

"Ominous words, indeed," Juliet whispered to Alexander once she thought they were out of the dear dragon's hearing and going up the stairs to her room.

He hastily nudged her into the bedroom, then crossed to stand by the window, where he leaned against the frame to look back at her. "I fancy you are thrilled to see your father again, to know that Marius is wrong and that your beloved father still lives—but what a damnable coil it presents."

"How true," Juliet replied, not taking offense at his language. The situation was indeed terrible. "Do you think we can continue to fool him?"

"What do I tell him when he asks to see our marriage lines? I lost them?"

Juliet frowned, walking over to the Windsor armchair to lean on the back. "Tell him you placed it in the vault at the Abbey."

"What if some kindly soul remarks about our supposed separation and reunion? Mrs. Ogleby is just the sort to do that little thing. Is that what I did before I came here? Have settlements drawn up, put the marriage certificate in the vault, arrange for your jointure and pin money? Perhaps I oversaw the master suite decorated just for you?"

Juliet watched as he turned to look out into the waning light. The set of his handsome face was harsh, as well it might be.

"Oh, Alexander, I am so dreadfully sorry," she cried softly. "If only Marius had not threatened to marry me off to Lord Taunton, we would not be in this pickle."

The lines on Alexander's face softened, and he moved to stand at her side, wrapping one arm about her shoulders. "You could not have imagined all that has transpired. How many people have a grandmother like mine, for instance? Or how many men have a Camilla Shelford chasing them? Your father is nothing more than the icing on the cake."

"If we think we have given a fine performance before, we will have to excel for Papa. He seems to be suspicious," Juliet said into the comfort offered by Alexander's shoulder.

"Remember, when he left England you were still in the schoolroom, a little girl," Alexander said, wrapping his other arm around her. "I imagine it is quite a jolt for a man to return expecting to find things as he left them, only to discover his daughter gone, he knows not where. Then, when he does track her down, he finds she has run off with some peer to Gretna and is now a married woman."

"But we didn't," Juliet reminded him quietly.

"Aye, there's the rub."

"I am twenty-one now, old enough not to require permission to marry, regardless," Juliet pointed out.

"But your birthday came after we wed, my pet," Alexander reminded her.

"Which we did not," she countered stubbornly and most needlessly. There was no reply to this obvious statement.

"I think you need a few new gowns. What with all the company, you must be tired of the same things," Alexander said, leaving her side to walk to the connecting door.

"The mantua-maker promised to bring the gowns I ordered as soon as she finished them. They ought to arrive any day. I imagine you could use a few things as well. You hardly planned for the sort of entertaining we have done."

"Certainly not a father-in-law and his new wife," Alexander said dryly, then entered his room and snapped the door shut behind him.

Juliet stared at the door a few moments, quite nonplused, then crossed to open the wardrobe to see what gown might do for dinner with her father, his new wife, and the dowager viscountess. The prospect was daunting, to say the least.

"The leaf green satin be the best one for this evening, ma'am," Pansy said as she entered the room to see Juliet holding out the moire.

"I suppose you are right. One of the new muslins will do well for tomorrow. Tonight had best be something nicer."

She changed, then wondered if Alexander would return—or would he merely go straight downstairs to the drawing room without her? She dismissed Pansy and sat down to wait.

He tapped on her door, then entered as she bid.

"You must think me a boor," he began. "I should never have said that about entertaining your father and his new wife."

"It is true, however."

"I wish the emeralds were here," he said obliquely. "Your father will think I am a poor sort of husband, not giving you proper jewels when he would know I could afford them."

"Alexander, they are in the vault in London, remember? And were we truly on a honeymoon, would I be needing something so grand as an emerald necklace?"

"And earrings, a brooch, tiara, and ring to match," he added morosely.

"Goodness! I suppose your grandmother will make some remark about them in that event," Juliet added wryly.

"Let us go down and face them the best we can then. You look lovely in the pearls, and since your father gave them to you, perhaps he will think it in honor of his return?" Alexander drew her along to the door, then paused. "Best have a dash of stars in the eyes."

She puzzled at this only a moment, for he answered her unspoken query by bestowing one of his heart-stopping kisses on her with all the expertise she supposed a rake might acquire.

"There now," he said with satisfaction, "I believe that did both of us good."

Juliet supposed she blushed to her toes and must look as flustered as possible under Alexander's warm gaze.

"You are very practiced at that, my lord," she said lightly in a very soft voice.

"Well, as to that," Alexander replied, looking a trifle uncomfortable and running a finger beneath the edge of his impeccably arranged cravat, "I suppose I am."

"I have heard that rakes make the best of husbands. I shall have to find one for myself, perhaps," she said, again in a light manner as they left her room to go down to the drawing room and their guests.

What Alexander might have said to that provoking remark was not to be known, for Julian Winterton and his new wife left their rooms at that moment to join Juliet and Alexander as they went down.

"What did you do while in Russia, Papa?" Juliet asked, wanting to know why her father had remained away for so long as well as thinking if he kept his mind on his own doings, he couldn't put his nose into hers.

Smelling faintly of sandalwood and dressed in excellent style, Lord Winterton escorted his wife into the drawing room before attempting to answer his daughter's most natural question.

"You know I went at the behest of the government," he began after greeting the Dowager Lady Hawkswood. "I was to tour Russia, making observations as to the condition of the country after Napoleon's disastrous invasion. I luckily found Helena while I was in St. Petersburg. A friend introduced her, and I was thrilled to discover she is a talented artist, most unusual for a Russian woman. We made a very excellent pair and rapidly found ourselves united in more than interests. Not only do I care deeply for her, but I had the advantage of an artist to make drawings of what we saw as we traveled." He exchanged a fond look with his wife, one that completely shut out Juliet.

"I wish I might see them," Juliet said, feeling terribly cut off from her father and his life.

"And so you shall, my dear," Helena inserted in her pleasant voice. "We were so pleased with the outcome—my illustrations and Julian's observations of the scenes we encountered—that a book will be printed with the most interesting of them. You will have one of the first copies."

Randall entered, acting again in the role of butler, to announce that dinner was served.

Juliet begged her father to tell them more of his travels, and so he did throughout the meal.

During a pause Helena darted a glance at Alexander and commented, "In Russia you would likely be called Sacha."

"They call men with his name that in England as well," the dowager added with a faint twist of her mouth. "I never liked it and made certain it was not allowed."

"How fortunate I did not mind," Alexander said with a narrow-eyed look at his grandmother.

Juliet smoothed over the exchange with a comment on the weather, and the dowager subsided. Alexander was more quiet than usual, and the conversation returned to Russia and the conditions Lord Winterton and Helena had found there. It sounded utterly dreadful.

"The cruelty of the French during their occupation was incredible. Yet the sight of the French prisoners, many of whom had lost fingers and toes, was horrible to see. Neither side won, if you see what I mean."

Juliet turned the conversation in another direction and wondered which side would emerge victorious when her father and Alexander met for a discussion on the marriage. She would not wager on either man to win.

Chapter 14

At the rap on the connecting door Juliet turned from the window to invite Alexander to enter. Her expectation of doom hung over her like a storm cloud waiting to break.

"Well, how do you feel this morning, meeting your father after several years?" he asked, sauntering across the room to join her. As always, he was impeccably dressed—this morning in nankeen breeches, a pale buff waistcoat, and a dark green coat, the tails of which were modest in length. With his hair arranged à la Titus he looked so dashing he made Juliet felt quite provincial; her hair simply styled and wearing a rather ordinary gown of green-and-white-striped muslin—never mind it was new.

"And with a new wife," she said, dragging her thoughts away from Alexander and how he looked. "He is much as he ever was. I believe I rather like Helena. She invited us to visit them. How odd—to be invited to visit my own home."

"I expect she thinks your home is with me," Alexander suggested. "It will be—even if we decide not to live together."

"What do you mean?" Juliet asked with great caution.

"You must know there is no possible way we can part now," Alexander said gently.

"I do not." Juliet's eyes flashed with amber fire. "I promised myself I'd not trap you into a marriage because of my foolish actions, and I won't," she replied with a stubborn set to her jaw.

"I see you wrote to your former governess," Alexander probed, evading the issue for the moment. "I franked the letter for you."

"Thank you. With Father home again, I decided it would be

sensible to let her know what has happened. I wrote her a brief letter after I came here, cautioning her not to reveal my whereabouts to Marius. I expressed a hope that after she completed her stay with her family she might wish to join me here, but I have heard nothing from her. She may have been so annoyed with me that she has sought a post elsewhere."

They both stared out at the gardens below for a few moments, then Juliet said in a hushed voice, "Alexander, whatever are we to do? I think Papa is suspicious."

"Why would you think that?" Alexander inquired. "I thought we gave a rather convincing performance last evening."

"That is just it—it was a performance. He is a very clever man, most astute."

"And that is not all of the problem, is it?" Alexander queried kindly, leaning back against the window surround, arms crossed before him while he studied his most unexpected wife.

Juliet sighed deeply, strolling away from the window and Alexander. "How perceptive you are. Of course it is not the whole of my problem." She spun about to face him, her hands clasped before her. "Alexander, I have *never* lied to my father before in my life. It bothers me greatly to do so now. I fear he can see guilt written on my face as clearly as if I put the word there."

"What can I say?" Alexander replied lightly. "We must wait to see how the day goes. I have asked your father's advice regarding the property I bought—Mr. Taunton's land and house. I suspect your father is the sort who enjoys giving suggestions."

"We must wait? And what of your grandmother? Every day she studies me as though she expects to see me in the family way," Juliet said, her cheeks flaming with the words, so intimate and full of implications.

"She will not say anything more. Ignore her looks if you can." Alexander left the window to cross to the connecting door. "Carry on as best you can, my dear."

"How well you do that—the little endearments, quite as though you meant them. I suppose you have had a great deal of practice at that as well," Juliet said with an apprehensive look at the man who shared so much of her life at the moment.

"You seemed determined to think the worst of me, Juliet," Alexander said. "But is it so terrible a thing if I have a bit of polish?"

"It is not that I think the worst of you, quite the contrary. I am made the more aware of my own lack of accomplishments in that line. I fear I am a very green girl," she concluded wistfully.

He returned to stand before her, looking down at her with a strange expression she couldn't fathom. "Do you not know a man prefers an innocent woman for a wife?"

"But I am not your wife," she reminded him.

He placed one finger on her chin, drawing a tantalizing line along the edge of it while he stared into her eyes, his own alight with some secret knowledge. "But that is where you are wrong, my dear girl." He bestowed a light kiss on her brow, then left the room before she could think of a retort.

When Juliet went downstairs, she discovered her new stepmother in the drawing room, looking at the piece of needlework over which Juliet had so carefully slaved.

"Lovely, my dear. How skillfully you have blended the colors for the flowers—quite as though they were real. Would you like to show me your gardens? Julian said you have done extensive work at Winterton." Helena gave her a persuasive smile that would have melted any resistance, had there been any.

The two women strolled from the house, watched by the dowager, whose puzzled expression contrasted with her impressive gown of plum sarcenet.

"Your husband's grandmother seems a bit of a dragon," Helena said hesitantly. "I trust I do not speak out of line?"

"You know she has offered Alexander an enormous sum of money on the birth of his first child?" Juliet inquired with a delightful blush. "It is so frightfully awkward."

"I can well imagine. It would give one the feeling of being under pressure." Helena strolled along, looking at the various blooms, then turned to add, "You are not, I think, in the family way as yet. You do not have the look of an expectant mother."

At these words Juliet's face turned a deep rose; she could feel the heat of her skin. Such frankness had not come her way before she pretended to be a wife.

"No, I am not," Juliet replied in a strangled voice.

Helena gave her a consoling pat on the arm. "Not to worry. Alexander does not appear to be the childless sort. I am sure he is not backward in his attentions."

Juliet wished the ground would open so she might escape this conversation. She turned away from her stepmother to look elsewhere, taking comfort in the knowledge that if Helena believed there was a chance Juliet might be expecting, at least there was the belief she was married. And that meant Papa likely believed it as well.

"It is like waiting for the tide," Helena said softly. "Nothing occurs before its time. When the tide is due to come in, it does, without any help from anyone or anything. The same is true for you, dear girl. When it is your time, then it shall be so. You must have patience, no matter how you may wish things otherwise," she concluded with a touch of Eastern philosophy, although delivered in a charming French accent.

There was no possible reply to this observation, so Juliet remained silent. Rather, she pointed out the modest topiary she had begun with Mr. Lumpkin's assistance.

"These are simple shapes, nothing fantastical. But I believe they give extra emphasis to the garden, punctuation marks, as it were," Juliet explained, more comfortable now she had managed to steer the conversation away from herself.

Before long, Helena excused herself and went off to find her husband.

Wishing to avoid the dowager, Juliet collected her needlework box and sought the solace of the pretty arbor Alexander had ordered constructed. In a year or two the vines would cover it. Now it stood rather bare, yet offering a refuge. With her needlepoint in hand, she enjoyed the peace, concentrating on placing neat stitches in the mesh.

"So here you are," Alexander said, joining her on the bench and sitting much too close for her ease. "I just left your father with Helena. He had some excellent recommendations regarding the new property."

"Good," Juliet replied, then wary, asked, "He is not coming out here, is he?"

"You must not allow your feeling of guilt to swamp you," Alexander admonished.

"Hush! Someone might hear you."

"Allow me to read to you. That ought to take your mind off your troubles," Alexander said with a hint of laughter in his voice.

Juliet paused, her needle in midair, wondering what on earth he could find to read to her.

He satisfied her curiosity by pulling a book from his pocket—a book she recognized as the one he bought at the fete. It was the book of poetry, and the thought he would remember how she had enjoyed her father's reading warmed her heart.

Alexander rose to pace about the garden while he searched the pages for something he wished to read aloud. Clearing his throat, he gave her a look she'd have deemed sheepish in anyone else less lordly. She resumed her stitching, hoping that she didn't make a hash out of the delicate design she'd so carefully worked to this point. Alexander read:

Whenas in silks my Julia goes,
Then, then (methinks) how sweetly flows
That liquefaction of her clothes.

Next, when I cast mine eyes and see
That brave vibration each way free,
O how that glittering taketh me!

"What do you think, Juliet? Did friend Herrick admire his Julia in an unseemly way? The flow of her garments about her body?"

"No, I doubt it, for he was a cleric, was he not?" Juliet said, her face only mildly pink. "He would not have behaved in an improper way. I do not recall that he married, however," she concluded with a delicate frown.

"Indeed, yes, in his way he was proper. I shan't bring you to the blush with a reading of 'Gather ye rosebuds while ye may' as I would like to," Alexander said with a chuckle. "But here is another verse you might appreciate."

A sweet disorder in the dress
Kindles in clothes a wantonness:
A lawn about the shoulders thrown
Into a fine distraction:
An erring lace, which here and there
Enthralls the crimson stomacher;
A cuff neglectful, and thereby
Ribbands to flow confusèdly
A winning wave (deserving note)
In the tempestuous petticoat:
A careless shoestring, in whose tie
I see a wild civility;
Do more bewitch me than when art
Is too precise in every part.

Juliet paused in her stitching, staring off into the near-distance for a moment before turning her gaze to an expectant Alexander. "Do you agree with him that a bit of disarrangement in a woman's clothing is bewitching?"

"Let me say that perhaps I find perfection a trifle over-whelming," Alexander replied with a grin. "For instance, I find you enchanting when I see your silly little cap at a tilt, or your shawl about to fall from your pretty shoulders. Could it be John Donne's sentiments are more likely to entice you? 'For God's sake hold your tongue and let me love' perhaps?"

"Alexander," she reproved, trying to look severe and utterly failing.

"No love? Another Donne, perchance," he said with a mischievous expression before he reopened the book and began to read.

Juliet listened as she heard the words from "Go and catch a falling star" read to her with curious intent. Did Alexander hunt for one who was true and fair, as the poet wrote? She made no comment when Alexander finished, although he seemed to wait for an observation from her.

What might have been said was to remain unknown, for at that moment Juliet heard the unmistakable sound of an approaching carriage. "More company? I vow, this place I thought so remote is like an inn."

"Look at it this way, the more people we have around us, the less likely your father, my grandmother, or anyone else is to ask disconcerting questions," Alexander pointed out.

"Do you really think the presence of another person will prevent your grandmother from voicing an opinion should she wish to make one?" Juliet questioned, putting her needlework aside after checking to see she had not made any mistakes. Her only error was in secluding herself in the garden and listening to Alexander read love poetry to her.

"Probably not," he admitted, walking at Juliet's side around to the front of the house and the arriving carriage.

A post chaise had drawn up before they reached the front of the house, the door had been opened, and a woman now stepped forth, looking about her with curiosity.

"Miss Pritchard!" Juliet exclaimed, hurrying forward to greet the surprising guest.

"It wanted only this," she heard Alexander murmur as she left his side. He walked around the two women to pay the driver of the post chaise, who looked anxious to be on his way after depositing the baggage on the drive.

"Juliet, my dear girl," this good lady exclaimed, her face composed, "what a lovely place this is you selected for your little retreat." Her gaze chanced upon Alexander and she halted, turning to Juliet for an explanation. "I understood you were alone and desirous of my company. I came as soon as I was able to leave my parents in good heart."

Juliet floundered, giving Alexander a beseeching look.

"Miss Pritchard, I have heard Juliet speak of you often," Alexander said in his most polished manner. "I am Hawkswood, Juliet's husband."

Miss Pritchard went pale, then a puzzled expression came over her face. "I was unaware you had married, my dear. You should have written me. I would have gone elsewhere. Your letter said you had left Winterton Hall to avoid an unwelcome alliance with a friend of your stepbrother." There was most definitely a question in her eyes and voice.

"I am sorry. I sent you a letter, bringing you up to date on the events that have happened lately. You crossed paths, it seems. I should have written before, but things have been at sixes and sevens here recently."

"What Juliet means to say it that we have been inundated with company. Marius and Lord Taunton, a friend of mine, a couple of others, followed by my grandmother."

"Papa came yesterday with Helena, his new wife. He met her in St. Petersburg," Juliet added in an aside. "But you must stay with us for a time. I'll not see you go so soon when you have just arrived," Juliet insisted, taking Miss Pritchard's arm to draw her into the house. "I wish you to meet Helena. And the dowager as well," Juliet added with a look at Alexander.

"The dowager is . . . ?" Miss Pritchard inquired of Alexander.

"The Dowager Viscountess Hawkswood. I doubt anyone has called her Charlotte since she was a girl," Alexander replied, exchanging a look with Juliet before casting a glance at the governess. He ushered her into the house, saying, "Welcome to our little household, Miss Pritchard."

Mrs. Bassett bustled forth from the rear of the house to meet the trio in the entryway, a question in her eyes as she turned to Juliet.

"My former governess, Miss Pritchard, has come for a visit. I wish her to stay in the Green Room, Mrs. Bassett."

Since that particular room was a very lovely one, lately occupied by Miss Shelford, the housekeeper immediately was given to know that the governess was held in high esteem. "Indeed, ma'am."

While Mrs. Bassett undertook to dispose of such luggage as the governess had brought with her, Juliet and Alexander brought Miss Pritchard into the drawing room where Helena and Julian Winterton were seated. Helena was writing a letter while Julian read a newspaper several days old, but nonetheless absorbing to someone desirous of catching up on news.

Upon the entry of Juliet, Alexander, and the newcomer, both

rose from their chairs, a hint of question on Helena's face that quickly disappeared as Lord Winterton greeted Miss Pritchard with civility.

"Miss Pritchard, this is indeed a surprise, but a welcome one. I may now express my gratitude for the care you gave my daughter in my absence." He said nothing for the moment regarding the elopement that presumably had occurred while Juliet was with Miss Pritchard.

"Ah, you were Juliet's governess," Helena exclaimed softly, coming to join them. "You must be most accomplished to have done so well," she said gracefully as she met the woman who was somewhere in age between Juliet and herself.

Miss Pritchard dipped a graceful curtsy, darting glances about the room, at Alexander, the others, and the room with curious, intelligent eyes.

"Whom have we here?" the dowager inquired, entering the room in a rustle of plum sarcenet.

"Miss Pritchard, Grandmother," Alexander smoothly explained, adding a rider to the effect that she had been Juliet's governess. This brought forth the observation that they were not quite ready for such.

"Have you considered the position of nanny, Miss Pritchard?" the old woman probed, a shrewd look in her gaze.

"Miss Pritchard is here on a visit, Grandmother," Juliet inserted. "She has been caring for her ailing parents and needs to recover her spirits."

"In my day, governesses did not take a rest at the home of a former charge."

"Then you were not acquainted with a governess as dear and accomplished as Miss Pritchard," Juliet countered, not about to endure any slight to her adored Miss Pritchard.

"Particularly one who was instrumental in introducing you to my grandson," the old lady retorted with a narrow stare at the bewildered Miss Pritchard.

"Come, you must be wishing for a rest and a change of clothes," Juliet said quietly with a slight tug on Miss Pritchard's arm. "Mrs. Bassett must have your room ready and things unpacked by now. I shall have tea sent up to you once you are settled," Juliet murmured as she hurried Miss Pritchard from the drawing room and up the stairs.

"Juliet," the former governess whispered when they had reached the upper hallway, "what is going on? I know you far too well to mistake that guilty expression on your face. You are up to something, and I would know what it is."

"I shall explain everything later. Just say nothing about that meeting. At the moment I shall settle you in your room and prepare for dinner. We dine at London hours, so change and rejoin us when you can."

The mystified governess entered her lovely room, quite as nice as she had known while at Winterton Hall, and resolved to find out precisely what sort of bumblebroth her charge had plunged into once her governess had departed.

Juliet left Miss Pritchard to settle into her room, returning to her own to change for dinner.

"This is an interesting turn of events," Alexander said from where he reclined on her bed. He propped himself on one arm while she came to a halt just inside her door, staring at him with horrified eyes. She hastily shut the door behind her. "Alexander," she whispered, "what are you doing in my room?" Much as she loved him, he was the last person she wished to see at the moment.

"Your father came upstairs with me, and I thought it best to continue the illusion that we are a loving husband and wife. He knows this is your room." Alexander lazily rose from the bed and walked over to gaze down at Juliet. "It is quite acceptable for husband and wife to come and go into each other's rooms."

"But . . ." Juliet objected helplessly, feeling quite as though she had been captured by the tide of which Helena spoke and even now was being swept out to sea. Alexander ignored her, turning to gesture to several boxes stacked on the far side of the bed.

"Some things came from Salisbury. If I make no mistake, they are from the mantua-maker. Shall I see the new gowns and assist you in choosing one for dinner?"

"Go away," she cried, upset that he was in her room. That she was secreted in her bedroom with a man not her husband—

never mind that she loved the dratted creature—while her father was just down the hall disturbed her dreadfully. If Papa knew the truth, he would be horribly disappointed in her, to put it mildly.

But, she also knew that he would march Alexander and her down the nearest aisle as quick as might be, and she didn't want that. Not that she didn't desire Alexander. She did. But she did not want him as a trapped and condemned husband.

Naturally, Alexander ignored her order—such as it was—and opened the first of the boxes, pulling a delicate caramel crepe gown—one that had been exquisitely decorated with embroidery—from the tissue in which it had been protected.

"I need look no further," he said, holding the gown up against a motionless Juliet.

She, quite unable to resist the magic in those dark eyes, meekly agreed to wear the caramel crepe. Only after he had left, retreating through the connecting door with a wink and recommendation that she not be long, did she toss the lovely new gown on the bed.

Fuming, she marched over to the looking glass. "You do not *look* like an idiot," she scolded herself. "Pity you are such a silly, craven soul." Yet, whether she liked it or not, she knew that his wishes would be carried out.

Pansy entered the room, silently going about the job of putting away the pretty new gowns and admiring the one Alexander desired Juliet to wear that evening.

Once Juliet had the gown on and she saw how well it became her, she decided Alexander was right. It was silly of her to cavil at his suggestion. Likely he only meant to bolster her spirits, what with her father, new stepmother, his grandmother, and now her past governess—a most skeptical lady—on the scene.

Pansy had completed dressing Juliet's hair in a rather fetching style with a number of ivory silk roses twined among her curls when another tap came at the connecting door. Not even raising an eyebrow, Pansy meekly departed, leaving Juliet in sole possession of the room.

"Enter," Juliet said, rising from the chair by her dressing

table. "I see you are ready to face inspection," she said when Alexander joined her.

"As are you, and most admirably by the looks of it. If we stick together as much as possible all through the evening, neither your father nor your ex-governess will have a chance to interrogate either one of us."

"I suppose she might feel duty bound to inform Father regarding my status," Juliet reflected. "Yet she would be loyal to me, I believe."

"Remember, we are as good as married in all eyes."

"Except yours and mine," she reminded him bleakly. "I shall have to talk with her sometime, for she will insist upon it. The important thing is to decide what to say."

"And she will catch you out in a lie, is that it?" Alexander asked with more perception than Juliet would have liked.

"Like Papa, she can tell if I prevaricate."

"Juliet, have you come to love me?" Alexander asked suddenly, the words darting to her heart like a spear.

Startled, Juliet turned her head slightly, hoping *he* had not the ability to detect her in a lie. "Of course not," she fibbed.

He took her chin to study her face, for her downcast eyes refused to meet his. "I see."

"You can see nothing," she retorted, her eyes flashing up, daring him to refute her.

"I see far better than you think," Alexander said with a pleased look. "We had best avoid all situations where you could be scrutinized, or it might prove risky." He escorted her to the hall door, then paused. "The good thing is that I'll always know when you attempt to hide the truth from me."

"You are a dreadful man," Juliet said lightly. But inwardly she decided she had best do as he suggested and not just from Miss Pritchard and Papa, but from Alexander as well.

They were the first down, followed almost immediately by Lord Winterton. Alexander fetched him a glass of claret while Juliet asked for more tales of his travels, figuring it a sensible idea to keep him from inquiring about her.

He would have none of her subterfuge. Looking at Juliet,

then Alexander, who had come to place a protective arm about her, Lord Winterton attacked.

"I should like to see the papers—all of them."

"They are at the Abbey," Alexander countered.

"Then why are you not there?" his lordship inquired suavely, persistently.

"Because, Papa," Juliet answered, "Alexander wanted me to see the house his grandmother left him."

"I believed you two at first, but there is something odd about your arrangement."

"Odd, sir? In what way?" Alexander dared to ask.

"That is it. I cannot put my finger on it, but Juliet does not look at me with an open face." Inspecting his daughter's visage, he added, "You are hiding something, but I'll be hornswoggled if I can think what it might be."

With greater relief than anyone could have suspected, Juliet greeted Miss Pritchard when she entered the room.

"I trust I am not too early?" that lady said in polite accents.

"I am most pleased to see you," Juliet said truthfully. Alexander was correct. With both Papa and Miss Pritchard in the room, neither was apt to attempt an interrogation. Juliet shared a rather warm, meaningful look with Alexander, one not missed by their guests.

Chapter 15

The following morning Juliet had sought refuge in the arbor when Miss Pritchard caught up with her.

Looking about her, Miss Pritchard declared, "What a pretty place this is." She joined Juliet on the bench, examining the needlepoint she had worked on in the slight shade offered in the arbor. "That is by far the nicest you have made. Well done, Juliet."

"Thank you." Juliet gestured to the arbor. "Lord Hawkswood had this made. I like it . . ." she said, recalling the love poetry Alexander had read to her not so very long ago before they were inundated with guests. She waited, wondering how long it would take Miss Pritchard to reach the heart of the matter. To stall, she inquired, "What is your Christian name, Miss Pritchard? I cannot believe I have never learned it," Juliet said with a puzzled frown.

"I do not encourage familiarity from my pupils, Juliet. As a matter of fact, my parents named me Horatia—a dreadful name I would as soon forget." Miss Pritchard wrinkled a pretty nose in distaste.

"I think it charming. Your parents were well when you left them?" Juliet anchored her needle in the canvas, putting the work aside to concentrate on what must be said.

"Indeed. Quite able to cope, thank you. I daresay the illness was a ruse to bring me home for a bit. However, I am pleased to be here with you now—even though I shan't be your governess or companion any longer."

"That is a matter I wish to discuss with you." Juliet looked about her to ascertain no one was close by. "I will have need of you before long, and I wish you to remain here until I leave."

"What is this?" Miss Pritchard asked quietly. "You are married now and will naturally be with your husband—will you not?" she added when she observed Juliet's expression.

"Do you recall my letter informing you that I was leaving Winterton Hall to avoid a marriage with Lord Taunton? I took Pansy and set out on a hasty journey south as far as Woodbury, where we encountered a bit of a problem." Juliet explained about the recalcitrant driver of the post chaise, being stranded in Woodbury, the overheard conversation between Mr. and Mrs. Ogleby, and Juliet's solution to her dilemma.

"Good heavens," Miss Pritchard inserted into the narrative. "What daring you displayed. Were you not terrified?"

"I was, but then things grew better. Mrs. Bassett was so kind to me, quite mother-hen-ing me to bits. Everyone appeared to accept me as the estranged wife of Lord Hawkswood with no difficulty. I adore gardening as you know and found these overgrown flower beds fertile soil for my talents." Juliet gestured to the beds overflowing with blooms. "I have been very happy here. I missed you dreadfully, but otherwise it has been an agreeable time."

"I know you did not meet Lord Hawkswood at my parents' home—as I overheard—so you could scarcely flee to Gretna from there; how *did* you meet him?"

Juliet briefly explained about Camilla Shelford, concluding, "She is an utterly wretched girl, quite obsessed with poor Lord Hawkswood. Small wonder he sought refuge here—where he hoped she'd not find him. What a good thing I could pretend to be his wife and scare her away, just as he helped me by preventing Marius from forcing me to wed Lord Taunton." Juliet waited for a reaction and had not long.

"You *pretended* to be his wife?" Horatia Pritchard exclaimed in a whisper, as she did when quite horrified. "Then you are *not* married to him?"

Relieved of her burden of secrecy with one she trusted, Juliet shook her head. "He is a dear man, but desires marriage no more than I do. Please understand, he has been kind and generous to me—protecting me from Marius, defending me from Miss Shelford, standing up to his grandmother when necessary."

"Good heavens, the offer of all that money from her," Miss Pritchard said in fainter accents. "He has not . . . that is . . . you are not, that is, my gracious, what a predicament!"

"Alexander has been the perfect gentleman, or at least almost perfect," Juliet amended, thinking of a few times he had teased her with his behavior, not to mention his smoldering kisses.

"What are you going to do, dear girl?" the former governess inquired in fascinated dismay.

"As soon as my father and Helena and Alexander's grandmother are gone, he will return to London and I will seek out a remote village where no one knows me. I could take an assumed name, and who would find out? Would you join me? Alexander promised to turn over all my dowry that Marius ordered released." She frowned. "Oh, dear, that is a problem I'd not considered. With Papa home again, Marius has no control over my money. Papa will demand to see settlement papers, and most likely the marriage lines."

"And there are no such things, are there?" Miss Pritchard murmured. "I can see no way out of it; you must marry Lord Hawkswood."

"That is what he says," Juliet said with a sigh, leaning back against the arbor, disheartened that her dear governess had no other solution. "But how can I? He left London, determined not to be trapped into an unwelcome marriage. It would be terrible to compel him into that very situation simply because I trespassed on his property, indeed settling in here as though I were truly his wife."

"You share quarters—at least I have seen him enter your room. How, er, intimate has the situation become?" Miss Pritchard inquired delicately.

"We talk, he has comforted me during thunderstorms—but never with impropriety." Juliet conveniently ignored being held close in his arms during that first storm as well as a few other things like the rosebud-trimmed nightgown. "I enjoy his company; we share many of the same interests—gardening, poetry, music. But he declared he'd no intention of marrying for years. I do not wish to trap so fine a man, then have him hate me for it the rest of my life."

"What about that vast sum of money the dowager offered in the birth of your first child? Pansy said it is the talk of the village." Miss Pritchard folded her hands in her lap while considering Juliet's dilemma, her eyes trained on a butterfly that drifted over the flowers.

"She will wait in vain," Juliet said dryly.

"He might well reconsider marriage in view of that money. It is a great sum, my dear. I have observed that for a good many men money will easily compensate for loss of freedom," Miss Pritchard said, a reflective expression crossing her brow.

"Somehow, I doubt it entices Alexander enough for him to change his mind," Juliet countered. "He has been most supportive regarding his grandmother, affectionately known as the dear dragon."

"I see." Miss Pritchard sighed, staring off into the distance for some moments. "I can think of no other out for you. With no money to your name, you have no alternative. I suggest you confess all to your father, the sooner the better. He is more apt to be lenient if this farce does not go on for too long."

"I cannot think he would wish this situation to be known abroad. Think of the scandal!"

"My dear, you and Lord Hawkswood should have thought of that a long time ago," Miss Pritchard said.

"I ought to have left the day he arrived, is what you are saying? I know that now, for what little good it does me. Oh, Miss Pritchard, never mind that I care for him deeply, I do not wish to force him to marry me."

Miss Pritchard merely shook her head at her former charge and said, "I trust your father will give me a reference in spite of this escapade? He would be within reason were he to deny me such."

Juliet shook her head in dejection. "I shall insist upon it. Come, let us seek out Helena and inquire about Russia. I would know more about St. Petersburg." She rose from the bench, then strolled to the house at Miss Pritchard's side in reflective silence.

There had to be another way out of this muddle. She tried not to think of life without Alexander and found herself on the verge of tears, which would never do.

Alexander moved on from where he had paused at the sound of Juliet greeting her former governess and companion, Miss Pritchard. He had wondered what Juliet would say to her, how she would explain the state of affairs, and in consequence had eavesdropped—something he normally would not stoop to do. But under the circumstances, he was glad he had. He had learned several vital bits of information. Juliet had been happy here before he came—certainly she seemed contented since then, particularly when they had been alone. And now he knew what he suspected was true—she cared for him, deeply, she said.

She was wrong about several things. And changing the situation would require a delicacy of hand and the greatest of tact. He strolled away from the sheltering hedge toward the stables, considering the best approach.

"St. Petersburg is an enchanting city, but then, I lived there," Helena said with a smile. "The houses are large and splendid; our streets are well lit at night and the city is well guarded. The river Neva is quite majestic, and clear as crystal. I have read that our main church, the Kazan, rivals that of Rome. The theater is not perhaps so very elegant, but the performances are most entertaining."

"I have heard the Hermitage is magnificent," Miss Pritchard, ever the teacher, interjected. They were seated in the comfort of the drawing room, and Russia seemed a million miles away. A gentle breeze wafted the sheer curtains in and out, bringing cooler air inside on a warm day, most welcome, indeed.

"True," Helena replied. "There are fine paintings and lovely furniture in the Winter Palace of the tsar, although I have not been there myself." She glanced at her new daughter, adding, "Something I think Juliet might enjoy is Troy Mountain. It is an unusual frame of wood, rising to about forty feet with a grooved railway leading from its summit to a great distance away. You enter a low carriage, then rush down the railway at great speed; it is quite exhilarating, to say the least. I have seen nothing like it anywhere else."

"You make it sound enticing," Juliet said, wishing her stepmother would continue her commentary on St. Petersburg. A stir at the doorway made it clear that was not to be.

Alexander entered the room, looking handsome and vital. "I propose we all go on a picnic. It is too warm a day to remain indoors. It is all arranged," he declared. "And I perceive you will all benefit from time in the open air. You as well, Grandmother," he added to the dowager dragon, who had followed him into the room.

She looked affronted, but could deny her grandson nothing, particularly when he had married just as she'd demanded, and to such a decent girl who loved him.

It was the first Juliet had heard of such a plan, and she quietly said so to Alexander when she had a chance.

"I thought it an excellent way in which to keep everyone occupied and from asking unpleasant questions." He paused, then urged her up the stairs to her room to collect her bonnet and parasol. Once inside, he asked, "You spoke with Miss Pritchard?" At Juliet's answering nod, he queried, "What advice did she give you?"

"You do not want to hear it," Juliet said stubbornly, selecting a bonnet from her wardrobe to avoid looking at him.

"Recommended you marry me, did she?" He strolled over to confront her where she edged away from him and toward the door.

Juliet's gaze flashed to meet his, her alarm unconcealed. "I said you'd not wish to hear it."

"I have said for some time that it is our only solution," he reminded her.

"And you are so eager to find yourself saddled with your unexpected wife," she snapped back in defense.

"I might be," he admitted, looking as though he was reconsidering the entire idea.

Since Juliet wanted nothing more than to be with Alexander forever, yet did not want to have him utterly hate her as a result, she took refuge in silence.

"Have you sought out your father as yet? What has he to say? Much the same, I'll wager," Alexander said, needling Juliet to the point of rashness.

"You, who fled London to avoid being trapped into marriage, would nudge me to say something that would place you into that very trap? How foolish," Juliet said, her voice muffled as she tied the bonnet ribands under her chin. She gathered her gloves and parasol, then paused by her door. "I am ready for whatever comes."

"But you worry," Alexander said, stepping closer. "I wonder why?"

"As do I, come to think on it," Juliet said in return, quite out of patience with the man for the moment. "You are an exasperating man," she said, surprising herself as well as Alexander.

"For God's sake hold your tongue, and let me love," Alexander said, pulling her close to him with an intent look in his eyes that confused Juliet even as it registered that he quoted Donne.

With a swiftness that totally surprised her, he bent, kissed her to breathless idiocy, then withdrew to study her face with a satisfied smile. "Think about that while we are picnicking, Juliet."

She stared at him in silence, wondering what went on in his mind. Her senses were all in disorder and she couldn't have made intelligent conversation had she tried.

They left her room, and he escorted her down to the entryway with exquisite courtesy. It was a good thing he did, for Juliet was not sure she could have managed on her own. Whatever possessed him to kiss her in *such* a way? One more second and she would have melted in his arms, and he could have done whatever he pleased—whatever that might be.

Alexander had organized the outing with his usual dispatch. Helena found herself sitting with Juliet and Miss Pritchard in the first carriage. Julian rode with the dowager, who had taken a liking to him—much to his dismay. Alexander rode his horse alongside the two carriages, ranging back and forth, talking amiably while keeping a weather eye on one and all. There was another vehicle, a fourgon loaded with baskets, simple picnic paraphernalia, and two maids to assist in serving.

Juliet wondered what his motive might be for the expedition. Surely there had to be a reason other than the weather.

She found out before long.

A luncheon of fruit and cold chicken, along with fresh bread and dainty little cakes put everyone in a good frame of mind.

Then Alexander said in a meaningful way to Juliet, "Why do you not take your father for a walk? I feel certain you have a number of things to discuss."

There was nothing to do but agree with every sign of delight, quite as though Juliet wished for nothing more than an intimate conversation—inquisition was more like it—with her father.

"Hawkswood seems to believe you wish to talk, Juliet," Lord Winterton said once they were away from the others.

Juliet twirled her parasol a little, taking note that no one could possibly overhear what she said—if she said anything, and she wasn't certain she would. "True."

"You have not been yourself," her father commented.

"But then, you have not seen me for some years. First, you went off to southern Russia, scouting for the government, I think you called it. Then, after Napoleon was safely out of that country, you went to the war area. Never did you think to come home. Is it unreasonable to think I have changed a little?" She was being evasive, but heaven help her, she had to be.

"I always knew when you were prevaricating, my girl. I believe you have been lately. It is Hawkswood, is it not? I should like to know where those marriage papers really are." He paused in their walk to examine his daughter's face. "Are the settlements properly done? Has he taken advantage of your stepbrother's lack of knowledge regarding such things?"

"This will not do," Juliet suddenly exclaimed. Standing on a knoll that overlooked the pretty picnic sight, she could see Alex offering fruit to Helena, while the dowager exchanged views—likely regarding the foolishness of picnics—with Miss Pritchard. Juliet could continue the deceit no longer.

So, she explained everything—almost. There were a few details she omitted—the kisses and the love poetry, mainly. As well, she said nothing of spending the night of the storm nestled in Alexander's arms. Somehow, she did not think her father would take kindly to any of those things.

Surprisingly, her father did not explode. Juliet suspected he was far past that state by the time she finished speaking.

"You mean you have been sharing that room as husband and wife all this time and you are not married?" he said in a dangerously quiet voice.

"Not precisely," Juliet said. "He has his bedroom and I have mine. We talk together in my room at times; he has comforted me during thunderstorms—you know how frightened I am of lightning and thunder. His mother died of a lightning strike, Papa."

"Pity, but that does not excuse his behavior, Juliet. You must realize he can do no less than marry you. You have been compromised beyond belief!"

"To do him justice, he insists upon the same thing," Juliet replied meekly. "And remember, he did not bring me here to do just that."

"Then I fail to see where the problem is. You must marry him, and he is willing to marry you. So?" Lord Winterton took Juliet's arm and continued to walk away from the picnic group.

"You forget the reason for his coming to Woodbury in the first place. He did not wish to marry that dreadful Camilla Shelford. She wanted to trap him into marriage any way she could. I'll not trap him, Papa."

"It seems to me as though he could have left at once when he found you in residence. For that matter, he could have insisted you leave his home. I wonder why he didn't?" Lord Winterton mused aloud.

Since Juliet had wondered the very same thing, she was unable to offer an answer to the query.

"I shall have a talk with him directly we return," his lordship said in his firmest, most chilly manner. Juliet had it in her heart to feel sorry for Alexander.

It proved unnecessary for Lord Winterton to seek a conversation with Alexander. He found Juliet and her father looking over a pretty view, both silent as they contemplated what had to be done.

"I expect you had best rescue Miss Pritchard from my grandmother, Juliet," Alexander said pleasantly, not at all as though he feared the coming chat with a man who looked at him as though he would cheerfully run him through with a sword.

"If you wish. Are you sure you want me to go?" she dared inquire. She looked from her irate father to Alexander, who seemed impervious to undertones he should have known might be present, and shrugged. Well, the best she could do was to warn him. "Papa knows all."

Alexander's brow went up as though to doubt she had actually revealed everything, and she could feel herself turn pink.

"Well," Lord Winterton said, impatient to have a discussion with his soon-to-be son-in-law now that he knew more of what had transpired the past weeks. "I may not know every little bit and scrap that went on between you two, but I am not blind, nor stupid." He gestured, and the two men sauntered off down the hill in a different direction.

Juliet watched them go, her heart sinking to her toes as she realized it would be most difficult to persuade her father to allow her a modest portion to set up a separate establishment— even as a widow.

It was a short conversation, she thought, when the men joined the picnic group before long. She studied her father's face, then Alexander's. How frustrating; she could tell nothing from either expression. Was her father furious because Alexander refused to "make an honest woman of her"? Or was Alexander angry because of the opposite, that he must?

She soon found out.

"Come along with me, Juliet. I would show you what your father and I discovered," Alexander said, holding out his hand to her. Miss Pritchard made a shooing motion with her hands. Neither Helena nor the dowager seemed to think it odd that a husband and his wife should take a walk together, alone.

Juliet knew better then to argue with him when he was like this—impassive and commanding.

The others reclined in the cool shade, enjoying the light

breeze and commenting on the heat of the day. Fans were much in use, and lemonade, chilled in the nearby stream, was sipped with relish.

"I trust it is a cool place, sir," Juliet said, her eyes snapping with suppressed annoyance at the way her well-planned life was being rearranged for her without any say on her part.

"You are furious, I don't doubt," Alexander said in a most conversational manner as he assisted her over a hummock of grass. They walked up the slight incline, then on to the stream, and here he urged her down on the bank to contemplate the languidly flowing water from beneath the shade of a large willow tree.

"I explained my side of the situation to your father. He seemed surprised to hear both our sides matched. You were truthful, I gather." Alex picked up a twig, twirling it about in his fingers before flicking it into the water to watch it slowly float away.

"I could go on with the lies no longer," Juliet said with a note of apology in her voice.

"I wonder you could at all. I believe you are not normally given to telling untruths." He looked at her then, questioning.

"No. I am usually a truthful person."

"So if I asked if you love me, you would be honest?"

"Unfair, Alexander," she said with a faint laugh at his audacity. "A lady does not reveal her heart so easily."

"Marry me, Juliet." He gazed at her with that blank expression he used at times when he wished to conceal his thoughts.

She sat motionless, trying to sort out her feelings. "You spoke with Papa. He told you what he felt must be done?"

"I have said before that we must marry. Now I ask you." He turned to look at the stream again, sending another twig on its way to the sea. "I think we would deal together very well. Shall I read you from Donne again? More romantic poetry?"

"No, no," she denied. Was that what it had been? That delightful hour in the garden with the love poetry? He had been softening her up for what he knew had to be done? She could not bear to wed the man she now loved with all her heart for so paltry a reason.

"Precisely what did my father decree?"

"He listened to what I had to say and then agreed that the sooner we married the better. I like to think he appreciated my offering to do the deed before he demanded it." Alexander debated on telling Juliet he loved her, deciding to wait. He wanted her on his terms, perhaps foolishly.

"You did? Why?" she asked, tossing her own twig into the stream to watch it sink to the bottom. Somehow, it seemed appropriate.

"As I said, we must and you know it. Society demands it of us. And would it be so very bad?" he asked lightly.

Not if he loved her, Juliet thought. "Society," she murmured. "A pox on Society. Were I to disappear from here, never to be seen by you again, what would happen? Would Society know or care?" she demanded.

"I would."

"You have done me a great honor, sir, but I fear I must decline your kind offer of marriage. And, since you make no other, I shall go." She rose with a quickness that caught Alexander off guard. In seconds she was off up the hill and over and gone.

Alexander rose slowly from the bank, brushing aside a willow branch as he tossed another twig into the water. It floated. "Three times lucky," he murmured. "You have not seen the last of me, my Juliet." He sauntered up the incline, then down to where Juliet had joined the others.

She plied her fan, sipped lemonade, and seemed to give no sign of what had occurred. But then, what had happened? Nothing more than he had expected. He must think of something else, for they *would* be married.

Chapter 16

Bunches of flowers were everywhere, by her bed, on the dressing table, in a bucket by the window—he must have run out of vases, Juliet decided, knowing full well who had invaded her room with all these blooms.

Breakfast had been such an ordinary meal; she'd decided to join Helena and her father, Miss Pritchard, and the dowager in an effort to please. It had been a quiet beginning to a normal day, if one could call *any* day that contained such a group of people in this situation normal. And then she had gone to her room to find this array!

There was a tag attached to the bunch of daisies in the bucket and, curiosity getting the better of her, she crossed to pick it up. "COME" was written on the square of white pasteboard, nothing more.

Puzzled, Juliet took the card and plumped herself on the little chair close by to stare at the pasteboard again. COME, printed in bold, slashing letters, the black ink seeming to jump out at her. She turned the card over to find nothing on the other side. That was all? *Come?* Her curiosity rising, she searched among the other bouquets to find nothing more. Not another word. Just that single word, COME. Bewildered, she took the card, thinking there was a mystery that might take a bit of solving, and tucked it into the small drawer of her dressing table. Perhaps the word had a deeper meaning that would occur to her later.

"Where'd he get all those flowers, ma'am?" Pansy inquired when she entered the room, the caramel crepe gown, freshly pressed, draped over her arms.

"I suspect he raided my garden as well as the one on the Taunton property he now owns," Juliet said, striving for an indifference she didn't feel. She purposely did not mention the mysterious card tucked into the flowers. No one was going to learn about that.

Leaving Pansy to tidy the room, Juliet hurried down to the garden; it was easy to see where Alexander had struck. A bit here, a bit there, and the bucket would be full. She wondered what would happen next.

"Good morning, my dear," Alexander said suavely from behind her, startling Juliet.

Spinning around, she gave him a confused look before tilting her nose in the air. "You picked my flowers," she accused.

"Wrong, my love. They are *my* flowers. This is *my* home, or had you forgotten? You may claim to be my wife, but the actuality is different, is it not? Shall we take a stroll?"

"I do not trust you," she said, nevertheless falling in step with him as he continued to saunter along the garden path, pausing to admire a cluster of daisies and mounds of early purple asters. Hollyhocks ranged along the back of a perennial border with lilies and hemorocalis, marigolds and a selection of other summer blooms in front. A hedge sparrow flew down to inspect the plants for insects.

Alexander tucked her hand close to his side, patted it gently, and smiled, saying nothing for the moment.

"Trust is such a tender word," he reflected aloud. "It brings to mind confidence, a certainty, a conviction. Do you have assurance in your chosen path, my Juliet?" Without waiting for a reply, which was not forthcoming, he continued, "On the other hand, you may rely on me, believe in what I tell you, pin your faith on my words."

"Words," Juliet said suddenly. "You tucked a card in those daisies. It had one word on it. Why?"

"Captured you curiosity, did it? You think I brought you a few posies?"

"I believe I have come to know you a little. Besides, who else would bring me flowers? And I doubt you do anything without a motive," she snapped back at him, sounding quite as frustrated as she, indeed, was.

"Ah," he said with a maddening smile, "then you shall have to uncover my motive, I perceive." He plucked a daisy, tucked it into her curls, and looked pleased with the effect it made. "I must say, it is nice to know that Mr. Wyllard is no longer to be seen lingering in the garden. Wise of you to send him on his way, my dear."

On that note, Alexander left her, striding briskly away as though he had accomplished his purpose in seeking her out. What it might have been perplexed her, and so she said to Helena when joined by that charming lady.

"Perhaps Alexander intends to keep you on your toes. I gather he means to confuse you."

Juliet could say nothing more without revealing the mysterious word on the white card, nor did she think it sensible to inform Helena of the flowers appearing in so intimate a location as the bedside. Juliet had no idea as to whether her father had revealed all to his new wife or not. And while Juliet might be curious, she did not wish to discuss the matter right now. It was enough to rail at Alexander for being Alexander. Poor Mr. Wyllard, once so favored, now totally ignored.

Remaining silent, Juliet turned her attention to the flower border, snipping off the dead heads of the yarrow with an absent hand, her mind elsewhere—on Alexander.

By lunch there had been no additional cards or any other mysterious events, and Juliet sat down at the table with a lighter heart. It remained so until the maid served her a plate of food. There was nothing wrong with the food; it was the crisp white card that peeked out from beneath a slice of bread that caught her eyes. On it was printed a single word—LIVE.

Hastily filching the card from her plate and whisking it into the reticule she fortunately had with her, Juliet found her pleasure in the simple meal destroyed. Alexander. It had to be he who had done this. But why? What was the significance of the word *live,* pray tell? Was it to remind her food was a necessity and that he was providing it? Had the word *come* intended to bring her to the garden so he might tease her?

Eating just enough so not to call attention to her lack of appetite, Juliet left the table as soon as she could.

Stealing up to her room, she crossed to the dressing table, opened the drawer, and took out the first card. *Come live,* the two words said—if they were meant to go together. Because they came in that sequence did not mean they were intended to be that way. She wondered when he would strike next. And where! Alexander was proving to be more devious than the worst of tormentors.

The remainder of the day passed in a suspicious haze. Juliet searched everywhere she went for an elusive white bit of pasteboard, but found nothing. Perhaps those two words were all he intended to vex her with?

Mrs. Ogleby and Mrs. Tackley, along with a pretty Lucy, newly engaged and proud of her lovely ring, called that afternoon. They seemed to find Helena intriguing, her faint French accent—for the Russian nobility spoke nothing but French—of enormous fascination. She, in turn, found them equally of interest. Miss Pritchard came in for her share of conversation as well.

Juliet was preoccupied, finding it difficult to concentrate on village gossip, speculations on Parson Richards wedding to the squire's daughter, not to mention news of the upcoming wedding to take place as soon as Lord Taunton could make arrangements.

"He is impatient, your bridegroom," Helena said, holding her teacup while studying the blushing Lucy. "I can see why; you are a very pretty girl. I trust it will be soon, so we may attend."

Mrs. Ogleby asked the question that popped into Juliet's mind. "Do you intend to leave shortly, then?"

"When matters are settled," Helena said composedly, which remark revealed practically nothing of their plans. It did remind Juliet that her father had insisted she be wed, and he was accustomed to having his way in all things. This would be one time he failed.

Mrs. Tackley inquired about life in St. Petersburg.

While Helena told stories she thought might amuse, Juliet's gaze strayed to the garden, where she could see Alexander wandering about, seeming of no particular intent. What was he up to now?

"Juliet, the tea," Miss Pritchard reminded gently, bringing a flush to Juliet's pale cheeks.

Pouring tea and offering tiny almond biscuits distracted Juliet, and she could only wonder about Alexander, what he would do next. He seemed to have taken over her mind, all her thoughts centered on him. He would drive her around the bend if this business with the pasteboards did not cease.

She approached the dinner table with caution, a reticule dangling from her arm just in case it proved necessary. As the meal was served—dish after dish, course after course—and nothing occurred, no little white pasteboard came to view, and Juliet gradually relaxed.

She and Alexander played a duet following dinner, the men deciding to forgo their port in favor of joining the ladies. Lord Winterton settled with Helena on the sofa, while the dowager claimed her favorite chair, the bergère. Miss Pritchard sat on the far side of the room, situated so she might watch everyone at once.

It took greater than usual concentration for Juliet to play; her eyes kept straying to Alexander. He sat at the clavichord, candlelight bringing forth hidden lights in his dark hair. His dark coat and pristine cravat succeeded in making his face stand out against the dim background. While a handsome man, he seemed gifted with unusual appeal this evening, and she wondered if it was the added mystery surrounding him that caused it. The realization that if she did pursue her intended course, she would likely never see him again struck her.

His eyes flashed up at her just at that very moment, and Juliet faltered in her playing, recovering quickly to conclude the piece with no more errors.

"We have played that bit of music before, and you showed no difficulty with it," Alexander said quietly for her ears alone when the others were deep in a discussion about the Russian theater as compared to London offerings.

"I was momentarily distracted," Juliet explained, wishing he did not stand quite so close.

"Shall I not look at you when we play? I won't if I disturb you," he said in that smooth manner he'd adopted of late when he wanted to vex her.

Without thought to what she said, she replied, "You *do* disturb me, far too much for my peace of mind." Then she heard her hasty words hanging in the air and longed to be elsewhere.

"How nice," Alexander said gently and strolled away from her side to pour himself a glass of sherry.

"I shall do violence to the man. I shall," Juliet whispered, a thread of sound.

Alexander turned to bestow an enigmatic look on her that all but compelled her to flee the room. When would he cease this assault on her senses? What could she do to stop him? Not a blessed thing, a wee voice in the back of her head replied.

Somehow Juliet scraped by the remainder of the evening without disgracing herself in any way. She couldn't have said what was discussed, nor if she received any odd looks. When possible, she took herself to bed, offering an incipient headache as an excuse.

She closed the door to her room, grateful to escape that expression in Alexander's eyes. She could not define it; she only knew it was dangerous and at the same time seductive.

Without waiting for Pansy, she hastily disrobed, put her things away, then walked to her bed, relieved she had been spared another card.

It was on her pillow, tucked into a scrap of lace, looking like a lover's missive. WITH. The bold black letters splashed across the card. She sank onto the bed, reaching out to touch the pasteboard as though it might burn her fingers. Her heart pounded, and her hand fluttered up to her throat. What did this mean? *With?* Why *with*?

With, live, and *come;* what significance did they have for Alexander? for her? She hesitantly picked up the pasteboard along with the scrap of lace and tucked them into the drawer of her dressing table to join the others.

Out of sight, out of mind did not work for her that night. She slept badly, waking when Pansy entered with her breakfast tray, knowing she must look a fright.

The maid beamed a broad smile at her mistress, bringing the tray to the bed when she saw Juliet was not inclined to rise "Special this morning, ma'am."

"I have little appetite; I slept wretchedly," Juliet said, running a distracted hand through her tousled hair. Her nightcap had ended up on the floor. Pansy picked it up, looked knowingly at Juliet, then left.

The tray held the usual pot of tea, slivers of toast, and raspberry jam, but directly atop her plate sat a small packet wrapped in lush white satin.

With trembling fingers Juliet undid the dainty riband that bound the packet, unfolding the satin hesitantly, as though something might leap forth to bite her. It was a miniature, handsomely painted by an artist with great skill. Alexander smiled at her with that disarming twinkle in his eyes.

She stared at the thing. A portrait? Slowly, fearing what she might find, she turned it over to see one small word printed on a pasteboard tucked into the back of the miniature. ME. She drew a relieved breath. Well, *me* at least made sense. She knew him so well he scarcely had to write his name, however unorthodox it might be to label the painting so.

Her heart slowed to a more normal rate. Here was something reasonable. A portrait, a nice thing to have were she to leave him forever. A memory. She paid no heed to the tears that slipped down her cheeks at the mere thought of never seeing him again. Why, it would be wonderful! She'd have peace!

Soggy toast and lukewarm tea did not provide a good start to a day. With Pansy's help she dressed hurriedly, hoping to escape the house and Alexander if possible.

The garden was devoid of people; only the hedge sparrow and a robin searching for insects disturbed the scene. She snipped off flower heads and pulled weeds, thinking gardening a tranquil pursuit and just what she needed.

Mr. Lumpkin ambled along the path, a ceramic jar in hand. "This be for you, my lady," he said, his voice rusty as though from disuse.

"Thank you," she said quietly, eyeing the jar with misgivings. Rising from where she kneeled, Juliet accepted the jar, wondering what on earth Mr. Lumpkin offered. As she looked down, she caught sight of a neat white card on top of the jar. BE, it said. Further examination revealed the jar contained honey. Well, this made sense of a sort, although the word *be* ought to have an additional letter. She didn't ask Mr. Lumpkin who had given him the honey; she knew. Alexander. Why honey? Did he think her his sweet? After slipping the little card inside the bodice of her muslin dress, she brought the jar to Cook. The card would join the others, even if the word had been misspelled.

Was there to be no escaping Alexander and his teasing?

"How are you this morning, Juliet?" Alexander asked when he encountered her in the entryway. "A trifle off color, I fear. Not sleep well, perhaps? We should do something about that." His smile was an intimate one; it seduced, beguiled, and made Juliet long to throw herself in his arms and beg him to do as he pleased with her. She might strangle him first, though.

"I am off for a bit of fishing. Harry Riggs said the stream offers nice little trout. I shall endeavor to bring some home to you." He touched her lightly on the cheek, then left the house.

Juliet hurried up to her room, hoping to avoid meeting anyone else. She went to the window, from which spot she could see Alexander striding across the grass in the direction of the stream. An afternoon of peace. He could scarcely tease her when he was away from the house.

Sinking down on the little armchair, she viewed her sanctuary, then noticed a paper on her dressing table. Curious, she rose and walked over to gaze at a drawing. It was of a man fishing by the stream. Not particularly well done, she could nevertheless recognize Alexander seated under a willow tree. Likely the drawing was intended to remind her of the very spot where he had proposed to her. Placed atop the drawing was another of the pasteboard words. MY.

My? How odd. It ought to have been me, not my. Puzzled at the error, Juliet placed the new word with the others, closed the drawer, and decided she might as well leave the shelter of her room. Alexander was here, everywhere he wanted to be. There was no evading him.

Again dinner was as normal as one might wish. Alexander had brought enough trout home for an excellent fish course for the six of them. True, the dowager made remarks about the streams at the Abbey offering larger trout, but that was almost to be expected from her. Miss Pritchard stated trout were always welcome, whatever the size.

The men enjoyed their port that evening, while the women repaired to the drawing room and a tray of tea brought in by a composed Mrs. Bassett.

Juliet looked at her with admiration. Nothing seemed to put her in a pucker; she was unflappable. The woman who had expected to care for a house in a remote village with not a sign of an owner, now had lords and ladies to cater to, all done with a serene face and effortless capability.

Again Juliet played a duet with Alexander, this time at the request of Helena, who professed to enjoy harp music in particular and duets in general.

Juliet managed to refrain from glancing at Alexander after she had plucked the first note, listening with care to the musical cues he offered and joining in with all the skill at her command.

"Well," her father said, rather jovially for him, "you two will be able to enjoy making music together through the long winter nights."

Juliet flashed Alexander a look of warning.

"Indeed, sir. Juliet and I are rather good at that sort of thing." Nothing was concealed in his words, but Juliet felt heat from his gaze that made her tremble.

With great effort she remained in the drawing room, joining in a light supper when the dowager demanded it be served, sipping her tea with what she hoped was a calm facade.

What would he do next? Another word, perhaps? What word? What did they signify? She wished she knew.

Eventually she could hold off no longer. It was time to go to bed; the others went first while Juliet helped Mrs. Bassett gather dishes, performing unnecessary tasks until Alexander sauntered over to look at the neat pile of napkins she clutched in her hands.

"Stalling, perhaps? Not afraid to face what is coming, are you, Juliet?" He stood close enough so she could feel his strength, sense his determination.

"Of course not. I am not sleepy," she said by way of reasoning.

"How agreeable," Alexander murmured before leaving the room to mount the stairs.

Once he had gone, Juliet tossed the napkins on the table and followed him, quickly entering her room. With a dubious glance at the connecting door, she hurriedly undressed with Pansy's silent help. She slipped on her voluminous nightgown, then climbed into her vast bed with a sigh of relief. Nothing more had happened. No white pasteboards, no words, and no Alexander. Pansy left with a whispered goodnight and Juliet was alone.

She snuggled cozily under the covers and was almost drifting off to sleep when she heard a creak—the door.

Sitting up, she whispered, "Who's there?"

"Alexander, my love. I have come to tell you the last word of that puzzling collection you had gathered."

"The words! You might have told me without waiting until now. Or it could have waited until morning," she grumbled. "What is it?" she concluded, trying to pretend she was not interested.

"Love. The quote is 'Come live with me and be my love.' "

"I might have known a rake would think of something like that. The answer is still no. Alexander, you know you ought not be in my room." She pointed to the door, wondering if he would meekly depart.

"But my love, everyone believes us married." He crossed his arms, looking somewhat smug.

"I did not invite you to my room," she protested.

"Or your bed. And that is the crux of the matter, dearest Juliet." He strolled to the foot of her bed, and in the faint light offered by a lone candle he had placed on her bedside table, she could see he wore his navy banyon. He also wore that determined expression. She wondered what he could say that might persuade her to agree with his solution to their problems. There would be no marriage without love on both sides; *she* was determined on that.

"Please leave, Alexander. Have you not teased me enough?" She watched him with care, wondering what he'd do.

"My love, I have not begun." He stared at her as though assessing her mind.

Juliet was thankful he kept his distance. He overpowered her senses far too easily when he touched her. And his kisses? They left her in no state to think rationally.

"I should miss you if you went away and left me behind as you have threatened to do," he said quietly.

"I should miss you as well," she whispered, a tremor in her voice. She couldn't deny him the truth about that.

He strolled around the room, coming to stand by the side of her bed, looking down at her with the odd light in his eyes that she had noticed on more than one occasion.

"There is but one answer for us, and you know it. We must be off to Gretna and I would that we go at first light."

"Tomorrow? But . . ." Juliet weakened. "Father? The dowager? Miss Pritchard?"

"They can well take care of themselves, I fancy." He pushed aside the covers, drawing her from the warmth of her bed and into his arms. "This is where you belong, Juliet, next to my heart. Can you deny it? Does this not feel like home and forever to you? Can you *honestly* tell me that you feel nothing for me, that you do not care deeply for me?

"No," she murmured softly, unable to lie to the one she loved. He tightened his arms about her and Juliet felt oddly cosseted.

"Juliet, would you marry me and be my love? I want you—not just to live with me and be my love—I want you to be my love, my wife, the mother of our children, the mistress of my home. Everything. And I want you forever."

He held her close and stood looking at her, not kissing her, nor did he attempt to seduce her—although he very might well have found it as easy as pie.

"You might have said something before," she said, illogically indignant that he had put her through such torment. Suddenly she halted her efforts to be released, staring up at his dear face with resolve. She would know the truth of the matter and now. Surely he would not lie to her.

"You say you want me to be your love, the mother of your children, but tell me Alexander, do you love me? It is not the money from your grandmother, is it?" She at last voiced the thing she had feared—that he found that incredible offer tempting, too tempting to ignore.

It was not easy to meet his gaze. What if she found the wrong message there? His lips might say one thing but his eyes would tell her the truth of the matter. She drew him toward the candle's light and waited.

He frowned. "I care not a jot for the money. I see I have failed miserably in my courting if you can possibly think that of me after this time. You doubt that I love you? I suppose that is possible, given your first opinion of me."

"I no longer think of you like that," she protested.

"Juliet, come morning we are leaving for Scotland and a parson and it will be because I love you and you love me. We will marry and raise a family and, God willing, have a good many happy years together. Does that satisfy you?"

"Oh. Indeed, it does." She digested this a moment, then said, "I will never leave you, Alexander, I promise."

He rewarded her declaration with suitable appreciation.

When Pansy entered the bedroom the following morning, she found Juliet dressed and ready to go out.

"You are up betimes, this morning, my lady," the maid said in surprise.

Juliet smiled. "Pack my things, all my things, every scrap you can find. We are leaving this morning."

Pansy stared at her mistress as though she hadn't heard right. "Leaving?"

Juliet nodded, going to the drawer in her dressing table to stow the collection of white pasteboards in her reticule.

"Your father and his lady? The old dowager? Miss Pritchard? They leave as well?"

Juliet shrugged and smiled mysteriously. "I expect they will leave when they wish."

The connecting door opened, and Alexander strode across the room to gather Juliet in his arms. "Good morning, love."

The maid was too proper to be staring at her mistress in the arms of the man she'd claimed to dislike, but this was no ordinary kiss or Pansy was a nodcock. She busied herself with pulling garments from the wardrobe, peeking around the door from minute to minute to see if they were done. They weren't for a long time.

"How soon can you be ready to leave? Take only what is necessary. Pansy can bring the rest along with Randall. He knows where to find us. Acceptable?"

"If you say so," Juliet replied, her subdued words belied by the love in her eyes. "You heard the man, Pansy. I would have a valise or two with the essentials, a few changes of clothes."

"The rosebud nightgown, as well, Pansy," Lord Hawkswood demanded nicely before he returned to kissing Juliet.

"Yes, sir," the maid said with a grin and set to work.

By the time Lord Winterton and Helena descended the stairs for breakfast, the traveling coach had drawn up before the front door and a modest pile of luggage was in the process of being stowed in the boot. The two elopers awaited them.

"We are off for Gretna, sir," Alexander said quietly to Lord Winterton.

"You persuaded her then? Last evening?" He looked at his daughter's pink cheeks and asked no more questions.

"My *wife* and I are taking a little trip to the north; Scotland, the lakes, other places of interest. We ought to be at the Abbey by Christmas," Alexander concluded with a satisfied smile.

"Your grandmother will no doubt be most pleased."

"We shall do our best, sir. We shall do our very best."